THE SILVER WAVES OF SUMMER

Kelp Books, LLC

"The Naked and the Dead" originally published in Mystery Magazine. "Lighthouse Scene for Miles" Originally published in Kelp Journal.

ISBN-13: 9781737322801
ISBN-10: 1737322803

Cover design by: Jaya Nicely
Library of Congress Control Number: 2021940548
Printed in the United States of America

CONTENTS

INTRODUCTION

A little over a year ago, I met up with Michael Scott Moore in Santa Cruz for a socially distanced surf session. We were fortunate in Northern California to have our beaches remain open for physical exercise during the pandemic. Between sets, I floated the idea by him of a collection of short stories with crime, surfers, and beach communities at its heart. A collection of "surf noir," we called it. And he thought it was a pretty good idea. It would have to have, of course, a painted cover to give it a fun, pulpy, midcentury feel. And so, the idea for *The Silver Waves of Summer* was launched.

When I got home, I quickly began the process of reaching out to writers much more talented than myself for a potential contribution to the anthology. It was met by all contributors with quite a bit of enthusiasm for the subject. These writers were genuinely excited to conjure up a "beachy" piece for the anthology. And after months of hard work from some of the most talented writers in the country, we pulled together a collection of eleven wonderful short stories, all nuanced in style and subject, but with the beach at their cores. We also tracked down and enlisted the mega talent, Jaya Nicely, for the incredible cover illustration.

Reading these stories as they came in was a pure joy, and I couldn't be any more thrilled with the collection you are about to read. We travel from a private nude beach on the east coast to the Monterey Bay, and down to Southern California where the action heats up. We even meet jazz legend Miles Davis at the famed Lighthouse Café. Each of these stories is a glittering gem to be savored in front of waves lapping at a seashore, or on your favorite Adirondack chair poolside this summer, and for all the summers to come.

David M. Olsen
Kauai, July 2021

IN THE BANK

By Antoine Wilson

The night was pitch-black and moonless. Fog rolled into the channel from the west, perfect weather for the pangas to make a midnight run for Tajiguas, as Felix said they would, if his information turned out to be any good. Buddy stood at the helm of the Sea-Tacean, his late father's hole-in-the-water, heading straight for the bank at a good clip, ear out for coasties on the radio, eyes on the radar screen, looking for any signs of this supposed easy haul. He'd never been seasick a day in his life, but his stomach was lurching now, out of fear, partly, but mainly out of excitement.

Felix had assured him this would be a piece of cake. He'd shown up with uniforms from a costume shop, zillion-candlepower spotlights, police beacon lights in red and blue, a whole box of gear. "These guys won't know what hit 'em," he'd said.

Now Felix was at the bow, scanning where the horizon would be with a comically oversized set of binoculars. What the hell was he thinking he'd see, other than a wall of fog? As if reading his mind, Felix turned and looked up at Buddy, gave him a thumbs-up while the sea spray shot off the prow to both sides of him like a flower opening to reveal what was inside... Sure, they'd had a smoke as soon as they were offshore, a little something to take the edge off, but it was strong stuff, stronger than Buddy was used to. They were ten miles offshore and the radar was empty.

Felix appeared next to him, trying to talk over the engine noise, and Buddy dialed back on the throttle.

"There'll be two or three guys," Felix said, his eyes flashing. "We gotta make sure at least one of them makes it out alive."

"Alive?" Buddy asked. "Why wouldn't they make it out alive?"

"If shit goes upside down."

"That's not what we talked about."

Felix patted him on the back. "Of course not. I meant just in case. Nothing's gonna go wrong, don't sweat it."

Buddy watched the fog swallow the black silhouette of Anacapa. It was just the weed, he thought, dusting him with paranoia. This would be like Felix said, an easy score, a onetime deal, four million dollars' worth of marijuana making its way up the coast, a drop in the bucket for the big boys, the guys who cut off faces and stitched them onto soccer balls, this was a numbers game for them, they expected a certain amount of—what had they called it when Buddy was working at Walmart?—*shrinkage*, that was the word. "A few flat-screens fall off the truck," Felix had said, "it doesn't make a difference in the big picture…" Of course Buddy didn't live in the big picture.

He'd been a professional surfer once, a bona fide contest surfer, a winner, even. Had surfed against MR, Pottz, Curren. But the contests he'd won had come before the whole thing was flooded with money, and by the time the sponsors were making it rain, he'd sunk in the rankings, falling off the bottom, watching everyone else cash in while he jockeyed for position at Rincon on a dinged-up twin fin, shivering in a wet suit one season too long.

So he resuscitated his father's flailing whale-watching and excursion-fishing business while the old man pickled himself into oblivion. It was Felix who'd tweaked the permits and obtained the dime-store insurance to make it possible. Then, inevitably it seemed, Buddy found himself with no time to surf. People were always asking him when he was going to get back in the water, telling him that if they could surf like he could, they'd be out every day. They didn't get it. They hadn't felt the cold touch of the brass ring at their fingertips, hadn't had to watch it ascend forever out of reach.

Right now, though, looking out over the black expanse of ocean, buoyed by the prospect of a new life, he wondered, How could he have ever left the waves behind? It had been a slow creep, his drifting away from the only place he really belonged...*feeling* a wave, anticipating it, finding the power in it, knowing when it was standing up behind him, when it would soften into a shoulder, when he should trim, when he should cut back—but these were just words. He knew, in a way that preceded language, he knew the ocean and its energy, could get in sync with it like nobody else, and yet he'd left it behind, had tried to absorb the lessons of the land, had naively reckoned he could always get back to it... It was right *there*, after all...

"Bingo!" Felix said, pointing at a spot on the radar. "Right? Bingo?"

"Could be," Buddy said.

Felix hovered over the radar screen in his preposterous costume, Navy officer whites, epaulettes sagging, medals on the front, a dress cap, scrambled eggs and all, hardly covering his shaggy hair. He looked more like a Third World dictator than whatever it was they were pretending to be.

Buddy flicked off the cabin light, the navigation lights, everything. They cruised forward in the dark, on a collision course with what was either a four-million-dollar payday or some dipshit lost in the channel.

The air cooled suddenly.

"We're in the soup," Buddy said.

"Feel like a pirate yet?" Felix chuckled. "Pull us alongside and we'll light 'em up."

The logistics of the interception eluded Buddy, but he had put his full faith in Felix ever since he'd asked Buddy, over way too many drinks on the beach in front of the Rudder Room, "What would you do if two million bucks fell into your lap?" and his thoughts had swelled with what that kind of money might mean for him, and for Jenny, of course; their fights had always been about money...

Felix put his hand on Buddy's back, which wasn't more than a hard knot of muscle.

"Brother," he said, "loosen up. These fools will fold in a second. We're dealing with *subcontractors* here. They'd rather be back on Playa Popotla, cracking cervezas and slicing up the catch of the day."

Buddy breathed deep. Felix knew what he was doing. The uniforms were ridiculous, but Felix had a way of doing just enough to get by, just enough to fool you, just enough to make it through. "Slippery," Jenny had called him. "Resourceful," Buddy had countered. When Buddy's surfing career evaporated, who was it who'd helped him navigate the working world, who'd set up the Walmart scheme, who'd greased the right palms to get his father's business running again? Buddy had learned the obvious lesson that being a natural in the water didn't mean shit in the world, but any lessons beyond that were slow in coming. In Felix's slipstream, he'd found a way.

From right next to him, he heard the click-click of a gun, a bullet being chambered.

"What the fuck, Felix?"

"Last resort, amigo, last resort."

"You said these guys wouldn't have guns."

"All the more reason we should."

Buddy didn't like it, but he couldn't argue with it, either.

The blob on the radar slowed. The smugglers were obviously trying to figure out where they were headed, landmarks and sky obscured by the thick mist. This was good. Buddy and Felix could capitalize on their confusion. Hopefully avoid getting rammed. Buddy wasn't sure the old tub could take that.

They were only a few hundred feet away, according to the radar. Buddy could hear the rumble of their outboard.

"Showtime," said Felix.

Buddy flipped on a switch Felix had mounted to a car battery up in the cabin.

The smugglers—there were three of them—put their

hands in front of their eyes, blinded by the mega candle-power spotlights.

Felix took the mic, said over the loudspeaker: "*Esta es la Guardia Costera de los Estados Unidos. Detenga el motor y levante las manos o nos veremos obligados a dispararle.*"

Buddy had no idea what it meant, but the men cut their engine and put their hands up over their heads, squinting into the light. The biggest one was bald, probably in his forties, with a mustache, and wearing a fisherman's waders. Another was similar in stature, a bit shorter, no mustache, full head of hair, Dodgers cap, jeans. They could have been brothers. Probably were. Both of them looked terrified. From what Felix had told him, a lot of these guys were your standard fishermen who had the bad luck of living where they did and owning the right kind of boat. They were invited to co-operate—or get capped. *Plata o plomo.* "Money or lead," Felix had said with a shit-eating grin. Buddy had found it funny, too, but now, looking at these guys, he felt bad for them. They didn't ask for this shit.

The third smuggler was a kid, maybe fifteen or six-teen, flat face, big cheekbones, acne. His hands were up, but his head was tilted to the side, and he didn't have the same deer-in-the-headlights look as the other two.

Felix got on the mic again: "*Acuéstese boca abajo con las manos detrás de la espalda.*"

Buddy watched the three men lie down on their stomachs, with their hands behind their backs. Felix headed to the rail to lash the two boats together. The plan was that he would keep an eye on the smugglers while Buddy hauled the bales of weed onto the *Sea-Tacean.*

Buddy cut the engine and made his way onto the deck. The night was strangely silent. Felix's collection of police beacon lights spinning in the thick of the fog lent a feeling of unreality to the scene. He hadn't realized the panga would be so big. A tarp covered what he assumed were bales of weed. Felix was on board already, holding his gun on the men, and waved Buddy over.

Buddy took a corner of the tarp and lifted. Four million dollars of compressed Mexican weed, grown somewhere in the middle of nowhere in Baja, bound for Who-Knew-Where, USA. He hadn't considered just how much manual labor would be involved, picking up the bales, tossing them aboard his boat, and wished he'd gotten in better shape ahead of time.

For some reason Felix seemed to be engaging the smugglers in conversation. No more of the don't-move-or-I'll-shoot business, just a steady stream of talk from him, answers from them here and there, names and places, it sounded like, though Buddy didn't speak Spanish, really, other than enough to pay off the cops.

"What are you talking to them about?" Buddy asked, walking back to grab another bale.

"Collecting some intelligence," Felix said.

"Playing Coast Guard?" Buddy asked.

"Getting our stories straight."

"Stories?"

"Drugs seized by Feds, they manage to escape, you know the drill."

"So they don't get murdered," Buddy said.

Felix looked at him straight on, his cap perched ludicrously on his head. "So we don't, fuckhead. *El capo* doesn't chase down weed seized by Uncle Sam. Privateers, on the other hand..."

"Jesus," Buddy said.

"Keep loading."

Buddy did as he was told. His back ached, his shoulders pinched, and despite the cool air, he broke into a sweat. He wished Felix would turn off the fucking light show; it was giving him trailers. Focus, he thought. Keep your eye on the prize. This would all be done in a matter of fifteen minutes. And thanks to Felix's foresight, nobody would come after them.

He thought about Jenny not having to bartend, not having to live with her parents, maybe she'd take him back, they could take a trip, a surf trip, warm water somewhere...

He heard a strange animal noise and realized one of the smugglers, the big bald one, was weeping. The kid picked up on this, and Buddy heard the words *nosotros* and *muertos,* then Felix again, with his Spanish, in the tone of reassurance Buddy knew so well.

"What's happening?" Buddy asked.

"Nothing," Felix said.

"Did he say something about them being dead?"

"Don't worry about it," Felix said. But Buddy could hear something slipping in his voice. "Just get it loaded."

Buddy was more than halfway done, clunking his way back and forth, his stomping around the only noise besides water lapping at the boats' hulls and the big smuggler's weeping. Then Buddy thought he heard the kid mumbling. Was he telling the big guy to keep quiet? Was he talking to himself?

He looked to Felix, who only nodded his chin at the weed still to be loaded.

After Buddy had loaded the last bale of weed onto the *Sea-Tacean*, he came around the cabin to a sight as unexpected as it was unwelcome. Somehow the fucking kid was standing there, Felix's gun in hand. Felix lay on the deck, facedown.

"Do as he says," Felix said.

No shit.

The kid said something in Spanish. Felix told Buddy that the kid wanted him to get down on the ground, too, hands behind his back.

Buddy did as he was told.

"How the fuck—"

Felix shushed him.

Buddy hadn't heard a thing. What kind of ninja skills did this kid have? Buddy should have known, from the way he looked into the spotlights—the kid had ice in his veins. All it took was for Felix to get distracted for two seconds, no doubt already spending his two million in his head...

Now the kid was yelling at the other smugglers. Buddy could only make out a few words, *la Guardia Costera* and *Playa Popotla* among them. Was he telling them to return with the same story Felix had told them? What was this kid's plan?

He might have been fast, but he wasn't that big. If

they could coordinate, Buddy thought, he and Felix could manage to get the jump on him.

The smugglers were standing now, listening to the kid, who kept his gun trained on Buddy and Felix. The big one kept blubbering.

"What's he saying?" Buddy whispered.

"If he goes back to Popotla," Felix translated, "they're going to kill him no matter what his story is."

Pop! For an instant Buddy thought he was shot. But it was the bald smuggler who went down. The kid had the gun back on Felix and Buddy in the blink of an eye. The other smuggler, the one in the Dodgers cap, dropped to tend to the big guy, but it was too late. He looked up at the kid, started the panga, unlashed it from the big boat, and gunned it, top speed, into the fog. The kid watched until it was long gone.

"You think that shit's gonna work?" the kid asked in English.

Who was he asking? Felix didn't say anything, and neither did Buddy.

"I shoulda capped both of 'em. Hanging it on the Coast Guard is corny as fuck."

Buddy and Felix remained silent. What did he expect them to say?

"I got another idea," he said. "You, up."

Buddy looked at Felix, who looked at the kid.

"The one who was moving bales."

Buddy stood. The kid's gun was pointed right at him. Felix was at the kid's feet. If he just timed it right... But how to signal to him?

"This your boat?"

Buddy nodded.

"I don't like that Coast Guard story, you hear me?"

"Okay," Buddy said.

The kid had the gun trained on Buddy's head, his finger on the trigger.

"I like a story where you rob a panga and then beach this floating piece of shit and get away. I like a story where everyone is looking for you. Thing is, *amigo*, they'll never find you, because—"

The kid was about to shoot—Buddy had never been more certain of anything in his life. He couldn't stand there and die. He leapt sideways over the gunwale, yelling, "Grab his feet!" to Felix just before hitting the frigid water, so cold it took his breath away.

He stayed under as long as he could stand it. Had to give Felix a chance. The air above was all lit up still with the spotlights and spinning lights and that nonsense. To take a breath would be to risk getting shot, but maybe Felix had taken the kid down already. Protected under the ocean's mirrored surface, Buddy prayed the kid didn't have a bead on him, and came up for a quick breath.

Pop! Pop!

Dammit. Dammit. Dammit. He'd have to swim toward the boat. If he could get under it and come up on the other side, maybe he'd have a chance. One of the spotlights was beaming all over the place now. Buddy got right up against the hull, came up for a quick breath, and swam under, feeling the barnacled belly of his father's old boat the whole way across. He came up against the hull, portside this time, no spotlights, and breathed deeply.

He had a moment to gather his thoughts. *Felix.* Where the fuck was Felix? If only he'd been able to cue him ahead of time, he could have taken the kid down. Felix would be pulling Buddy aboard right now, the kid dispatched with, everything fucked up but on balance hunky-dory.

After a minute, the kid yelled, "Come up, fool, take a breath."

He was still on the other side of the boat, swinging gun and spotlight around.

"Where the fuck are you, *pendejo*?" the kid mumbled.

Buddy listened carefully. At some point the kid would get wise, come around the other side. But what about Felix? He still had time to make a move. If he was still alive, that was.

Suddenly all the lights went out. Everything was black.

Buddy kept his hand against the *Sea-Tacean*, listening.

All he could hear was water lapping against the hull. Ghostship vibes.

Nothing, for what seemed like an eternity.

Then Felix's voice: "Fuck it, let's go."

The running lights came on, illuminating the fog again. The boat started with a rumble. Then it was underway. Any thought of hanging on was quashed by the sight of the kid's silhouette at the stern, gun in hand, scanning the water.

Buddy went under and stayed under as long as he could. Felix's words echoed in his mind. *Fuck it, let's* go. Had he imagined them? Had he maybe heard the kid and thought it was Felix? But who would have been piloting the boat? By the time he surfaced, gasping for air, the boat, his father's boat, was already only an outline in the glow of running lights receding into the fog.

Felix had sold him out. From the start. *What would you do if two million bucks fell in your lap?* As if Buddy had been a panga guy, *plato o plomo*, or, in this case, *plato y plomo*. No wonder Buddy had felt bad for the scared-shitless smugglers, the men who'd rather be fishing and drinking cervezas —he was one of them, he wanted the same for himself, if only he'd been able to see...

Too late now. As long as Felix and the kid were smart about where they converted all that weight to cash, everything would go down just as the kid said it would, a robbed panga, an abandoned *Sea-Tacean*, and everyone from the cops to the narcos looking for prime suspect number one, a burned-out ex-pro surfer who made the score of a lifetime and disappeared...

To be enshrined as a folk hero for the two-bit dealers, Isla Vista stoners, Oxnard locs...shrouded in speculation about new names, offshore accounts, countries with no extradition treaties...then, eventually, obscured, his legacy gone the way of his body, sapped of heat and energy, swallowed into the pitch-black immensity of the cold Pacific...

But what was this? His father, sunglassed and up to his chest in crystal blue water, warm water, and Buddy on his hands and knees on a board the size of a dinner table, and his father saying, *Ready, Buddy, hold on...* and the white water coming for them, not big enough even to get Dad's hair wet, and the push, first, from Dad's hand, timing it a little early, then a wobble as the board left Dad's fingertips, then the white water propelling him forward, and *Stand up, Buddy, stand up...* as he rose to his feet and realized where he was and what he was doing, threw his hands up in the air, his first claim, lost his balance and went over the side, his first wipeout, into the water, plunging under the surface, making no move to surface, understanding instantly that from that point on, nothing else would matter like this...taking it in, that feeling, that understanding, and then his father's hand, lifting him...

Antoine Wilson is the author of the novels *Mouth to Mouth, Panorama City*, and *The Interloper.* He is contributing editor of the literary journal *A Public Space* and lives in Los Angeles with his family.

OFF THE 405

By Naomi Hirahara

"Ah, there it is." From their Oldsmobile Cutlass, Noriko Shimizu pointed to the familiar, tattered, red flag next to Lifeguard Station Number Six at Huntington Beach.

Every late summer the Shimizus, the Hoshidas and the Babamotos took their annual beach trip to Orange County. They all lived in San Gabriel Valley, a landlocked disk of land that held the smog against the low, purple range of Southern California mountains.

The Babamotos, who had the largest brood at four children, were responsible for snagging the best location on Huntington Beach, which was one of the few with fire pits. The family came early, before noon, even, to unload their beach chairs, umbrellas, bags of charcoal briquettes, and coolers filled with Coors, Cactus Cooler, and 7UP. The oldest children would then display a red flag as a sign of where the other families should park and meet.

Noriko's husband, Fumio, a cigarette hanging from his mouth, grunted. This had been the most noise that he had made during their drive from Monterey Park from the 10 to the 710 to the 5 to the 405. He never had been that talkative, but lately his conversation had decreased to a mere dribble.

Their daughter, Judy, sitting in the back of the Cutlass,

had been quiet as well, her nose in a book. Her weekday routine after coming home from high school was to escape to her room and close the door firmly behind her. What did American fifteen-year-old girls do alone in their bedrooms? At that age Noriko had no bedroom of her own, not to mention no privacy. She spent many afternoons of her World War II years in Tokyo hiding in bomb shelters, her neighbor's breath hot against her neck and somebody's knees touching hers.

Since she wasn't needed at home these days, Noriko had decided that she wanted to learn how to drive. Fumio took her out a few times, but their last session was a disaster. She had made a right turn on a red without checking whether an oncoming vehicle would be making a left onto the same lane. It turned out that one was, nearly causing a collision. The driver in the other car had blared his horn while Fumio screamed at her, saying that she had no sense. When they returned back to the house, Noriko wondered if he was only referring to driving or perhaps to life itself.

Finding an open parking space between a Wagoneer and VW Bug, Fumio parked, and the three Shimizus piled out of the Oldsmobile. The sun was already intense, and Noriko patted down her straw hat that she had purchased from Thrifty's. She retrieved a box of inari-zushi, vinegared rice packed in light brown, fried tofu pockets, from the back seat while Judy hugged her striped beach towel close to her chest.

Fumio pulled on a pair of sunglasses to shield his trademark hooded eyes. Those reptilian eyes made him look interminably sleepy. His hair was becoming thin, but the strands remained jet black. He wore a cotton shirt, his swim trunks, and zori, the ubiquitous rubber kind with uncomfortable toe straps that were held to its base by circular knobs.

They walked past white families with their intense smell of either Coppertone or coconut-infused Bain de Soleil. The older ones rested underneath umbrellas while the younger ones and the ones who wanted to be younger baked themselves in the direct blaze of the sun.

The Shimizus entered into their spot, which was configured in the same way as previous summers. The cooler was positioned closer to the parking lot, while a metal, collapsible table held hot dog buns, large ketchup and mustard bottles, and potato chips. A watermelon floated in a tub of water from a melting block of ice. The fire pit had not yet been lit yet. They would wait until everyone's arrival.

"Hello, hello," Shoko Babamoto greeted the Shimizus with flapping hands. Even at the beach, she wore her frizzy hair pinned in a bun. She wore no hat; her skin was dark, but not as dark as the men's. A spray of freckles dotted her nose and upper cheeks.

"You made it." Shoko's husband had a gravelly voice that reminded Noriko of yakuzas depicted in Japanese movies. He had a large gap in between his front teeth, perfect for him to hold his filtered Tareyton cigarette.

Noriko placed her department store box of homemade inari-zushi on the table next to the hot dog buns. She found it easy to be with the Babamotos. The couple had given into the chaos created by their four children, especially the three boys. Practically nothing bothered them. Their laissez-faire approach to child-raising inspired Noriko, who was more burdened by the minutiae of daily human interaction. Even now she watched as her daughter shyly approached the Babamoto girl. They were about the same age but went to different schools and only saw each other during these annual gatherings at the beach. Soon they were headed to an unoccupied spot to start building their giant sandcastle.

The Hoshidas arrived late, as they always did. They had no children and came in an old truck camper. The husband liked surf fishing and had retrieved a fishing rod and white pail which once held five gallons of soy sauce from the back cab. The wife, Ginger, followed, a visor shading her angled cheekbones. There was a sharpness to Ginger, in both her appearance and personality. Her tongue could be sharp, sometimes cutting Noriko's confidence to shreds. Ginger was a Kibei Nisei, like the men, born in America and raised in Japan, while Noriko and Shoko were full-fledged immigrants who couldn't speak English well.

Judy and the Babamoto girl had returned to their beach

site to grab 7UPs from the cooler.

"Hello, Auntie Ginger," Judy said, her towel tied around her waist. She wore a pink bikini tube top that had skinny straps that went from the center and tied around her neck.

"Oh, Judy, what a cute bathing suit." Only for Ginger, Judy untied her towel and revealed her bottoms too. Oh, how many hours did Noriko spend in the department store waiting for Judy to make her decision of what suit to wear. And by the time she decided, she had refused to let Noriko even see it on her.

Ginger continued to chat so easily with Judy that Noriko couldn't help feeling jealous. Ginger was a secretary at a high school and was used to being around teenagers on a regular basis.

After the girls had left and the three women settled back in striped lawn chairs, Noriko announced, "I'm learning how to drive."

"Why now?" Ginger asked, pulling down the lip of her visor. "You could have helped Fumio sooner if you knew how to drive."

Ginger's words stung. She was right. Why had Noriko waited this long?

"It's fine." Shoko patted Noriko's exposed lower arm. "You're doing it now. Maybe you can even work. Judy will be off to college soon."

Noriko nodded, but not in agreement. Work meant only one thing—housework like what Shoko did or maybe working in a Japanese market. Because what could a woman who could only speak Japanese do in America?

The men sat closer to the surf so that Ginger's husband could easily cast his line into the waves and wait for perch to tug at the cut-up sand crab that he had attached to the hook. Their shirts were now off, and they all sported striking, almost comical farmer's tans; their faces, necks, and lower arms the color of almost-burnt toast. In their low-slung swim trunks, their lean, sinewy muscles developed from cutting lawns in a hundred-degree weather, sometimes six days a week, were in full display.

Noriko secured the hanging string of her hat underneath her chin and walked to the shore.

The girls were forming a house with the wet sand while the Babamoto boys were deep in the surf on worn Styrofoam boards or bodysurfing. Soon Mr. Babamoto ran and dove into the sea with his sons. The yelps of children in the water punctuated the roar of the waves. Everyone seemed to have a place on this beach. Everyone except her.

When Noriko looked back at where the men had been sitting, she saw that her husband was gone. And then to Shoko—she was pulling out a watermelon that had been soaking in a metal tub.

Noriko trudged back to their site, sand gripping hold of her wet feet.

"Where is Ginger?" she asked.

"Bathroom. That time of the month. Rotten luck, huh?" Shoko said, cracking open the oblong watermelon with a knife from Japan.

Noriko nodded for no specific reason. More out of habit. Sometimes she nodded to indicate that she had heard what a friend was saying. But sometimes it was like breathing. She was unaware that she was doing it.

She drifted in and out of conversation with Shoko, thinking about the pointlessness of her life. Judy would be off to college someday soon. Noriko hoped that she would first attend East Los Angeles College and commute from home. But lately Judy exhibited the same restlessness as her mother. Actually, all three Shimizus seemed to be drifting away from each other like unconnected buoys floating in the water.

Noriko rose and helped Shoko salt the slices of watermelon and place them on paper plates.

It had been a good watermelon with firm flesh and a brilliant red color. Shoko had chosen well.

Shoko poured the charcoal briquettes into the pit and doused the pile with lighter fluid. Noriko began to open the packages of hot dogs. She couldn't help but to wonder what was taking Ginger such a long time to change her tampon. But perhaps she had soiled herself. Noriko took a deep breath. That was it. A flood of empathy washed over her. How could she be so suspicious of her friend? They had known each other ever since Shoko had introduced them about twelve years ago.

"I have to go to the bathroom. I'll be right back," she called out as Shoko pushed a lit wad of newspaper into the pile of briquettes.

Even though Noriko was wearing closed-toe tennis shoes, she gingerly entered the dimly lit beach bathroom. It was plain concrete with disgusting, slippery floors.

No one was in line, and she quickly bent down to check the occupied stalls. No red-painted toes in white sandals. No sign of Ginger.

Maybe she had gone to the camper to deal with her woman problem. Or maybe she went to take a quick nap in the narrow bed above the cab. It was a tiny space that only someone around five feet could sleep in. And even then, you needed to scrunch up your legs to your chest.

Noriko quickly urinated, making sure that her bare buttocks did not touch the filthy toilet seat. She had even placed the paper on the seat even though she wasn't going to sit on it. Just like her constant nodding, it was a habit with no reason.

There was no soap to wash her hands, so she dampened her fingers with a weak stream of lukewarm water from the faucet. While doing so, she gazed at her smear of a face in the metal panel across from her where a mirror would have been in any other bathroom.

Released from the concrete restroom building, Noriko absorbed the expanse, now crowded with even more people. She decided to walk by the camper, just to check if Ginger may need her assistance. Her arm brushed against some car side windows as she walked in between some parked cars before the camper was in view, parked in a far row. It was a Ford camper truck, a mint-green body with a white top.

A set of keys hung from the back door of the camper. Ginger had multiple keys hanging from a chain, as if they were medals of her work at a high school. *Oh, you silly*, Noriko thought. *You need to be careful, Ginger. Any stranger can come and steal your keys*. But then she looked down and saw them.

Fumio's slippers. Thin, white top with a blue bottom. She knew that they were his because his big toes were freakishly large and quite distant from the rest of his toes. They left deep, distinctive impressions on his slippers.

While Noriko was absorbing Fumio's slippers tossed next to Ginger's white sandals outside, she heard noises coming from the camper. She pressed her ear against the door. She recognized the grunts. The camper, in fact, was even starting to rise up and down. She should just open the door and confront them. She imagined Ginger's pert breast smashed into Fumio's face, his eyes wide open, which was the case only right before he climaxed.

Noriko started turning the knob. But no, she couldn't bear it. And what could she say?

Those two had enough verbal skills to turn the situation back on her and make her feel guilty. Somehow she would be the culprit, the guilty one who allowed all this to happen. And what if she and Fumio did get divorced, which she sometimes secretly feared? What would happen to her? Her family in Japan wouldn't take her in. And Judy. Judy would probably blame her too.

She carefully removed the heavy set of keys from the knob and then opened the driver's side door. She eased herself up to the seat. There was a pillow on the passenger side, and Noriko pulled it up behind her back. She leaned to the side to find the ignition and slipped the car key into it.

As she abruptly backed out of the parking lot, the grunting and moans immediately ceased. In its place, "Hey, what's going on?" It was Ginger's perfectly enunciated English.

"What the fuck—"

The camper shook as bodies jumped from the sleeping nook. There was a narrow window from the camper to the driver's seat. The plastic pane slid open. "Noriko, stop!"

She sped out of the lot.

As she made a hairpin turn onto a main boulevard, bodies toppled down. It took a while before Fumio's face appeared back in the window.

"Wrong way!" he yelled. "Wrong way!"

Noriko wasn't stupid. She saw it. The sign, DO NOT ENTER. But it only gave her more courage to put her foot all the way on the gas pedal, jump the curb, and speed onto the off-ramp to the 405.

Naomi Hirahara is an Edgar Award-winning author of multiple traditional mystery series and noir short stories. Her Mas Arai mysteries, which have been published in Japanese, Korean and French, feature a Los Angeles gardener and Hiroshima survivor who solves crimes. Her first historical mystery is *Clark and Division*, which follows a Japanese American family's move to Chicago in 1944 after being released from a California wartime detention center. Her second Leilani Santiago Hawai'i mystery, *An Eternal Lei*, is scheduled to be released in 2022.

SUMMER OF '86

By Tod Goldberg

This all happened in the 1980s, back when it made financial sense to rob a bank, but long after I knew there was no getting away with it.

I'd been out for about six weeks, sleeping in my childhood bedroom in Walnut Creek, trying to figure out what the next fifty years of my life might look like with a felony conviction and penitentiary time on my record, when my twin sister, Sarah, called. At the time, she was living with a guy calling himself Hank Niculescu, who operated a bike rental and repair shop right on the beach in Pajaro, which was convenient for everyone involved until Hank disappeared.

"Come down for a couple weeks," Sarah said, "and I'll pay you to watch the bike shop. Then when Hank gets back, you can either stay or go or heist a casino, whatever your next move is."

"I don't know anything about bikes," I said.

"You think Hank does? He's got a guy who fixes them. You just need to be out front, smiling, and collecting money. It's not orthopedic surgery, Mitch."

"So then why do you need me?"

"I just thought you'd be about sick of Mom by now," she said.

I looked out the kitchen window. Mom was in the

front yard, planting azaleas around the birch tree. They'd be dead by June. July at the latest. Nothing she ever planted around that tree ever lived. But she kept trying, year after year. It kept her busy. She'd had her own troubles over the years, so keeping busy was paramount. Mom spent twenty years as a public defender, but she lost her license after she got nicked for running a Ponzi scheme with the ladies who lunch—which was fine. She made better money working more as an "advisor" than as a lawyer. I found her a steady clientele.

"We've been going to a different restaurant every night," I said, "getting to know each other again. She's developed a special predilection for steak houses that used to be train cars."

"What a dream," Sarah said, "you're dating Mom."

"Any idea where Hank ran off to?"

"Somewhere he didn't have any enemies would be my guess."

"You seem all torn up."

"Every day he's gone," she said, "I hate myself a little less."

Sarah sold real estate for an operation that built condos in Pajaro Dunes, which meant she got in on the ground floor and had a sweet three bedroom on Pelican Point, looking right into Monterey Bay. Pajaro was nice, but it wasn't Santa Cruz or Capitola, at least not yet, so Sarah had a side thing going buying depressed properties, which is how she got to know Hank, since she also owned the beachfront stand and repair shop Hank worked out of, which is why she needed me. If she wanted to keep collecting rent, what with summer coming, Hank being gone was not optimal for business. She didn't feel right trying to hire someone for her boyfriend's business, but I was family.

In the morning, I'd wake up, go for a jog on the beach, take a swim, and then make my way to the shop, all before 8:30 a.m. Hank's guy, Porter, would be there around 9:00 a.m., usually with coffee for both of us, and we'd open up. Porter would tune up the rental bikes, get them all lined up out front in a precise rainbow—if you fucked with the indigo bike and put it on the wrong side of violet, you were risking your life—and then would spend the rest of the day out back, working on bikes the locals brought in for repairs in his immaculate shop, which was basically a garage attached to the stand. The stand had been a hundred different things over the years—a sno-cone shop, a floatie rental, a time-share info booth—but after Sarah bought it, she fixed up the garage, and now it was all real nice. I ran the cash register, read the *Chronicle* or whatever paperback I found on the beach, and tried to be pleasant to the tourists.

Which is how it was one afternoon, a few months into my stay, when I was at the counter, reading *The Thorn Birds*, and a detective named Garrison walked up, introduced himself, then asked, "That a good book?"

"I didn't know there were so many sheep in Australia," I said.

Detective Garrison looked past me, into the shop, where Porter was working on a beach cruiser, caught his eye, then came back to me. "My wife read it when it came out," he said, "then read it again when the miniseries came on. I've never done that before. Read a book twice. You?"

"In prison, I read everything twice. It was either that or start in on the dictionary."

"What were you in for?"

"Bank robbery," I said. "But you know that."

Garrison smiled. "How much you make off with again?"

"I did all right."

"That's not what I asked," Garrison said.

"But that's what I'm telling you."

Garrison took a notepad from his pocket, flipped through it. "So you're the girlfriend's twin brother, that right? Mitch Lenney, three-to-seven, out in under four?"

"Yep," I said.

"Lucky you," he said, "have your sister's boyfriend go missing, and you slide right into a nice job with an ocean view."

"It's always been like that for me," I said. "Everything lines up just right for my success."

"Your sister," he said, "owns this building, but she's not legally responsible for this shop. She and Hank, they're not married."

"You also the bike shop police?"

"My point," he said, "is that Hank comes back and thinks the till is short, you're looking at another fall, your sister isn't."

"I'm not worried about that," I said. "The criminal life is not something that interests me. I'm about staring at the Pacific and reading fine literature now."

"Hank's ex-wife and kids are looking for him. Or for his child support and alimony, anyway. You could see if they want to take over."

"How much does he owe?"

"About a grand a month for three months," Garrison said, "and then a grand a month for another fifteen years."

I opened the cash register, counted out what we had. I pushed the stack of cash toward Garrison. "That's about five bills," I said. "I'll get more tomorrow, if you want to come back."

He pushed the stack back. "I'm not your bagman," Garrison said.

"It's for the kids," I said. Thing is, I meant it. The idea that Hank had stiffed his kids was not some shit I was into. Not that Sarah had ever mentioned Hank having kids either. Which was a problem.

Garrison scribbled something in his notepad, ripped the page out, handed it to me. "Write a check," he said, "mail it to that address." I said I would. "Weird thing," he said, "wasn't even the ex or the kids who reported Hank missing initially."

"Divorce can be like that," I said.

"Wasn't your sister either," he said.

"If you love someone, set them free," I said. "That's what we were taught as children. But if you see our dad, tell him Mom would like the station wagon back."

"When did you meet Hank?" Garrison said.

"Never did," I said.

"Last anyone saw him," Garrison said, "was the end of January. The twenty-seventh he wrote a check for a gallon of Pedialyte at the Alpha Beta. Where were you then?"

"I was living up the coast with a Nazi named Mark Tucker," I said. "We had a little place together in a housing development called Bastille by the Bay."

"Everything is a joke to you?"

"No," I said. "I'm just over here trying to sort out my life. And interacting with cops is not high on my list of things to do. It's not personal."

"That's good," Garrison said. "I don't know how I'd sleep if I thought it was about me."   This made me laugh. I kind of liked that fake-ass, tough-guy cop humor, perhaps because I knew a fair number of cops. You grow up in the suburbs, you end up growing up with a bunch of guys named Travis or Trevor or Trent who wind up wearing the badge.

"You should get out of town," Garrison said. "This is not a good place for you."

"Yeah? Where to?"

"Somewhere your sister and your mom aren't," he said.

"You've done some research."

"Your whole family," he said, "is suspicious. This is your one best shot with me."

We stared at each other for a long moment, until I said, "We could just start pissing."

"I wouldn't go whipping anything out, if I were you," Garrison said. "That's how a guy like you ends up with one in the chest."

Porter came up to the counter, shook Garrison's hand. "Any luck finding Hank?" Porter asked.

"None yet."

"You will keep looking?"

"No law against an adult leaving town."

"I am suspicion," Porter said.

Porter had an accent that was hard to place. Vaguely Eastern European, the English language hung in his mouth in unusual ways, so that you couldn't tell if he'd lived here twenty years or fifteen minutes. I couldn't tell if it was real or a bit.

"Hank's been leaving town in the middle of the night most of his life. If he'd bothered to keep up with his child support, I doubt I'd even be involved."

"I only know him as my boss and friendship," Porter said.

"Something breaks, I'll let you know," Garrison said.

Porter thanked Garrison, then went back to his bikes.

"Piece of advice, Mr. Bank Robber?" Garrison said. "Keep good ledgers, hate for you to have to move back in with your Nazi buddy." He picked up *The Thorn Birds*, flipped to page 406. "This is where it heats up."

"Couldn't have them thinking I had anything to do with it," Porter said. It was after seven, and we were eating broiled steaks at the Del Monte Café, waiting on Sarah. She was already twenty minutes late. "So I place the missing call. Me and Hank, we've been friends a long juncture." Porter paused. "Well. Not friends. I mean. We have been knowing each other a long time. It would make sense I was concern."

"Where'd you meet?"

"You see these warehouses? My family? We owned half of them. Croatians made this area." The Del Monte was on Walker Street in Watsonville—Porter lived in an apartment just above it—across the street from blocks of vacant produce packing plants. If you could get a time machine and roll back to the early 1900s, when the Del Monte opened, the streets would be packed with workers coming off their shifts, gaslights illuminating the freshly lain Southern Pacific tracks. Now, the sun had been down for thirty minutes, and the Del Monte was the only building still lit on the block, the cooks and servers the only humans moving for miles. "We owned all the fruit packing. Then Smucker's and Nestlé, those cocksuckers, they start undercutting us, then the farms, they become corporate, then the railroads pave over their spurs and move their lines."

"Things change," I said.

"Thank you for your understanding cliché," he said. Porter was a little drunk, so I didn't reach across the table and smack him. Also, he had a good six inches and a hundred pounds on me and looked like the kind of guy who got into fights for fun, not anger, which was, frankly, the last kind of guy you wanted to fuck around with. I was also in a place in my life where I was avoiding violence as a rule. It wouldn't last. "I tell you this not from some desire that you should know my woes. You ask me where I met Hank. I'm telling you. I fell into a depression, which led to habits." He cut the rim of fat from the remnants of his steak, dropped it into the empty husk of his baked potato, poured a couple shakes of A.1. into the potato skin, too, then picked it all up and ate it like a taco.

"If you're still hungry," I said, "order some dessert."

"I'm not hungry," he said. "I eat when I am anxiety." He finished chewing. "I grow drugs."

"What kind?" I said.

"Marijuana," he said, like he was talking about apples. "But lately? I am growing poppies very successfully, learning how to extract opium and making heroin, much trial and error, but much success."

"Out in the open?"

"I look like a fool?" Porter asked. He tapped the window again. "Produce warehouses have strong ventilation and plumbing and no windows. And if there is problem? State flower of California is the poppy. Easy to explain." Porter leaned across the table. "Even the failure has been successful enough to be lucrative for people who are addicted, though admission is that there have been some bumps in the streets. When Hank was disappearing, I had the sense that heat would be turned on me at some point, so I say, well, get ahead of this problem before they begin to look at me. And so, I made that call. I am not sorry."

"Did you wait until the bank robber took over the bike shop, or did you alert the authorities right away?"

Porter said, "I may have taken the liberty of time to make my decision."

Fucking hell.

"I met Hank in rehab. I was his sponsorship."

"Guess that didn't take," I said.

"I have not touched drugs in ten years," Porter said.

"You're drunk," I said, "and you're cultivating illegal substances."

"Different commitments," he said.

"I don't think that's how it works," I said.

"And yet you are the person who goes to prison, and I am freedom."

Sarah slid in beside me. The waitress came over, and Sarah ordered a steak and a Tom Collins, and then I asked for another steak, for our pal Porter, since he was eyeing my gristle. When the waitress left, Sarah said, "Porter tell you about his warehouse of shitty heroin yet?"

"Yeah, he mentioned it."

"Great," Sarah said. "Did he tell you how it killed Hank yet?"

"No," I said, "he left that part out."

Porter shuffled in his seat. "We are telling your brother our secrets? There is no approval process?"

"Sarah," I said, "what have you done?"

"I fucked up," she said, and then pointed at Porter, "by helping *that* fuckup."

I should have left right then. Garrison was right.

Later that night, Sarah was busy working on some contracts, so I sat outside on her little patio, smoked a cigar, ate from a bag of marshmallows, listened to a couple have sex on the beach, and thought about what Porter and Sarah ended up telling me: Hank was Porter's main heroin and opium focus group, which worked fine until he OD'd after Porter shot him up with his latest batch. He couldn't exactly call 911, so he called Sarah instead, and the two of them decided the best course of action, which was to get rid of Hank's body and then pretend he ran off. Sarah thought she'd report him missing after I got into town, her thinking being if the cops did come to look into things, they'd find me, get suspicious, find out I had an ironclad alibi, and that would be that.

That my sister had planned to use me as a red herring didn't make me happy, but truth was? I admired the hustle. But then Porter beat her to the punch. Which made her look suspicious to the cops, particularly since she had no idea Hank had an ex-wife and children.

Which I did not admire.

Around midnight, Sarah opened the slider and came out, a drink in her hand, just in time to catch the couple from the beach walking back to their car. They waved at me as they went by.

"Friends of yours?" Sarah asked.

"I think I just heard them planting their family tree."

"Do you remember back when there were, like, six serial killers working out here?"

"Of course," I said. This had been in the late '60s and early '70s, when we were just kids, and Mom still had the beach house in Capitola. "Why?"

"Those two would have been on the news in the morning," she said, "missing their heads or something. Mom thought maybe that's what became of Dad."

"That he got killed?"

"No, that he was one of those maniacs running around hacking people to death. Ed Kemper or something."

"He'd have been caught by now."

"Yeah," Sarah said. "But I do wonder where he is, if he thinks about us, all that shit." We'd had this conversation a thousand times, so I stayed quiet, particularly in light of the night's news. Plus, she knew my opinion: if Dad wanted to be in our lives, he would be. Also? I thought maybe Mom had buried him under the birch tree. "And hence, all of my romantic notions explained." She raised her glass out toward the ocean in a toast. "To Hank, the love of my life."

"How did you not know he had an ex-wife and kids?"

"He never mentioned them," she said.

"You never did that thing where you go over all your old, significant relationships?"

"Hank didn't like to hear about my past," Sarah said, "so I kept out of his."

"Why don't you just tell the police what happened and let Porter deal with his own shit?"

"I could." Sarah nodded. "I could. And I thought of

that."

"But?"

"I helped him get rid of the body, so that's a problem."

"Porter wouldn't dime you on that," I said. Well, he might. But I knew enough guys inside that I'd solve that problem, quick, before any trial.

"The other complication is that we own the warehouses."

"You and Porter?"

"No," Sarah said.

"You and Hank?"

"No," Sarah said. "We. You and me."

"Jesus fuck, Sarah," I said. "I own the warehouses?"

"You told me to get rid of the money. I got rid of the money."

"I didn't mean," I said, "enter into a criminal conspiracy with the money, Sarah."

She waved me off. "They were basically abandoned, so our LLC grabbed them up for next to nothing," she said. "End of summer, we'll own them outright. Porter's been a very good tenant. It's not a crime to rent a warehouse to someone who then uses them for criminal behavior."

"Unless," I said, "you abet the criminal behavior."

"They could put me on the rack, and I'd never admit to knowing," she said.

"You think Porter feels the same way?"

"I could make him feel the same way," she said.

"That would be a great way to show the cops you're in mourning."

I offered her the bag of marshmallows. She reached in, took out three, popped them in her mouth one after the other.

"Do we have any graham crackers?" she asked.

"I'll look," I said. I went inside and started opening cabinets, finally locating a box of Golden Grahams on the top shelf of the pantry, standing upright on a yellow lazy Susan. When I took them down, I found what Sarah surely wanted me to find: a loaded .357. I brought both back out to the patio, set them down on the little beveled glass table. "Here you go."

Sarah glanced at the gun, then opened up the box of crackers, took out two, grabbed up another handful of marshmallows, put them all in her mouth at once.

"You ever shot a gun before?" I asked.

"Not at a person," she said once she'd swallowed down her concoction.

"Keep it that way," I said.

"It's Hank's," she said. I looked it over. It still had the serial number on it. Which was a surprise. "He told me if anything happened to him, to get rid of it."

"And yet here it is."

"I don't think he meant if, like, Porter and I got rid of his body after he OD'd on Porter's skunk scag."

"You need to tell me now if Hank's the East Area Rapist or something."

"No," she said. "Of course not. He'd never hurt a woman."

"Just the other half of humanity?"

"He's an honest man now," she said. "I mean, before he died, he was beginning to be more honest."

"This is not good," I said.

"Little brother," Sarah said, "I cannot lie to you."

"Except for all the times you have."

"Cannot does not mean will not," Sarah said. "Benefit of being in the world four minutes longer than you. Earned wisdom." She finished her drink, then threw her tumbler toward the crashing waves, the glass landing with a thunk about fifteen yards away. "In my mind, that was going to be more dramatic." She squeezed beside me on the chaise lounge, put her head on my shoulder—it was how we looked in Mom's first sonogram—and tried to cry. "I don't miss Hank," Sarah said. "He was an ass, okay? Hank was an ass. But he loved me, and I miss having someone who loves me. Is that pathetic, Mitch?"

"Yes," I said.

"Well, it's true." Sarah sniffled. "How come you didn't ask where we put Hank's body?"

"Because if I know," I said, "I'm liable to tell the police

ten, fifteen years from now when I get wrapped up in some new, worse fuckup and need a way out. You don't want that." Sarah agreed, she did not want that. "And this way, I won't fail a polygraph either."

"If what Garrison told you is true," Sarah said, "all Hank's ex and kids need is some money? And then it's no problem anymore."

"Hank owes a grand a month for another fifteen years," I said. "You have that kinda cash?"

"Not on hand, no," Sarah said. "Could you get your hands on that much money?"

"I'd be shoulder deep in dye packs," I said, "plus, I'm not robbing a bank to keep Porter out of prison." Still, I couldn't have those kids on my conscience. I wedged myself out of the chaise lounge, tucked the gun in my waistband, and hopped over the low patio wall and headed toward the water.

"Where are you going?"

"To think about how I can get you out of this dumb shit you're in," I said, "and how to make sure those kids of Hank's aren't irrevocably fucked up. So please, don't fire or fuck Porter before I get back."

Hank's ex, Mary, lived in a bungalow across the street from the Saltwater Sands Hotel in Aptos, along with her two kids, a daughter named Kyle and a son named Hank Jr., who went by Deuce, because that's the kind of people they were. She worked for the hotel, painting portraits and landscapes for tourists, so when I stopped by with a check, the babysitter told me where I could find her.

Mary was stationed on a bluff above the beach, with a perfect view of the Cement Ship—the wreck of the SS *Palo Alto*—which hadn't moved in about sixty years and was now more art installation than maritime accident. She had a corona of six easels before her, each with an unfinished portrait on the canvas. The weird thing was that the background for each was already done—the Cement Ship at the golden hour —with a hole in the middle, where the finished human would go. She moved from canvas to canvas, filling in details: a nose here, an eye there, a wisp of hair. Back and forth. Not exactly da Vinci, but everyone has a process.

"It's not like on TV," she said eventually.

"What do you mean?" I said.

"Not every artist has to be tortured," she said. "Not every painting needs to be an expression of pain and suffering. Sometimes, the beauty is in the work itself, the actual labor. The conveying of the person."

"How do you remember what they looked like?"

"I can close my eyes and see them as easily as I see you."

"That's quite a skill," I said.

"It pays a third of the rent," she said. She looked at the envelope in my hand. "You here to serve me a summons or something?"

I handed her the envelope. "It's what Hank owes you."

Mary sat down in her paint-stained director's chair, opened the envelope, took the check out, held it up to the sun. "Looks legit," she said. "And who are you?"

"Mitch Lenney. I'm running Hank's bike shop while he's gone," I said. "My sister, Sarah's been involved with him for a while now."

"Your sister couldn't show up herself?"

"Sarah was concerned there might be some animosity," I said. What she'd said, specifically, was she didn't want to end up pulling some bitch's hair over a dead man.

"Sarah Lenney?"

"Yeah."

"She leaves calendars with her face on them in my mailbox all the time," she said.

"Yeah," I said, "she's a real estate agent."

"Is that a good job? Selling things you don't own?"

"She likes it."

"Maybe I'll try that when I've lost all hope," Mary said. "When's Hank coming back?"

"That, I don't know," I said. I explained to her about how Garrison had come to see us, which is when Sarah found out Hank had children to support and an ex-wife who needed her cut, too. Mary listened carefully, then said, "So Hank doesn't know you're paying me?"

"No."

"She seen him?"

"Not in months."

Mary stuffed the check into her bra. "His kids could use a phone call if he happens to pop his head up," she said. "They haven't heard his voice in a long time."

"Since when?"

"Christmas," she said. It was May. "Be an asshole to me, fine. But don't ruin your kids' lives. No matter what stupidity he got up to, he always has sent his money. Even, I guess, once he started shacking up with your sister. No offense intended." She paused. "Well, no. Some offense intended, but it's misdirected, I understand, since it's not like it's her fault Hank neglected to mention his fucking ex-wife and kids."

"My sister thinks maybe he relapsed," I said.

"He would need to be clean to relapse," Mary said. She shook her head. "When he was using at his worst, he still was a pretty good father to Kyle. I mean, as good as he could be. He's never really gotten to know Deuce too well. But still, he's always provided. That's why I feel worried about this."

"Well," I said, "we're keeping the shop open. So, you're taken care of, you can let your attorney know."

"For how long?"

"I guess forever," I said.

This made Mary laugh. "Nothing lasts forever," she said, "and nothing survives the fall and winter on the beach. That's why Hank got into all that other shit."

"What other shit?"

"Oh come on," she said. "He's been in and out of jail half his life." She got up, started back on her canvases. I watched her for a few more minutes as she worked. It was kind of mesmerizing. She stepped back, looked at her work. One of her portraits was of a woman with long, black hair that fell over her shoulders and who looked like the singer Crystal Gayle, if Crystal Gayle had broken her nose and jaw.

"Was that lady in a car accident or something?" I asked.

She pulled Crystal Gayle off the easel. "Guess I'll start that one over." She ripped the canvas into pieces, dumped them in the trash. "It's not just about the money," she said. "His kids hardly remember him at this point."

"How old are they?" I asked.

"Three and five," she said.

My own father was already out of the picture by the time I was six. That turned out great.

"I could call them," I said.

Mary stopped painting. "What?"

"If they don't remember Hank," I said, "what could it hurt?"

"For you to pretend you're their father?"

"I like kids," I said.

"Do you know how deeply fucked up that idea is?"

"I have some sense," I said.

"You don't even know me," she said. "Why would you do this?"

"You seem like you could use a friend."

"I'm not looking to hook up, if that's what you're thinking," she said. "I mean, you're nice and you're handsome, but this is too weird to be functional even for me, okay?"

"Not what I was looking for," I said, though Mary did have her appeal, if you were into women who dressed like Stevie Nicks and sort of looked like her, too. Which I was.

"Do you have a pen?" she asked. I did. She gave me her number. "Call around seven. Just ask them about school or their friends or whatever. Don't mention the cat. I accidentally ran her over, and now I'm trying to find one that looks reasonably similar," Mary said. "My whole life is a wreck."

For the next two months, every other night at seven, I called Deuce and Kyle and shot the shit. I usually called from a payphone in front of the Safeway, or the one inside the Beachcomber, or just from the shop, because Sarah could not bear to hear me pretending to be Hank. Even when Mary wasn't home, Kyle would answer the phone, and we'd just pick up where we left off. Deuce, being three, didn't have much going on, but Kyle was a little chatterbox, and I enjoyed hearing her thoughts on life.

Did I tell them to have sweet dreams and gold stars?

I did.

Did I start to drive by their place at night sometimes, just to make sure everything was safe and sound if I knew Mary was out?

I did.

Did I tell them I loved them?

I did.

It got to be that I stopped worrying anything bad was going to happen with this whole deal. The bike shop was making money, Porter's other business was making money, Sarah was selling condos like mad, June turned to July to August, and the beach was full almost every day, the smell of Pronto Pups and suntan lotion and saltwater breezes, enough to make me think I'd finally figured out how to live with all this shit behind me.

Then Detective Garrison showed up again.

I'd just hung up with Kyle—she'd gone to a birthday party that morning—and little Deuce—he was starting to get into Matchbox cars—and was sitting at the bar at the Beachcomber, having a beer, trying to will the A's not to lose to the Mariners—when Garrison copped the stool beside me, ordered a beer for himself, and quietly watched the game.

"What do you make of Canseco?" I asked. The game was delayed, a summer storm rolling down the coast, lightning sparking just long enough to scatter the players into the dugouts.

"Future of the game," Garrison said. "Power, speed, pretty good arm, big personality. Just what it needs."

"He's got a twin too," I said.

"No shit?" Garrison said. "I'm more of a Giants guy."

"Yeah," I said. "It's funny. He's terrible. Ozzie. Still in A-ball. Can't get out."

"There's something here about nature and nurture," Garrison said, "but I'm not smart enough to figure it out."

The bartender came by and dropped off a bowl of peanuts then, so I ordered a shot of Jack and got one for Garrison, too, since I wasn't sure where this was all going, and ordered a round for the two guys I made as Garrison's backup sitting over by the jukebox.

After we took down our drinks, Garrison said, "Turns out Hank has parents."

"Here I thought he was a test-tube baby," I said.

"Nice people," Garrison said. "Live up in Napa. They were surprised to hear how involved he's been in the kids' lives lately, particularly in light of the missing person's report they put out too. Turns out, they don't know him as Hank Niculescu, because that's not the name they gave him, so they reported him missing as Henry Nichols, which is his actual name. Low priority, fella has a criminal record and five different names, different police departments are actively ignoring the case, so it takes a while for anything to come of it, until Mr. and Mrs. Nichols get the grandkids for July fourth and hear all about dad's exploits working for the FBI."

"You never embellished a story for a kid?"

"Maybe my own," Garrison said.

"These kids," I said, "just need something that makes their dad seem cool."

"And you picked federal law enforcement?"

"Kids don't remember shit. So I said something dumb one time, big deal. And I gotta tell you, Kyle said Grandma called her fat, which ruined the whole holiday."

"Between us," Garrison said, "Grandma is running about a quart low these days. Grandpa, on the other hand, stormed the beach at Normandy and is ready to storm the beach at Pajaro to put one between your eyes."

"Is it against the law to talk to a child on the phone?"

"You're a felon, Mitch," Garrison said, "pretending to be their father."

"Their father is a felon," I said.

He reached into the breast pocket of his jacket, came out with a couple photographs, set them on the bar. "That you parked out front of their house?"

It was. He knew it was. You could see my face pretty easily, since I had a flashlight so I could read, in one photo, *Raise the Titanic*, in the other, *Shogun*. Both were fucking terrible.

"Mary's been spending a lot of nights out," I said. "Someone needs to take some responsibility with these kids. And anyway, what's the crime? I'm not getting any benefit from it. I'm just helping Mary out. She agreed to it. Practically suggested it."

"That's the thing," Garrison said. "I had to ask that same question. What benefit is my friend the bank robber getting from sharing a delusion with those children? So now I gotta tap the phone, I gotta trace calls, I gotta spend a good amount of time examining who you are, how much money you stole from that bank in Walnut Creek, and where that money went."

"Straight to my debts," I said.

"Yeah," Garrison said, "I saw that. Nothing flashy. No cars. No houses."

"I didn't rob Fort Knox," I said. "I robbed the Crocker next door to Gemco. And I apologize for not getting a letter from the Wah Ching gang saying they were in receipt of my final payment for gambling debts. But as you can see, I'm alive, so the money was received."

"You got five grand from that Crocker," Garrison said. "The Wah Ching wasn't putting out hits for five grand. So my guess is that the Crocker wasn't your first job. It was just the one that got you put away."

"And so you think I did thirty-eight months just to get out to harass children? Please. Ask Mary. She'll tell you."

"I did," Garrison said. "She was real surprised to learn about your criminal record. She'd like you to stop calling her children, as of about twenty minutes ago."

"Fine," I said.

"And she'd like you to stop bringing over the support money," Garrison said.

"Fine," I said.

"And this parking shit," Garrison said, "Mitch, you ever heard of stalking? You could be in county right now for that."

"That what those backup guys are for? You taking me to county?"

Garrison took a deep breath, then chuckled in a way that didn't seem to indicate he was in the least bit amused. "No," Garrison said, finally, "I'm not. Because inexplicably? I believe you. You're too smart to be in something this dumb." He stood up then, finished off his beer. Waved at his backup. They got up, left. "Hank's probably dead," Garrison said once they were gone, just like that, a simple statement. "He's never gone more than sixty days, under any of his aliases, without having some police contact, so unless he's in a coma or chained up somewhere, he's dead."

"What kind of shit was he involved with?"

"You really don't know?"

"Sarah's a straight edge," I said. "She thought he was just a beach bum."

Garrison ordered another shot. Took it down. "All right listen. Cop to robber? He's a suspect in a dirtbag-on-dirtbag shooting up near Tahoe. He was going by Nick Hankston up there," Garrison said. "A grow house got robbed. Assailant shot the proprietor in both knees and ran off with a bunch of cash."

"Surprised anyone bothered to call the cops," I said.

"Local cops think it was the shooter who called, worried the guy would bleed out and he'd be on the hook for a murder. Neighbors ID'd Hank's Ford truck, but half of the damn county was in and out of the place buying weed, driving beat-up Ford trucks. He admitted he'd been up there, but then so did everyone else. Cops didn't have enough to hold him."

"Not even on his fake identity?"

"He called himself that," Garrison said, "but all his paper was legit. You can call yourself whatever you want these days."

"Lucky," I said. "The guy die?"

"Nope," Garrison said. "But he's got the mush brains from loss of blood. He's useless. Couldn't or wouldn't ID Hank, couldn't tell if he stole ten bucks or a million." He picked up the photos of me out front of Mary's, tore them in half, dumped them in an ashtray. "So, I know you didn't kill him. But I suspect, if it's someone local, you know who did.

My advice to you, Mitch? Get a lawyer, come to the station, give a statement. Those kids are young enough that they'll think they had a pretty great relationship with their father for a few months, so don't beat yourself up. Twenty years from now, they'll work it out in therapy."

"Therapy won't fix everything," I said. "Trust me."

"Hank's parents are going to court. They'll be taking possession of the bike shop soon as a judge gives them the okay. My guess is a week. Maybe less. Steer clear. This isn't your problem."

"Season's about over anyway," I said.

Garrison looked up at the TV for a moment. Dave Kingman was up to bat for the A's. The rain delay apparently up. "You know what I never liked about baseball?"

"What's that?"

"You never know," he said, "how long it's going to take for someone to lose."

By the time I broke into Porter's apartment the next day, the coast was being hammered, sheets of summer rain coming down from Fort Bragg to San Simeon, along with gale-force winds and lightning. It had been a few years since the last El Niño, so no one was panicking about landslides just yet, but Californians are terrible with rain; they lose all sense of time and space and reason, so the streets were empty.

I called Porter that morning and told him they were red-flagging the beach (which was true), that even the surfers were coming in (which wasn't true, those dudes were bigger lunatics than the motherfuckers I met in Quentin), so he could have a day off. And then I made a bag of PB and Js and camped out down the block from the Del Monte, waiting for Porter to make his move. It wasn't until two that afternoon that I saw him exit the building pushing a bike, no umbrella, just a garbage bag over his clothes, and take off across the street toward his warehouse.

I went around the back of the building, which housed the café on the bottom floor and then four tiny apartments up above. I found the power meter behind a thick hedge, cracked it open with a screwdriver, popped the meter's face off, broke off the plastic receptors, and screwed it all back together. Two minutes, in and out, the whole building was dark. PG&E would need to come out to fix it. Which they weren't about to do in the rain. I picked Porter's lock in about thirty seconds—it was nothing more than a push button, the door, the lock, the whole building, more antique than safe house—and let myself in.

Porter had decorated his shitty one bedroom with a couch, a tiny TV, one well-tended house plant, fifteen bikes, and then five garbage bags and three suitcases packed with most of his earthly belongings: a stack of jeans, half a dozen denim work shirts, a black blazer, way too many Eagles records, and plastic bags of heroin. If it were the consistently good kind of heroin, it would probably have a street value of a couple hundred thousand dollars. Maybe half a million.

But it wasn't. It was bags of heart attacks and strokes and living like a vegetable.

Still, whatever Porter had planned with the rest of his life, making a quick getaway was clearly a part of it, and he may as well have had uncut diamonds with him. He also had about five grand in cash, which I went ahead and took.

I did fifty push-ups and then called Porter's warehouse. He answered on the seventeenth ring. Which was good. It gave me time to do a couple jumping jacks.

"Where have you been?" I said.

"Right here," he said. "You said we were closed."

"I've been calling your place all day!"

"Okay, okay," Porter said. "Catch your breathing. What is problem?"

"Cops came and arrested Sarah. Kicked in the front door and pulled her out by the hair."

"She needs to keep her mouth closed," Porter said.

"I'm losing my mind over here, Porter," I said.

"Okay, okay," he said again.

"Have you been talking to the cops?"

"No, never."

"Because they said they already had you in custody. Are you already out?"

"No, no," Porter said. "They lie. They are allowed to lie. It is constitution that cops are legal to lie. I am right here. I am not in custody. We are speaking. Come to the Del Monte. We have steak and figure this out. Come in one hour of time."

I told him I would. Even though Sarah's condo was only about fifteen minutes away, the fucker.

I hung up and watched out the window for Porter to ride up, which he did about ten minutes later. He picked up his bike and began to climb the stairs, so I stationed myself beside the front door, Hank's gun wrapped in a pair of Porter's jeans to muffle the sound, and when Porter walked in, I shot him in the side of the head. Porter was dead before he hit the ground, but I buried another bullet in the wall, just in case the cops needed a clean slug.

I put one more in his face for talking shit that day in the restaurant.

The day after Labor Day, Sarah and I dragged a cooler of beer and a couple chairs and towels out to the empty beach to work on our tans one last time. The bike stand had been closed since Hank's parents took it over a month earlier, since they didn't have anyone to work it, what with Porter dead. They were still paying rent—it had been a good summer, before everything went south—since their lease wasn't up until December. Sarah wasn't planning on renewing with them. We had our own idea. Artisan s'mores, available all year long. We'd be rich.

Around lunchtime, Detective Garrison came walking over the low dune behind us. He'd rolled up his slacks and had his dress shoes tied around his neck. Beach people are different, even the cops.

"There's Donnie and Marie," he said. I put down the paperback I was reading—*The Bourne Identity*—and opened the cooler, let Garrison pick a bottle of Anchor Steam. He looked around, like he was worried someone would spot him, but then he said, "It's actually a nice place when all the tourists leave, isn't it?"

"I sold twenty condos this summer," Sarah said. "Take in the view while you can."

"More people, more crime," Garrison said. "Good for my business." He took a long swallow of his beer. "I wanted you to know, before you saw it in the paper, we got a ballistic match on the gun used to kill your friend Mr. Porter. Turns out it was used in a shooting up near Tahoe last year that Hank was a suspect in." Garrison kept his eyes on me.

"So my Hank is still alive?" Sarah said. "Is that what you're saying?"

"Or his gun is," Garrison said. He finally glanced at Sarah. "His parents are choosing to believe he's still with us, so that's the premise I guess we're going with for now."

"What do you believe?" I asked.

"I believe you two are neck deep in some shit you're never, ever gonna get out of," he said. He pointed his bottle toward the bike stand, which was only about fifty yards away. "That nice garage you got? When did you renovate that?"

"January," Sarah said. "Hank did it himself. You can go pull the permits."

"I did," Garrison said. He picked up *The Bourne Identity* and flipped through the pages. "This realistic?" he asked.

"No," I said. "You might like it."

"Ludlum's usually pretty tight. Lots of action and fighting. Not a lot of bullshit talking."

"I'm having a hard time getting into it," I said.

"You might try reading some classics," Garrison said. "Maybe start with Edgar Allan Poe. 'The Cask of Amontillado.' That's a good one. See where it takes you." He pocketed *The Bourne Identity*, finished his beer, took another beer, but didn't open it. "Porter, by the way? Grew up in San Jose."

"No shit?"

"That accent was made up. His parents teach horticulture at San Jose City College. They'd like to get into his warehouse, see if there's any plants to salvage. They had no idea he'd developed such a green thumb." Garrison watched the crashing waves for a few seconds, then regarded us both, a strange look on his face. "Personally? I don't really give a shit about Hank. This planet is better without him on it.

Same with Porter, if I'm being honest. Neither of them is worth a squirt of piss in my view. But it's not up to either of you to decide that. So if I were you? I'd keep a real close eye on that garage. Hate for there to be a robbery or fire or a busted plumbing line that required any kind of police or city action around it." He cracked open the second beer, tossed the cap into the sand.

"You'll be on the lookout to see if Hank uses that gun anywhere else, I trust?" I said.

"Oh, I'll be watching real close," Garrison said, "soon as I get back from vacation. Wife and I are taking a cruise around the world."

"When do you clock out?" Sarah asked.

He looked at his watch. "Two beers ago."

"Enjoy the book," I said.

Garrison said, "I'll bring it back to you up north next summer."

"I think you'll find me right here."

"I wouldn't bet on it," he said. "Have a nice fall, you two."

Garrison disappeared back up the dune. For a long time, both of us were quiet, busy trying to figure out what the fuck just happened, until Sarah said, "You smell that? Is something on fire?"

Tod Goldberg is the New York Times bestselling author of over a dozen books, including *The Low Desert, Gangsterland*, a finalist for the Hammett Prize, *Gangster Nation, The House of Secrets*, which he co-authored with Brad Meltzer, and *Living Dead Girl*, a finalist for the Los Angeles Times Book Prize. His nonfiction and criticism appear regularly in the *Los Angeles Times* and *USA Today*, among many other publications, and has been widely anthologized, including in Best American Essays. Tod lives in Indio, CA and is a Professor of Creative Writing at the University of California, Riverside where he founded and directs the Low Residency MFA in Creative Writing & Writing for the Performing Arts.

MOBY'S DOCK

By Steve Wynn

You'd think a hacksaw would slice through resistant objects more easily than that.

I was in good shape. I was in a mad panic. I was drunk as well, which always gave me a little extra, unfettered strength like one of those moms in the *Weekly World News* who lifts a Buick off her trapped baby. And yet, I was having quite a time of it. Each swing of the blade dug just a fraction of an inch, incurring more sweat than progress. The gloves didn't make it any easier. It took nearly an hour, the longest hour of my life, before I had finally rendered a pile with no piece larger than what fit in a midsize Hefty bag, just like the ones contained in a box to my right. I filled each bag, making me chuckle nervously as I remembered my first job in junior high school as a bag boy at the Safeway supermarket on Pico Boulevard. How far I'd come!

The bags were filled, and I was dripping with sweat, smelling of funk. I loaded them all into the trunk of my cobalt blue '65 Ford Galaxie and drove to the dumpster behind Webster Field, keeping one hand over my left eye to stave off the swirling double vision, and a besotted eye on the speedometer, making sure to drive neither too slowly nor too quickly. I'd have a lot of explaining to do if I got pulled over.

I knew Webster Field would be deserted at 2:00 a.m.

and I pulled into the parking lot, turned off the engine and lights, and waited ten minutes to make sure there was no activity before skulking from the car, tossing the bags into the dumpster, and then getting back into the car, driving away and making sure that nobody was there to see me as I headed north on Sawtelle Boulevard, and back home, singing loudly and quite tunefully, thank you, to "Rock You Like a Hurricane" as it blared with intermittent static on KMET. I was home free.

I divide my life neatly into the time before and after my last visit to Moby's Dock, a bar at the end of the Santa Monica Pier. It was my favorite bar, and I could never understand why it wasn't more crowded. The happy hour special of a shot of well booze and a pony Budweiser for two bucks couldn't be beat. The jukebox played Sinatra and Dino, and you could watch the sun set over the Pacific Ocean from the tables that lined up along the picture window at the westernmost end of the bar. On the days when I was feeling a little flush, I would order a tequila sunrise, trying not to think of the Eagles, and would watch the last rays of the sun play games with the tropical colors in the glass before taking my first sip. In the two years since reaching the legal drinking age, I had probably been to this bar a hundred times, and nobody had spoken a word to me besides the bartender's shuffle of "What'll you have," "How's it going, buddy," and "Nice weather we're having."

My job at the Fotomat on Wilshire Boulevard covered my nut, which was pretty much my drink tab, gas for the Galaxie, and family packs of Top Ramen. I was living rent-free in my dad's basement just down the road from UCLA where I'd dropped out in my sophomore year. My dad wasn't thrilled, but he still felt bad about divorcing my mom when I was in high school, living out the cliché of running off with his buxom secretary who dumped him less than two years later. The side entrance of the house led to the basement, which means we would often go weeks without seeing each other, and our only communication was the sheepish mumble and furtive shrug of two dogs who knew they'd been bad and were afraid of getting whooped again. He wasn't about to evict me. I think he liked having me around. Even if he had fallen from grace, he had not even come close to reaching my level, and thus, I must have made him feel good about himself. Unlike me, he was earning well over minimum wage, after all.

Working at the Fotomat wasn't too bad. I had been at the same booth since high school, and I felt lucky to have a job where I could be alone, get my work done, and listen to Vin Scully on my transistor radio during the long lulls between customers with whom most of my interaction was limited to "110, 220 or Instamatic?" or "Gloss, high gloss, or matte?" Then you would fill out the envelope, toss the film inside and seal it up, toss it into a mesh bag and wait for the pickup at the end of your shift.

The pickup was also when the developed photos would get dropped off. You'd take the envelopes filled with photos or slides and organize them by name in the shelf opposite the cash register. The entire inside of the booth was about ninety square feet, side to side, top to bottom. You could fit about ten of those booths in the average prison cell. I know, I'd done the math.

There were training and motivational sessions every few months, which were a waste of time, but you got paid by the hour, so I didn't complain. My fellow employees would mostly talk about all the salacious photos they had uncovered. Boobs, butts, blow jobs, each guy trying to top the next one over what they'd seen. One guy who worked at the Fotomat in West Hollywood, the largest gay neighborhood in the city, said that at least half of his photos were of nudity and sexual activity. I don't know. I never looked at a single one of my customers' photos. Maybe I felt it was wrong. I hated the idea of someone doing that to me, not that I had ever taken a nude photo in my life, but as someone who hates to even have someone listen in on a phone conversation, I shuddered in horror at some kid watching me in my most private moments.

Or maybe I was just lazy and happy to listen to the Dodgers and FM rock radio.

Sometimes I'd work the night shift, but mostly I tried to get the day shift so I could be off at five o'clock and over to Moby's in time for happy hour where I'd get my modest buzz on, spending no more than five or six bucks, and be home in time to watch a little TV or listen to records before passing out. It was an easy, uncomplicated life and, aside from the occasional album purchase or rock club show, I didn't feel I needed much more to make myself happy.

Since breaking up with my high school sweetheart a few years before, I hadn't given much thought to dating. On the other hand, I gave a lot of thought to sex. I was barely out of my teens, after all. But the dating part of the equation gave me the shivers. It was all too much work only to lead to inevitable disappointment, much like when Misty had left me for that stoned-out surfer. Was that what she had wanted all along? He listened to Pablo Cruise, for Christ's sake. No thanks. I took care of my own needs; my life was simple. And with each solitary day, I felt more and more adrift and craved companionship, closeness, and idle chatter less and less.

All of this is why I was fully unprepared for her. She drove up to the booth in a gold '69 Challenger with Roxy Music's "Country Life" playing from the cassette deck. I could see it was a Pioneer, the one I'd wanted to buy before settling on the less expensive Radio Shack option. I thought she looked a little like Cherie Currie, the singer of the Runaways, whom I'd seen the week before at the Whisky a Go Go. She turned down her car stereo to give me the film.

"Matte or gloss?"

"Do they take the same amount of time?"

"Matte takes an extra day."

"I'll go with gloss, then, that's fine. Hey, is that the Clash playing in your booth?"

"Yeah. *London Calling*. It came out on import yesterday."

"Cool. I heard that 'Stand by Me' song on the radio. It's great."

"It's the hidden track at the end. It's actually called 'Train in Vain.' Okay, here's your ticket—you can come back tomorrow any time after three, and your photos will be ready."

Off she went. If that was flirting, then I guess I'd been doing it all wrong, but she did seem to look at me a split second beyond what was functionally necessary for the transaction before peeling off down Twenty-Third Street. I felt a tingle of flush and expectation, the kind I had neither felt nor wanted to feel for some time. That night at Moby's Dock, I had an extra shot and pony beer just to settle down a bit.

She was back the next day. I saw the gold Challenger approaching as it entered the parking lot, and I made sure to have her photos ready for when she pulled up. I took a glance at my reflection in the window of the booth and, more importantly, at what was playing on my cassette machine, and felt good about "Songs the Lord Taught Us" being the soundtrack as she drove up to the window.

"Cool. The Cramps. I saw them last year at the Starwood." She was wearing Ray-Bans, and her dyed-black hair was slicked back from her face, setting off the paleness of her skin. "Lux Interior is pretty crazy on stage. Have you ever seen them?"

"Yep. I was at that same show. That version of 'Surfin' Bird' seemed like it lasted over an hour, right?"

She paid with a five-dollar bill for her photos and then handed me another roll of Instamatic 110 film. "Can I get these back by tomorrow?"

"Yeah, sure. Matte or gloss?"

"I forgot. Which is faster?"

"Gloss."

"Okay, then gloss it is. Enjoy the tunes," she said as I took the film canister and handed over the claim slip before she gave me a toothy, slightly nicotine-stained smile. "We should hang out sometime," and then drove off, the Dodge leaving a white plume of smoke which made me think of the Pope who had just died weeks earlier.

I had a lot on my mind later that day at Moby's Dock, and I didn't particularly like the feelings I was having. My life had gotten simple and focused. I enjoyed the discipline, the simplicity, and also the lack of complications that romance, compromise, wasted time, and also the inevitable breakup brought, which I knew was all part of the game. The pain had been too much before. I didn't want any more pain. I had better things to do. If only I knew what they were.

I timed the tequila sunrise perfectly with the sun setting over the Pacific Ocean, knowing I'd have my last sip, rattling the ice cubes and slurping the syrupy residue just as it got dark and, more importantly, as happy hour was ending. I wished they had peanuts today like they had the day before, and I decided to hit up Arlene's for some greasy chili fries on the way home, figuring it might lower the level of tension I was feeling, my usually blank slate of a mind waylaid by an imagined listening party with the girl in the Dodge. Maybe it was time to open myself up a little bit.

I finished the drink and made my way to the Galaxie, chili fries, and the new Echo and the Bunnymen album that I had bought the day before, that waited for me at home.

She came back the next day at the beginning of my shift just as I was counting in the register. "I know I'm early, but I was passing by on my way to work, so I thought I'd see if the photos came in yet."

"Nothing yet. They usually don't come in until around three."

"Oh, right. Well, hey. Maybe you wanna come by later this evening after work and listen to some records together. You could bring the photos by, if you don't mind."

I was taken aback but didn't show it in my response, "Well, I don't normally do house calls but yeah, sure. Sounds like fun."

"Cool." She handed over a slip of paper that she had already prepared with her name, address, and phone number. "My name's Jenny, by the way. Come over around eight? Is that good for you?"

"My name's Daniel. And yeah, that sounds great."

"Awesome. See you then."

The car pulled away, leaving me with a nervous rumbling in my stomach. It must have been the chili fries.

The daily delivery of photos was dropped off by the Fotomat van that afternoon, and I settled in to filing them all in the drawer by name while Vin Scully called the sixth inning of a day game against the Padres. I saw her envelope, and as I said aloud, "Don't do it, don't do it, don't do it," I opened the envelope, carefully pulling away the sticky adhesive so that it would be easy to reseal without detection.

The photos were all taken in a backyard of what appeared to be a very nice house. In swimwear of varying degrees of modesty, people were waving from a pool, standing by a grill waiting for hot dogs, or sitting under a tree. She wore a white bikini that held my glance for longer than I felt was proper, but that ship of propriety had sailed. I moved on to other photos of kids, babies, and what appeared to be very conservative-looking parents. They seemed like a nice family.

At Moby's Dock later that day, I found myself ordering a third shot-and-beer combo. It felt good. I was no longer afraid. Maybe I'd meet her dad someday. We could talk about baseball. Dads like baseball. The last sip of the pony Bud gave me the illusion of clarity and courage, and I called her from the pay phone by the cigarette machine.

"Still okay if I drop by?"

"Sure, come on over."

I drove down Pico, turning right on Centinela, and followed the increasing numbers until I got to her address, just beyond Washington Boulevard. It was a true tropical apartment, tiki lamps and colored lights illuminating the stucco façade, and I thought about "Sex Beat" by the Gun Club. "You make my tropical apartment bed your sacrificial pool." Maybe it would be a good night.

She opened the door and had what I knew immediately was Martin Denny on the stereo. The apartment smelled like a mixture of vanilla and Pine-Sol, making me think of freshly lit candles and furtive cleaning. She wore a Dead Kennedys T-shirt.

"Can I offer you a drink? I've got beer, wine, some vodka and tonic."

"Vodka tonic sounds great. Hey, nice tunes. My dad used to play this record all the time."

"Mine too. I feel like it goes with this apartment building somehow, don't you?"

Her dad. My dad. Backyard barbecues. My mind started doing that thing that happens after a few drinks, shuffling through a deck of mental synapses and impulses, like a shifty dealer in Las Vegas. I couldn't focus and tried to remember the photo with the bikini. That worked for a second before I started thinking of freshly manicured lawns and kids playing on rubber, horse-shaped rafts near the edge of the pool.

We made our way through the small talk of jobs, high school, favorite movies, and the second side of the Martin Denny record hadn't even ended when she leaned over to kiss me. Her hair smelled like cilantro. Her tongue moved in my mouth in a mechanical, counterclockwise direction which made me think of the snake I had used to unclog my shower drain the week before.

My mind started racing. Clogged drains. Cilantro. Dads with hairy beer bellies serving plump, grill-marked hot dogs. Wondering if her turntable would automatically reject the tone arm when the side was finished or if we'd hear the click-click-click of the retaining groove. The sickly taste of cheap tonic water. Cilantro. Vanilla. I tried to focus on the bikini in the photo and instead got my dad telling me about the receptionist who wasn't coming back.

"Look. I gotta go. I'm really sorry." I was sweating.

"Wow, are you sure? Are you okay? I can make you some coffee if you want."

"No, no, no, everything's okay. I just remembered I have to pick up something at the store before they close. Hey, thanks for the drink. I'll see you around."

The length of Sepulveda from Washington up to Sunset swirled, doubled, and blurred, and I fixed my eye on the speedometer to make sure not to vary from the speed limit, the hand over my left eye helping with the focus. I shouted while the radio played. "Fucking idiot, fucking idiot" and other varieties of self-incrimination all the way until I pulled into the driveway of my dad's house, pulling around to the side on a little slope by the entrance to my basement apartment.

I turned off the lights and the engine, exhaled with relief and leaned back in my seat, closing my eyes and trying to recap what had just happened when I realized the car was moving. I had forgotten to put it in park, and the Galaxie rolled slowly and easily down the slope toward the weeds and dirt and a tree that had been planted the year before. The tree never stood a chance, my front grill knocking it right off its root, and the entire length, just about the same height as me, ending up on its side like a melodramatic death swoon in a bad B movie.

My dad rarely came around to this side of the house, but I couldn't exactly leave a fallen tree, violently ripped from its roots and stump, sitting there until he happened to come by one day, leading to questions and difficult alibis. No, I had to get rid of the evidence. This bit of warped logic was crystal clear despite or maybe because of the mix of vodka, whiskey, and beer in my system.

The hacksaw and Hefty bags were easy to find in the garage, and within an hour, the lifeless corpse of a tree was chopped into small pieces, placed in the various bags, and I was on my way to Webster Field. My dad never asked about the tree. Maybe he never saw it or maybe he just didn't want to know.

Two years later, a big storm hit the beaches of LA, and most of the Santa Monica Pier was destroyed, leaving only half of Moby's Dock with the rest tumbling into the Pacific, a mess of shot glasses, barstools, and a jukebox to be cleaned up and hauled off in the coming weeks.

I watched the footage on the news and turned to Jenny sitting next to me on the new couch we had bought the week before. "Wow, I sure used to love that bar" I said as the tiki lamps and colored lights undulated outside the window of our apartment, making me think of sunsets and chili fries.

Steve Wynn was a founding member of The Dream Syndicate whose 1982 debut album "The Days of Wine and Roses" is one of the building blocks of the indie rock scene that began in the following years. Since then he has released 32 studio albums as a solo artist and as a member of Gutterball, The Baseball Project and the revived Dream Syndicate who reformed in 2012. He has written over 500 songs, some of which have been covered by the likes of REM, the Bangles, Yo La Tengo, Concrete Blonde and Luna. "Moby's Dock" is his first short story.

THE NAKED AND THE DEAD

By Charles Ardai

The sign said, "WELCOME TO HEAVEN." It also said, "PLEASE REMOVE YOUR CLOTHES HERE."

Beneath the sign was an open doorway through which I could see a long row of metal lockers. Next to the doorway was a high counter, and behind the counter was a man who appeared, for all practical purposes, to be naked. He wore a wristwatch and, heaven help me, a bow tie.

"Name, love?" he said.

"Susan Jaffe."

He checked a list of names on a clipboard and apparently found mine. "All right." He pushed a register and a pen across the counter to me, along with a plastic card key. "Sign in, then you can change." He indicated the lockers with a flick of his head.

Funny euphemism, I thought as I signed my name. Change. As though one walks out wearing anything at all.

I hesitated at the blank under the heading "Reason for Visit." I wrote in "Assignment" and passed the book and pen back across the counter.

"Go on," he said, this time flicking his head at the key.

"Thank you, no," I said. "I'm here on business."

"On business, on holiday, on orders from your doctor, all the same to us," he said. "No one passes this point without undressing."

"You don't understand," I said. "Mr. Brown asked me here specially."

"Indeed." The man pointed to the list on his clipboard. "That's why your name is here. And more power to you. But no one can go on the beach if they're not naked. It is a rule, miss, of which I am certain you can see the necessity."

I couldn't, really; there wasn't much I could understand about nudism. Seemed to me like a bunch of grown men and women—men mostly—acting like naughty children and getting nasty sunburns in the process. Paying private club fees for a chance to strip on weekends and lie around in each other's sight. Then spouting high-minded nonsense about "naturalism" when called upon to defend themselves on the talk shows.

And the people who did it were businessmen and politicians, aging stars of stage and screen, familiar voices from the radio, even progressive men of the cloth, out of theirs. Not to mention an otherwise respectable man like Geoffrey Brown, who ran this place but had neglected to mention that fact to me until the current situation arose and he decided he needed my help. Geoff knew me from a screenwriting workshop we'd both participated in; when we'd had to tell the group something about ourselves, I'd said, "Private investigator," and he had said, "I own a recreational club." He'd said nothing about naked men in neckties then.

"May I speak to Mr. Brown?" I set my lips in a tight imitation of the man's smile.

The man pressed a button on the counter and spoke into a telephone receiver retrieved from underneath. "Mr. Brown, there is a young woman here who wants to speak with you. Yes. She is reluctant to undress. Susan"—he looked at the clipboard again—"Jaffe, sir." He turned to me. "Mr. Brown will be right out."

By now I would have been quite prepared to see Geoff Brown emerge from his office stark naked, but he came out dressed in a polo shirt and short pants. The short pants were bad enough for a six-foot-tall man well into his fifties, but they were better than seeing him in less, and when the desk clerk came from behind his desk and I saw that he was indeed naked, I had to turn away to keep from laughing.

"Can't be embarrassed, Susan," Geoff said. "Not if you're to investigate this situation."

"I'm not embarrassed. I'm amused."

"Well, you can't be amused, then. Not if it means that you can't look a man in his eyes just because he's naked below."

"His eyes are not the problem."

"Well, it's his eyes you've got to look in. And trust me, he'll be looking in yours."

"That's fine with me," I said. "I won't make your guests uncomfortable if I can avoid it."

He looked me over. "Well, you can't avoid it wearing that."

"Wearing what? Clothes?"

"Perhaps if you at least changed into a light-colored swimsuit."

"I will wear what I am wearing. It's not a matter I wish to discuss."

"Do you want to be conspicuous?"

"I want to be dressed."

Geoff shook his head. "It's no good. The reason Heaven works is that everyone knows everyone else will be naked. It's based on trust. Even one exception could ruin the whole thing."

"The reason Heaven works," I said, "is also that your clients know they won't come across a corpse as they stroll along your beach. Only several of them did just that yesterday morning. If they can handle that exception, they can handle seeing a woman who isn't naked."

"Susan, please," Geoff said, but he could see that he wasn't persuading me. "I'll be undressed, for God's sake."

"Is that supposed to encourage me?" I said. "Look, Geoff. You want to undress, be my guest. You want to hire someone else to investigate the murder, that's also fine. But if you want me, you get me as I am. Do we understand each other?"

Geoff agonized over the decision, then grabbed a key off the counter and headed for the lockers. "If you insist. Come along."

The man behind the counter glared at me as I passed.

The locker room was empty when we went through except for an old fellow drying himself with a towel. He didn't look up. Geoff selected one of the lockers, pulled off his shirt and pants, threw them in, and locked it with the key. He stood before me for a second in a sort of silent challenge, a test of my sensibilities that I met with an impatient stare. Seeing no blush creep into my cheeks, Geoff was apparently satisfied.

He traded the key for a towel at a window; I saw that both key and towel had a *2* printed on them. The man behind the window filed the key away in an envelope with Geoff's name on it and stuck the envelope in a cabinet.

Geoff stopped just before the exit to the beach and faced me with a serious expression. "Are you quite ready?" he asked.

I looked him in the eyes. "Quite."

"Very well," he said. And, swinging the towel over one shoulder, walked through.

It was just after noon. The beach was practically empty as everyone lay or sat in the grassy shade above the long strip of sand, waiting out the hottest part of the day. One brave and stupid woman lay face-down on a beach chair under the full glare of the sun, her rear end and shoulders already lobster red. I wondered whether she was asleep and, if so, whether I should wake her.

Geoff took care of this for me, stepping out into the sun and squatting by her side. He whispered something in her ear and touched her shoulder, leaving yellow-white finger marks on her skin. She rolled over and sat up with a jerk. Her uncooked front was an almost translucent white, not unlike my complexion. I could've warned her that with skin like that, she'd burn as soon as she stepped on the beach. But by now such a warning was unnecessary.

While Geoff helped her pull her chair into the shade, I took a tube of sunscreen from my shoulder bag and applied it liberally to my forehead, cheeks, chin, earlobes, and hands. Then I turned up my collar and buttoned it at my neck.

The woman stopped in front of me, hands on her scorched hips, and stared. She wasn't the only one staring, I noticed, and no one was being very discreet about it. Odd, I thought, but revealing: these people, who claimed to be free from the ogling gaze, lost no time ogling an outsider themselves. I stared back at the woman as I wiped the extra lotion off my palms onto a tissue.

I held the sunscreen out to her. "Want some?"

The woman turned to Geoff. "What's with her?"

He looked me up and down as though noticing for the first time that I was clothed. I waited to see what story he'd tell.

"She's my cousin," he said, "and she's shy."

"Hell," the woman said, "I'm shy too. You can't stay shy when you come to a place like this. Make her take off her clothes."

"She will."

"She'd better." The woman stalked off.

Geoff walked me a few yards down the beach. "You see?"

"Oh, I see plenty," I said. And I did.

There were perhaps a dozen men and a half dozen women on the beach. The average age was closer to the current Fahrenheit temperature than the centigrade. I thought I recognized one of the men from television's *Nightly News*, but I couldn't be sure at this distance, and I felt little inclination to go closer. One of the women bore a startling resemblance to Sophia Loren. But it couldn't have been.

I realized after a bit that I had my arms crossed over my chest. I uncrossed them and let them dangle by my side. They felt uncomfortable having nothing to do there but play with the clasp of my shoulder bag and dart in and out of my pockets. I was self-conscious despite myself.

"You'd feel more comfortable," Geoff said, "if you were naked."

"I'd feel more comfortable if all the rest of you were clothed."

Geoff clucked and led me along the beach.

The beach was something of a ragged L shape, running along one long wall and one short wall of the rectangular main building. Small shower huts closed off each end of the L, and a tall chain link fence around the buildings completed the beach's isolation. There were no trees, though there was a certain amount of stiff undergrowth near the fence. For shade, the beach was peppered with gaudy umbrellas the size and color of small circus tents.

The beach's other border was with the sea—actually a large bay with another beach visible on the horizon. A few powerboats churned up the water in between, but they could come no closer to Heaven than the floating barricade of buoys and nets about fifty feet offshore.

Geoff stopped after we made the turn onto the base of the L. "This is where the body was found," he said.

We were facing the sun, so I put on my sunglasses.

"Mr. John Nash of Albesar University, professor of English literature and one of my original members. One bullet in the back of the neck. We found him wrapped up in his towel. Until someone turned him over, everyone thought he was just asleep."

"Who turned him over?"

"I did."

He knelt in the sand, let a handful run through his fingers. "You'd never know a man was murdered here. Already when we found him, the blood had washed away." He shook his head and patted the sand down.

"No blood on the towel?"

He looked up. "Oh yes. Blood on the towel, of course."

"His blood?"

"Presumably. The police said it matched his type."

"His towel?"

Geoff nodded. "Number six."

I took out a small notepad and wrote the information down. "Who is number one?"

"God, Susan, you sound like that old TV show."

"Well?"

"Who do you think?"

"I would think you, but your towel has a big number two on it." I pointed to the number stitched into the fabric in the middle of his towel.

"You know I'm married, Susan."

"Your wife is number one?"

"In this and in all things," Geoff said, rising to his feet again. He started back the way we had come. "Come on."

"Wait. I want to look around." I went into the shower hut. It was an empty, damp, gray cinderblock affair with a dripping showerhead on each wall. Plain as plain gets. The fence a few feet behind the bunker was similarly functional: tight links of carbon steel with concertina wire on top and *No Trespassing* signs hung every few feet for good measure.

The bunker butted up against the wall of the main building near where they met. I noticed a door. I tried to open it, but it was locked.

"You can only open that door from the inside," Geoff said.

"What's it for?"

"Convenient access to this part of the beach."

"Not very convenient if you can't get back in," I said.

"We did that for the sake of security. One entrance is safer than two."

"Evidently not," I said.

It took a second for Geoff to grasp my meaning. "No, evidently not," he said finally.

I walked to the water, removing my shoes and rolling up my cuffs along the way. The wet sand by the surf was tightly packed and held my footprints only until a wave came to wash them away. I walked into the surf. The bottom was visible almost all the way out to the buoys. "Is it always this shallow?" I asked.

"More or less."

I walked back out. When I stepped on the dry sand, it coated my feet like breading on a piece of meat. I sat on a lounge chair and brushed off as much of the sand as I could. Geoff stood over me and told me the rest of the story.

"Nash only came up during the week, never on weekends. He always sat here, at this end of the beach. Liked his privacy. He used this entrance so he didn't have to pass Martin to get in. Martin's the fellow out front."

"The one with the tie."

"Right." Geoff chuckled. "Looks ridiculous, doesn't it? But he likes it, so what can I do? Anyway. Nash evidently came here around eight or nine in the morning yesterday. There were three other people on the beach at the time, but they were all on the other side. At nine thirty, we heard a loud report, like a gun going off. I say it was like a gun going off now, but you only think of that afterwards. At the time, we assumed it was a backfire from the highway or something along those lines. I know I did. I didn't come out here until ten, ten fifteen. Tried to wake Nash up, noticed the blood on the towel, unwrapped him—and there it was. A big, bloody hole in his throat. So, I called the police.

"They took him to the morgue, searched the area thoroughly, took the other people on the beach in for questioning. Inspector Morris took my statement, for the little it was worth. And they've started an investigation. But I wanted you to take a look at the matter as well. You see, as much as I hate to admit it, it has to be that one of my members is a killer—no one else could have gotten in. Or if someone somehow *had* managed to get in, certainly no non-member could have gotten out again, not without being noticed. No, it was one of us. I just want to know which one it was."

It was a hell of a problem. I was glad it was Geoff's, not mine. Except, of course, that now it was mine too. "Were you and Nash friends?" I asked.

"Friends, no. Barely acquaintances." Geoff shrugged. "He was an original member, but that just means he bought in early. I barely knew the man. Of course, I'm horrified that he was killed. But no more so than if any other member had been. I don't really get to know my members as much as I should. It's one of the things I have regretted for some time."

As he talked, I put my shoes on; the sand on my feet was now dry and came off easily. When he paused, I looked up to watch the activity on the beach across the bay. The people there looked like stick figures splashing about, flailing on tiny surfboards, parasailing on long tethers attached to speedboats—more active, at least, than this geriatric haunt. No death there.

"What's that beach?" I asked.

"It's called Beachhead International," he said. "It's a Club Med knockoff. American students mostly, on holiday. Only slightly more expensive than the Caribbean and not as hot."

"They ever come over here?" I asked. "Students, I mean."

"Susan, Heaven is not a hotel. We are a private club. You have to be a member to come here."

"Of course," I said. "No offense."

"Sometimes," Geoff said, accepting my apology with a nod, "on weekends, when our younger members are here, you see them watching through binoculars. Or some kids will buzz us—you know, in a parasail. Race up to the buoys, hooting and whistling, drop their trunks as they pass. What happens, often enough, is that they drop their trunks too far and the trunks fall off into the water, and then they end up flying back to their beach naked. Which usually puts them off doing it again too soon."

"It sounds moronic," I said.

"American teenagers. What can you expect?"

I nodded. "But live and let live, right, Geoff? People have to be free to do any fool thing they want with their vacation time. I mean, isn't that what this place is all about? Is it less silly to walk around naked than to fly across the bay and drop your trunks?"

"You don't have to approve of what we do here," Geoff said icily, "and you don't have to do it yourself. But you shouldn't mock it. I am paying you to investigate a murder. That is all. So investigate." He stood up and walked away.

I do have a tendency to push too hard. I ran after Geoff and apologized. After a second, he apologized, too—I'd hit a sore spot. He took ribbings all the time, from the press and from his friends, and he didn't need it from me. Fair enough. So I eased up on him and got down to business.

Kelly Link *was* from the *Nightly News*. He anchored the six o'clock report on weekends and was flattered that I recognized him.

Maintaining the charade he'd begun earlier, Geoff again introduced me as his cousin. Link smoothed back his pearl-white hair, crossed his legs, and patted the grass next to him. I sat. When I looked up again, Geoff was gone.

"So, what do you do?" Link said. "Are you in your cousin's line of work?"

"What line is that?" I asked.

"Well, it's obvious you're not a naturalist, but I thought you might run a club...or something. One of his, maybe. Or your own."

I knew what kind of club he would have liked me to run. His eyes, struggling valiantly not to stray beneath my shoulders and repeatedly failing, told me that. If his gaze had had fingers, my clothes would have been off me before I hit the ground.

Nudists always say that nudism has nothing whatsoever to do with sex. Don't believe them.

"No, Mr. Link. I'm a writer."

"Novels?"

"Journalism."

"Society?"

"News," I said.

An unhappy look crossed his face—or perhaps merely a look of wariness, as though he were afraid that I might want to talk shop or, worse yet, hit him up for a job.

"I write for the *Globe Dispatch*," I explained. It was the truth. Detective work paid only half the bills in the best of times, and these were hardly the best of times. But my investigations provided occasional scoops too juicy for the *Dispatch* to pass up, and what they couldn't bear to pass up they paid for, sometimes quite nicely.

"I see," Link said. "So you're here about Nash."

I nodded. Better to let him think I was writing a story than that I was investigating the case. It made the difference between his being a source and his being a suspect, wherein often lies the difference between receiving the grudging, anonymous truth and a big, fat, self-protecting lie. "My editor said there's an angle because Nash was riding out a storm at the university," I told him. "Unpopular comments he made, offending the students or something of the sort. You know kids."

"I do," he said. "Have two of my own, both teenage girls." Link was lost in thought for a moment. "Sarah's dating an Albesar boy. I wonder if he knew Nash."

"Did you?"

Link blinked. "Did I—"

"Know Nash."

"Hardly," Link said. "Tiny, old, fidgety man who never mixed. I'd see him sometimes at the water's edge, from a distance. If he saw you watching him, he'd dart back and disappear. Not that I watched him, you understand."

"Of course," I said.

"When he came around to this side of the beach to leave, he would walk through without a word to anyone. And we said nothing to him, at least after the first few times. We respect each other's privacy here, Ms. Jaffe."

Which was a joke, since he was still darting glances at me as though it were I and not he who was naked. I followed Geoff's advice and maintained eye contact at all times. Not that I had any inclination to do otherwise, or that Mr. Kelly Link would have been anything less than delighted if I had.

"Seems odd that a quiet, private man like Mr. Nash would be the center of a controversy for offensive remarks," I said.

"Oh, Nash was an old-line conservative. Students today are all for multiculturalism, homosexual rights, tearing down the Western canon, all that rot. It's even reached Albesar by now. Nash probably said something as offensive as 'We mustn't throw away our copies of Shakespeare just because he was a white man.' Scratch the story beneath the surface, and I'm certain that's what you'll find."

"Perhaps," I said. "And yet the question remains, who

murdered him?"

"I have some thoughts about that," Link said.

"Were you here when it happened?"

"Didn't your cousin tell you?"

"No."

"Well, I was. I was the one Geoff ran to first when he found Nash's body."

"Really!"

"Yes. You see, I was sitting over there." He pointed to the end of the beach nearest the corner of the L. "If anyone had passed me, I would have seen it. No one passed me all morning. I'll swear to that in court. If it comes to that."

"But if no one passed you and no one could get back into the building without passing you—"

Link shook his head. "No. You miss my point. No one passed me until Geoff came running out and told me about the murder. At that point, needless to say, Geoff passed me."

The thrust of Link's theory suddenly became clear. "Surely you don't mean that Geoff killed him?"

"I don't mean anything. I am merely pointing out what I observed. You are his cousin. I don't expect you to draw the same conclusions I have drawn. But they are, nevertheless, my conclusions."

"But if you think Geoff is the killer," I said, "why didn't you tell that to the police?"

Link shrugged. "Your cousin runs a fine club. He and I have never exchanged anything other than congenial words. Nash was a man I never cared for, and I certainly am not going to put Geoff's head on the block in his defense. So, your cousin is a murderer—didn't I say that we respect each other's privacy?"

I disengaged myself politely and moved off down the beach, away from Kelly Link and his theories. I didn't think until it was too late to ask him what had become of the gun —that is, what Geoff had done with the gun if he had, in fact, been the killer. According to the articles I had read in the paper, the police had dredged every inch of the shallow water and had combed quite thoroughly through the sand in search of the murder weapon. They had even dismantled the beach umbrellas and the showerheads in the concrete huts. Nothing had turned up. Any theory that failed to account for the missing gun, as Link's appeared to, fell far short in my estimation.

The sun was a little lower in the sky now, and the sunburned woman I had met before was back on the beach. Having succeeded in roasting her back, she now lay with her front exposed. I was glad to see a sheen of sunblock on her skin, at least.

She turned her head to me as I walked past.

"Ms. Brown!" she called. "If that is your name."

"It's not," I said. "My name is Susan Jaffe." I extended my hand, which the woman took and shook. My hand came away not quite greasy or oily, which I might have expected, but sticky.

"Mine is Eleanor," she said. "Eleanor Crane. And I apologize for shouting at you earlier. I was in a good deal of pain at the time."

"And you're not now? I don't understand how you can lie on your back, the way it's burnt."

Eleanor waved my concern away. "Aloe vera, my dear. Aloe vera. Apply thickly within half an hour of receiving a burn, and the pain recedes to nothingness. I am a great believer in aloe vera."

That accounted for the stickiness. "It's good to know," I said. "I'll buy some the next time I come down here."

"I don't see why," Eleanor said. "You'll get no burns dressed like that. I don't see why you don't just put on a veil the way the women do in those Muslim countries and complete the outfit."

My jaw dropped. "You make it sound as though lying out here naked, inviting skin cancer, which I daresay aloe vera will do nothing to heal, and being stared at by randy old men is some sort of feminist statement."

"In its way, it is, my dear. Going naked is empowering. It says to all those men who stare at us on the street, whether we wear long skirts or short, sheer blouses or thick ones, 'Go on, stare all you like, you don't control me.' Beside which, it feels good—I even like the feel of a bit of sunburn. It reminds me that I'm alive."

I shook my head. "I hope you don't take offense, but I think that's the most foolish thing I have heard in a long time. About the sunburn, particularly, but all of it, really."

She gave me the once-over, raising her head from the chair a little to do it. "If you could see yourself, dear, dressed top to toe in long sleeves and long pants on a beach in the middle of summer, you'd know which of us is foolish. But you may think what you like. Frankly, I don't understand what you are doing here at all if you don't want to undress. It's like going to the movies but keeping your eyes closed and your ears plugged up with cotton, if you ask me."

"I'm not here for the beach," I said. "I'm here for the murder."

Eleanor's eyes opened wide. "The murder? In what capacity?"

"I mean to write it up for the *Globe Dispatch* tonight. Journalism is one of my vocations."

"Then you must have had a good conversation with our Mr. Link," Eleanor said.

"Good enough. He seems to think that Geoff committed the crime, however. I must say—"

"It's preposterous," Eleanor said, lifting herself up on her elbows. "Geoff is the gentlest man I have ever met. And even if he weren't, he had no reason at all to kill Nash. They barely knew each other. And even if he'd had a reason, how could he have done it? I saw him come running over, and he was carrying nothing at the time. He was as naked as I am. The police searched the beach, the umbrellas, everything each of us had with us, the area near the fence, and they found nothing. Nothing! It's what newspaper writers would call an impossible crime. You can quote me on that if you like."

"No crime that has been committed is an impossible crime."

"Quite right, of course. So quote me on something else. I'd love to get my name in the paper."

"Well, who do you think did it?" I asked.

"I told you—I think it's an impossible crime. Maybe sprits descended upon us. Or maybe aliens. Why not say it was aliens, my dear? Or is your paper not the sort that prints that type of story?"

"It's not," I said. "Not yet anyway."

Before I left Eleanor Crane to the joys of sunburn, I asked her to point out the third person who had been present when Nash had been shot. Geoff had told me her name —Elissa Wald—but had not pointed her out to me the way he had Link and Crane.

Crane scanned the beach back and forth and back again; then she looked out to sea and, with a satisfied mm-hmm, pointed to a woman in the water.

The woman lay face-down on an inflatable raft, but whereas Eleanor had a sunburn that rivaled the color of the old Soviet flag, this woman had a remarkable tan, dark and golden, like a perfectly cooked turkey in a television advertisement. She was out of place in at least one other way as well: she looked young, no older than twenty-five. Barring myself, I think she was the only person under fifty on the beach.

I considered how I might attract Ms. Wald's attention. I even thought briefly of commandeering one of the inflatables that lay unused at the end of the beach and floating out to her. But that seemed impractical as well as potentially messy, so instead, I stood at the water's edge and called her.

She heard her name after I had called it three or four times. She looked up, shaded her eyes with her hand, and stared at me. I imagine that I did look foolish; perhaps she even thought I was a mirage. She put her head back down and closed her eyes.

"I want to talk to you," I called. "Ms. Wald, please come in. It's about John Nash."

That got a response: she looked up again, then rolled off the raft and began a swift underwater breaststroke back to the beach. She swam in almost all the way, until there was perhaps no more than six inches between her and the sandy bottom. Then she brought her knees up under her and stood suddenly.

I'd had no idea how tall she was—from a distance she'd seemed of average height. But now, as she wiped the water out of her eyes and wrung out her hair, I realized that she was at least a foot taller than me, which put her at about six foot three. Though I had more than ten years on her and was fully clothed to boot, I suddenly felt a bit overmatched. She stared me in the eye with a sullen expression, and I thought of what Eleanor had told me, about nudity being empowering. I decided that it wasn't pure rubbish after all. I certainly wouldn't have felt so much an unwelcome intruder had this girl I'd dragged unwillingly off her raft at least been wearing something.

"Listen," I said, "I'm sorry to trouble you, but I'm writing up the Nash murder for the *Globe Dispatch*—"

"Fine," Elissa said. "What do you want from me?"

"I understand you were here yesterday when it happened."

"I was here, yes."

"I thought you might want to give me your version of events."

"Not really," she said. She turned away and looked out across the bay. She squinted against the sun and crossed her arms over her chest.

"Do you have any idea who killed him?"

"I said I don't want to talk about it."

"Did you know Nash well?"

She spun around, and now the look in her eyes wasn't sullen; it was enraged. "How dare you interrogate me? This is a private property. I don't recall seeing you here before, and I seriously doubt that you acquired a membership since yesterday. So go away—you have no business here."

"I am a"—I almost said *friend*—"cousin of Geoff Brown's. He invited me."

Elissa shook her head. "Still gives you no right to bother me."

"No. That's true. If you don't want to talk, I can't force you. However, if you did know Nash in some way, I'll be able to find that out. You were here when he was killed and now you won't talk to me—how do you think that will look in the paper?"

"You little bitch," Elissa said. She sized me up. "I bet you'd do it too."

I nodded.

"All right," she said, "try this on: I did know Nash. I was his student. For a term he taught me great literature. Then he found out I was pregnant and almost put me out of his class. Then he found out I'd had an abortion, and he did put me out of his class—not only that, he led the charge to have me thrown out of school. Which was successful, I might add."

"I'm sorry," I said. "That's awful."

"Yes, it is. I'm not at all sorry the man's dead. I sometimes thought of going over to his side of the beach and killing him myself."

"Really?"

"But the fact is that I didn't kill him. You can print that in your paper, if you like: 'Wald Not Sorry He's Dead but Someone Else Got to Him First.'"

"No, that's okay," I said. "I am sorry to have bothered you. I'll respect your privacy." The phrase caught in my throat, and I realized it was the same one Kelly Link had used.

"Good," she said. Suddenly she was in the water again, and before I knew it, she was back on the raft, glistening under the sun.

Strange girl, I thought. I thought of Nash as Link had described him, always making his way off the beach without talking to anyone, as quickly as he could. Surely he knew that Wald was a fellow member; surely he'd seen her on the beach; she cut quite a striking figure. Maybe his haste to get off the beach unnoticed stemmed from more that bashfulness—maybe a part of it was shame, or perhaps fear. I wouldn't have wanted to confront Wald if I'd been him.

I decided it was time to find out a little bit more about this man.

"Isn't it a bit odd," I asked, "that Nash was such a conservative and a nudist as well?"

The old man across the desk from me nodded, his gray fringe of hair shaking vigorously. But then he said, "No, not at all. There is a long tradition of naturalism in this country going back at least three centuries. And of course, the ancient Greeks found nudity entirely unobjectionable. I am not a naturalist myself, but I see no contradiction in Nash's positions. At least not in *those* positions."

I turned to a fresh page in my notebook. "How much do you know about the controversy surrounding Professor Nash?"

"His office is right across from mine. Two weeks ago, a dozen students picketed up and down the hall with signs that read 'Nash is a fascist.' How much more do I have to know?"

"And why did the students think he was a fascist?"

"Oh, probably because he was." He pulled out a cigarette. "Mind if I smoke?"

"Not at all."

Professor Overdeck lit up. Soon his head had a second gray-white wreath around it. "It's hard to say how much of Nash was bluster for the sake of bluster and how much of what he said he really believed. Once he confided to me that he liked to get the students angry with him because it ensured that they were engaged with the material he was teaching them. I don't agree with this tactic, but then I don't like going naked on the beach either. To each his own."

"What was it, actually, that Nash would say that would get the students angry?"

"Everything." Overdeck tipped a quarter inch of accumulated ash into a coffee cup on his desk. "That Albesar had been a better institution when there were no girls there. That the boys studied better when they didn't have girls around to distract them. Which is true enough."

"True?"

"I'm all for progress, Ms. Jaffe. But every act has costs as well as benefits, and it would be foolish to ignore the one out of zeal for endorsing the other."

"What else?"

"That the underclass is partly responsible for its condition and wholly responsible for its fate. That the state owes no debt to the poor and unemployed, for they contribute nothing to the state. That equal distribution of wealth is a fantasy on the order of the Fountain of Youth; that is, unattainable, and undesirable even if attainable. That power in the hands of the few is better than power in the hands of the many."

"And he said all this in the context of his literature classes?"

"Why are you surprised? These are all subjects that come up in literature."

"I suppose." I was getting a clearer picture of the man, but not one that brought me any closer to being able to figure out who had killed him. "How about moral issues?"

"Such as?"

"I talked to a girl who claimed that Professor Nash engineered her expulsion—"

"Elissa Wald."

"Yes. She said Professor Nash led the fight to have her thrown out of Albesar because she had an abortion."

"Nash was a strange man when it came to the subject of sex. He was a passionate opponent of abortion."

"But surely a student cannot be expelled for having an abortion."

Professor Overdeck raised his shoulders and turned his palms out.

"It wouldn't be legal," I said.

"You are correct, of course. Ms. Wald's grades were borderline at best, and she'd had trouble with other students more than once. There were perfectly valid reasons to expel her."

"But?"

"But there are other students in much the same situation who have not been expelled. So, she is justified in asking why she was singled out."

"What is your opinion?"

"I'm not sure my opinion matters. But I'll give it to you anyway, take it for what it's worth. The father—we never knew who the father was for certain, but it was generally believed to be Ronald Bryce. The two of them had certainly spent a great deal of time together. And young Bryce had been one of Nash's favorites—until he started socializing with Ms. Wald. I think Nash resented her. Bad enough that she herself had minimal interest in what he was teaching, but to take away his best pupil as well—that was just too much. He called her a succubus, a lamia, and worse than that."

"He said this to her?"

"I certainly hope not." Overdeck dropped the stub of his cigarette into his cup. It sizzled briefly before going out. "But he said it to me, and we were not especially close. He made no attempt to hide his dislike of her."

"Would you call that professional behavior?"

"No, but I would call it typical of Nash."

I glanced down at my notes. "That young man, Bryce, how might I find him?"

"I'm sure the department has his telephone number. You might have some trouble reaching him, however."

"Why is that?" I asked.

"A week after Elissa Wald returned after having the abortion, he left school. He hasn't been back since."

I tried Bryce's number and got an answering machine. The machine instructed me to leave a message but hung up as soon as the tone sounded. That meant that the message cassette was full, and that meant Bryce hadn't listened to his messages in some time.

There are ways to find a person other than the obvious, though, and given my profession, I know more than a few of them. I got the numbers of his classmates, asked professors who his friends were, spoke to those students about where they had seen him last. I asked Elissa, who answered bitterly that she of all people wouldn't know where he was, since she hadn't heard from him in months. His parents were out of the country, and their staff had no information to give me. I ran down twenty dead ends, maybe twenty-five, maybe fifty.

But eventually I cast my line and snagged something,

a girl who said she'd seen Bryce on the coast. She drove me to a hostel, from the looks of it a home primarily for moneyed tourists. It was just down the road from the Beachhead International resort I had glimpsed from Heaven, and I decided to look around there after talking with Bryce—if I could find him to begin with.

I examined the register; his name was not on it. I scanned the balconies at the front of the building, but none of the reclining sunbathers matched the photo I'd copied from Bryce's class album. Then I walked around to the back, and there he was, in a lounge chair on a balcony two stories up.

I called to him and said I bore a message from Elissa Wald. He grimaced and hesitated but finally threw down a key, and we were soon seated across from each other in his minimally appointed bedroom.

"Coke?"

I shook my head. He took a bottle out of a Styrofoam chest in the corner, twisted off the cap, sent it spinning out the open window and over the wall of the balcony. Then he sat down. He was a stocky, muscular boy, not nearly as tall as I'd expected from knowing that he'd squired Elissa Wald for the better part of a semester. But you never know. His eyebrows formed a thick, black bar across his face, giving him an air of intensity, but otherwise you wouldn't have thought him a scholar. He was wearing an unbuttoned, short-sleeved shirt and blue boxers covered with pictures of surfboards. A pair of formidable barbells near the foot of the bed got plenty of use, judging by the size of his forearms.

"I lied," I told him right away. "I have no message from Elissa."

"So why did you say you had?"

"It's the only name I knew you would respond to."

"And you are…"

"Susan Jaffe. I'm a newspaper writer working on a story about the murder of John Nash."

He nodded. "Then you will certainly want to talk to Elissa. She hated the man."

"I have, and she has admitted as much."

"Well, that's Elissa. She'll hide nothing."

"So I've seen."

"Then you've been to Heaven?"

"Yes."

"Anything for the story, eh?"

I ignored the comment. "Tell me something, Mr. Bryce. Why did you drop out of Albesar?"

"Drop out? Bite your tongue. I am on extended holiday. They'll take me back when I'm ready to return."

Given his parents' net worth, an idea of which I'd developed in the course of my hunt for him, I was sure this was true. "It's good to know you haven't given up on scholarship entirely. Professor Nash would've been disappointed."

"Please. Nash was a horse's ass, and I told him so on more than one occasion. That's why he liked me. I'd say it to his face, and we'd laugh about it. It wasn't that he liked my interpretation of Wordsworth or Shelley. I'm not saying he didn't—but the reason he took me under his wing was that I was willing to debate with him, man to man, rather than picketing outside in the hall or smearing his name under an alias in the school paper."

"I understand that you didn't spend much time with him after you started seeing Elissa."

Bryce fixed me with an odd stare. "There are only so many times you can have the same arguments with an old man who isn't going to change his mind. I really don't enjoy debate for its own sake. After a while, I gave up."

"When you started seeing Elissa."

"Around then, yes."

"Some people say Nash resented Elissa for taking your time away from him."

"He took me drinking after class one day and told me she was a bloody whore." He took a long pull on his Coke, finishing the bottle. "I'd say he resented her."

"And that he devised her expulsion for this reason?"

"Listen, Ms. Jaffe, what are you trying to do? Build a case against Elissa? I'll save you the trouble. I can't think of anyone who had a better reason to kill him, and from what I've read about it, she's one of only a few people who had the opportunity. I assume she killed him. If that's what you wanted to hear me say, now you have."

"You're a cold man, talking that way about your lover."

"I'm an honest man, and she's not my lover, she's my ex-lover."

"Was it your child, then, the child she aborted?"

He tapped his fingernail against the soda bottle. I'd thought to slip the question in, get an answer before his guard went up. Now, in the sudden silence, I realized that his guard had been up all along.

"I've been told that it was," I said.

"People talk," Bryce said, "and you can't change their minds. So it isn't worth arguing."

"Then it wasn't your child?"

"Like I said, it's not worth talking about. People will believe what they want to believe."

"What do *you* believe?" I asked.

"I believe it's time for a swim." He stood up. "I think we've talked about this plenty. I'd like to table the topic for the day."

"Where do you swim? At the resort?"

"Beachhead, yes."

"I was just on the way there myself," I said. "I'll come with you."

He looked less than delighted. "I hope you have a suit on under that. Strip down at Beachhead and you'll catch more glances than you did at Heaven."

"Oh, I'm not going to swim," I said, "just walk on the beach."

"Fine," he said. "Suit yourself."

From this side of the bay, the people at Heaven might as well have been clothed. Now they were the stick figures, walking along their crooked, little stretch of beach, paddling rafts around on the far side of the buoys.

The crowd at Beachhead paid them no attention except for occasional pointing and laughing. Even this was no guarantee of voyeuristic intent, since pointing and laughing were everywhere; people pointed at the snack hut, at the parasailers overhead, at the lifeguard's post, at each other. I saw no binoculars or telescopes trained on the other side of the water. Nor did I see any parasailers returning with their trunks around their ankles, though I did see almost as curious a sight, a lad who must have weighed two hundred fifty pounds strapped into a harness and dragged out over the water. I was surprised when he became airborne—I would have expected him to sink. They towed him out halfway to the buoys, then turned and came back, and all the way he never rose more than twenty feet above the water.

Ronald Bryce had outpaced me as soon as we left the hostel. He was in the middle of the beach before my foot even hit the sand. I wasn't sure why he was so eager to get away from me, though several possible explanations suggested themselves. Maybe he didn't like talking to reporters—most people did not. Or maybe he thought he'd said too much against Elissa. They were ex-lovers, but that didn't mean he wanted to see her go to prison. Or perhaps he was afraid that she *wouldn't* go to prison and would see his accusations in the paper—if she had killed Nash, it made sense for him to be afraid of her.

I walked along the beach until I reached him. He was in conversation with two girls and another boy.

"Following me, Ms. Jaffe?" Bryce asked.

"I didn't want to leave without saying goodbye."

"Goodbye."

"It almost sounds as though you want me to leave."

"We're not friends. You're a reporter; you got what you wanted out of me. I told you I'm not saying any more. So sure, I'd be delighted if you left."

"Ronald!" one of the girls said. "Don't be rude."

Bryce shrugged. "Goodbye, *please*," he said. Then, to the girl: "Happy?" She smiled at him flirtatiously, and he grabbed her around the waist, lifting her off her feet. She kicked a little, but he didn't put her down and she didn't really seem to mind.

"Any messages for Elissa?" I said.

He turned back to me. "Confession is good for the

soul," he said. "Tell her I said that."

I didn't tell her—but I told Geoff Brown. We were sitting in his office. The curtains were drawn so we couldn't look out on the sun as it settled over the water. This was no time for admiring a sunset.

"Will they release her?"

"If I personally guarantee her, I believe they will. Until the trial."

"You would do that?"

"She is one of my members. I can do no less."

"On what grounds did they arrest her?"

"She had an opportunity and a motive for the murder. Link and Crane had opportunity—as, I suppose, did I— but no motive. This makes Elissa the prime suspect, even if they don't know how she carried out the murder."

"And she denies it."

"Yes."

"Link comes to no one's defense except Link's. He doesn't want to get embroiled in a scandal. He thinks it would tarnish his image even to be associated with this club, much less this murder."

"And Crane?"

"Eleanor is not...let's just say that her testimony carries very little weight with the police. She is too apt to say something that makes her sound like a lunatic. Which she is not, by the way. It's just in her nature to attempt constantly to shock people."

"So, in the absence of any better explanation—"

"They locked Elissa up, that's right. Their first clever notion was that she must've gotten on one of the inflatable rafts, paddled around to the other side of the beach, shot Nash, squeezed the gun into the inflatable through the inflation hole—don't ask me how—and paddled back. They abandoned that one after checking all the rafts, though."

"No gun."

"No gun," he agreed. "Then they thought she might have hidden it in or under one of the buoys. So they searched the buoys."

"No gun?"

"No gun. Now they're trying to come up with some other explanation. But they're confident that she is guilty."

"Ronald Bryce seemed pretty confident too."

"Yes," Geoff said. "It's becoming quite a consensus."

"Tell me something," I said. "Do you think she killed him?"

He shook his head.

"Neither do I."

"But, Susan, in my case it's sentiment talking. Look at this." He pulled out a file from one of his desk's drawers, opened it to a typewritten list. "She's been coming to Heaven even longer than Nash. Her mother used to bring her when she was a child." The page listed the first dozen or so members of Heaven: Lydia Brown, Geoff Brown, Arthur Tannaos, Caryn Wald, Elissa Wald, John Nash, Kelly Link, Damon Carter, Lionel Bryce, Kyle Williams, Samuel Shaulson, Tyrone Clerk. "I saw her grow up. I can't imagine her killing anyone."

One of the names on the list caught my eye. "This Lionel Bryce, is he any relation to Ronald?"

"I don't know," he said. "Could be. Lionel stopped coming years ago. I believe he passed away."

"I wonder."

"Bryce is hardly an uncommon name."

"True. But I still wonder."

I chose an empty corner of the locker room and changed into the bathing suit I'd brought with me, plain white and inoffensively conservative. It had seemed like the best compromise and not very likely to attract attention.

Eleanor Crane smiled at me when I stepped out onto the beach. "One step closer, my dear."

I nodded to her. We were the only ones on the beach this early in the morning. The rafts were lined up in the surf, bobbing slowly. Some had deflated overnight. I chose one that hadn't, climbed aboard, and clumsily pushed off. I lay down on my side, then turned over on my stomach to steer. The headrest of the float came up in front of my face, so I couldn't see where I was going. But I didn't have to see.

I dipped a hand in the water on either side of the raft and pushed myself toward Elissa.

I saw her off to one side. She was lying on a raft herself, glistening in the morning sun, turning slowly as she swept the water with one hand. I tried to bring my raft up next to hers but came up behind her instead. I didn't slow down in time, and we collided.

She started. "What—"

"Sorry," I said.

"Oh. You."

"I'm glad to see you out here," I said.

"Why?"

"Because it means you're not in jail."

"Geoff got me out. I'd've thought you'd know all about it. It was in the papers."

"I don't read the papers. I just write for them."

"So what are you writing now? A follow-up piece? 'Murderess Skinny-Dips after Her Release'?"

"I don't believe you're a murderess."

"Why not? Everyone else does."

"Not Geoff."

She shrugged. "He probably does too."

"No," I said. "He really doesn't. He hired me to find out who killed Nash. If he thought you were guilty, my job would be over. It's not. He still wants me to find out who killed him."

"I thought you were his cousin. I thought you were a newspaper writer."

"Well, I am a writer. I am also a private investigator. I am not his cousin. That was a lie."

"So why should I believe you now?"

"Because I believe you."

She shrugged again.

"I found Ronald Bryce. He's a good-looking guy."

"Yes."

"Can I ask you some questions about him?"

"Please don't."

We floated for a while in silence. Across the bay, a powerboat started up and came toward us, trailing a parasailer. As this one came closer, I could see that he was holding a video camera and aiming it down at us. Elissa turned over onto her stomach, put her head on her arms. "If I had a gun now," she said, "I'd be a murderess and never regret it."

The powerboat made the turn and started to head back to its side of the bay. The parasailer lingered overhead for a few seconds, finishing his long, lascivious arc. He shouted something—at me, I suppose, for not being undressed enough for his liking. But he was too high up for the words to be fully audible. It was better that way.

Elissa turned over again, pulled a bottle of suntan oil out of one of the raft's dimples, and reapplied it to her chest and legs.

"Does that happen often?" I asked.

"Every day."

"So why do you come out here and lie naked, knowing that they'll come and gawk at you?"

"I've been coming here for almost twenty years," Elissa said, "since before there was anything at all on the other side of the bay. I like it here. I'm not going to stop coming because of them."

"I understand."

"Do you?"

"I think so," I said. "You're a stubborn woman. I mean that as a compliment. You stick with what you believe in, and you finish what you start."

"That's right."

"The same way you stayed with Ronald. People told you not to, Professor Nash told you not to, he told other people you were seducing his best student—"

"I don't want to talk about this, I told you."

"But you loved him and you kept seeing him. You even got pregnant by him. It was his baby, wasn't it?"

Elissa didn't say anything.

"But then you had an abortion. Why? Did you finally give in to the pressure? Did it get to you after all?"

Silence.

"Why won't you talk to me about it?"

"You said it, I'm a stubborn woman."

"At least tell me this: Do you know if Ronald was re-lated to Lionel Bryce, who used to be a member here?"

"Lionel was Ronald's uncle. He died a few years ago."

"Thank you."

"For what?"

"For answering one of my questions."

Elissa turned to face away from me.

"Will you answer one more?" She didn't say any-thing. "Who do you think killed Nash?"

Her voice was soft. "I don't know."

"Did you see anything that morning? Anything un-usual?" I waited. "Please, it's important."

She rolled off her raft and into the water. I saw her brown form streak through the water toward the shore. When she surfaced again, she was thirty feet away, sitting in the shallows with her back to me. I paddled to her, slid off the raft, and knelt in the sand.

"Get away from me."

"I want to help—"

"You want to pry. You want to get a story and put it in the papers for everyone to see. You're like that guy with the camera, only you're worse, because he'll show his video maybe to a few of his friends and that's all, but you want to show me to everyone. You want to expose me—and a hell of a lot more than just my body."

"I don't want to expose anyone except John Nash's murderer."

"Then leave me alone!"

"Okay," I said. I walked out of the water and toward the main building. I thought I heard Elissa crying behind me, softly, but I didn't look back.

Even with sunblock, I'd burned a little. I lay awake, uncom-fortable on my stomach, worse on my back, unable to fall asleep. I should have bought some aloe vera, I told myself. But I hadn't, and now it was too late.

I got up and ran cold water in my bathtub, closed the drain, waited for the tub to fill. Then I climbed in and soaked. The pain dulled. It was temporary relief, but I'd enjoy it while it lasted.

As the burn receded, though, I realized that it was not the only reason I'd been unable to fall asleep. My mind buzzed with all the interviews I had conducted, all the information and half-information I had collected. I couldn't help thinking of Elissa sitting half in and half out of the water, sobbing like a forlorn mermaid. I did believe she was innocent. But how could she be? There had only been four people present at the murder scene, and three of them had had no reason to commit the murder.

But, at the same time, how could she be guilty? Nash had been killed by gunshot, and she had no gun.

I thought about Nash, the tiny slip of a man at the center of everything, a tyrant in his classroom but a timid gnome in his private life. I thought about his jealousy for Bryce's affection, his cruelty toward Elissa. He had denigrated her to others, and I could hardly imagine that he hadn't done so directly to her face as well. Had he told her that she'd ruined Bryce's life? Had he tormented her into having an abortion? Not intentionally, surely—he opposed abortion. But had he done so nevertheless?

I thought about Nash's corpse bundled up in his towel like a little package. I thought about Geoff's finding it, unaware of what it contained. I thought about the gunshot they'd heard that had sounded like a backfire, about the one-way entrance into Nash's side of the beach, about Martin, with his wristwatch and necktie, watching everyone come in. Everyone but Nash.

And then, all at once, I understood how it had been done. And I thought I knew why.

I stood next to Geoff, who stood next to Elissa. They'd both dressed for the occasion, which is to say that they had put on clothes. Elissa's short wrap didn't cover much, but it was better than nothing, and I didn't catch Inspector Michael Morris staring once. Well, maybe once.

But when the boat started up, all of our attention was focused on the horizon. It came toward us, trailing its human cargo at the end of a parasail cord. The cord was nearly horizontal, the parachute billowing out behind like a great, red-and-white balloon.

The driver of the boat aimed directly at us and didn't turn aside halfway across the bay as the boats usually did. He sped right up to the line of buoys and made a tight turn only at the last instant, sharply reversing direction and then stopping.

We all took an extra step back from the shore. I heard Geoff's gasp.

The man in the parachute's harness kept sailing toward us, the rope that held him to the boat describing the arc of an enormous circle. He flew over the buoys, over the water, and finally over the beach.

Now we could see that he had his elbows hooked around the parasail lines and that he held something in his arms: a bundle wrapped in a towel I had borrowed for the occasion. With a heave, the man released the bundle when he was at the midpoint of his arc. It landed at our feet.

Suddenly relieved of the extra weight, the chutist was jerked upward and, in an instant, rose forty feet into the air. Now he was at proper parasailing height. The boat started up again and began towing him to the opposite shore.

Within seconds he was just a speck in the sky.

Morris unhooked a walkie-talkie from his belt and spoke into it. "Thanks, Simon. You can bring him in."

Geoff bent and looked at the bundle. It was a towel wrapped around a life-size CPR training dummy, borrowed from the police. Not just any towel, either—the towel had a large number six stitched in the middle.

"My God, Susan. Even his towel. But how did you get that?" He turned to Morris. "Did you release it to her?"

"No, I just asked your towel attendant for it," I said. "It was right where it should have been. Nash never checked it out."

"But we found it—"

"No. What you found was towel number nine. Lionel Bryce's towel."

Geoff closed his eyes. "And who had Lionel Bryce's towel?"

"Lionel Bryce did, until he died. Then his nephew, Ronald, must have found it among his effects."

"That's unbelievable. It's too much of a coincidence." Geoff shook his head. "What if Lionel had been number eight —or number ten?"

"Then maybe Ronald would never had gotten the idea for this scheme. Maybe he would have thought up some other way to kill Nash, or maybe he would have done it the same way, only he would have left the towel out. But the fact was that his uncle's towel could double for the towel of the man he wanted to kill—an enormous coincidence, I agree. And one he couldn't pass up."

"So, Ronald killed Nash," Geoff said.

I looked at Elissa, who was hugging herself tightly and staring at me. There was rage in her eyes, though whether it was directed at Ronald or me, I couldn't say. "It's the only explanation that makes sense," I said.

"It doesn't make sense to me," Inspector Morris said. He lumbered over to us, kicking up divots of sand as he came. "I'm not saying you're wrong about the fact—this was a convincing demonstration, Ms. Jaffe. Bryce must have lured Nash somewhere else, possibly to his hotel, shot him, and then flown his corpse over here."

"Exactly," I said. "Martin didn't see Nash come in that morning, but Martin never saw Nash come in any morning— Nash habitually used this entrance."

"Hold on, Susan," Geoff said. "There's a big difference between carrying a dummy and carrying a dead body."

"I don't know what Nash weighed," I said, "but he was a small man. If you'd seen Bryce, you wouldn't doubt that he could carry him."

"But the gunshot we heard—" Geoff said.

"The one you first thought was a backfire? My guess is that it was a backfire."

"Fine," Morris said. "I'm not questioning the how. And I even believe you about the who: Bryce's towel is as damning as a piece of evidence can be. But why? Why did he kill Nash? That's what doesn't make sense."

"Elissa," I said, "would you like to explain it?"

She shook her head.

"Then I'll try. Bryce wanted Nash dead, and he wanted Elissa to be blamed for it. He wanted them both to suffer. Why?" I gave Elissa one more chance, but she wasn't talking. "Because," I said, "they killed his child. She got pregnant by Bryce, but under tremendous pressure from Nash about having sabotaged Bryce's future, she had an abortion. A week after the abortion, Bryce left school. He still hasn't come back. That's how strongly it affected him. Clearly, he wanted them both to pay.

"He must have known that Elissa would be charged with the killing—that's the only reason he could have had for this elaborate scheme to plant the corpse on the beach. His bit of foolishness was shooting Nash. If he had strangled him or broken his neck, there would have been none of this confusion about a missing murder weapon. And no one would have doubted that Elissa could kill him in one of those ways. She's twice his size."

"That's fine," Morris said, "except—"

"Except that it's not true."

Ronald Bryce came onto the beach flanked by two police officers, each gripping one of his elbows. Bryce's hands were crossed and cuffed behind his back. A third officer led another handcuffed man, this one scowling. I recognized him as a speedboat driver I'd seen at Beachhead, presumably the one Bryce had hired to tow him when he flew over with Nash's body.

Bryce looked at me and then at Elissa. She turned away from him.

"Please," she said. She sounded as if she were about to cry.

"Your reasoning was sound, Ms. Jaffe," Bryce said. The sound of gloating rang in his voice. "It isn't your fault that you were proceeding from faulty premises."

"Ronald, don't," Elissa said. "Haven't you done enough?"

"You see," Bryce said, "it wasn't my child she aborted."

"Then whose?" Morris asked.

"It was Nash's."

The sound of the surf was the only sound we could hear. That, and Elissa's sobbing, muffled when she buried her face in Geoff's shoulder.

"Nash's," I said. "But when did he—"

" 'When did he,' " Bryce said mockingly. "When didn't he? This is a man who got off on exposing himself to young girls, and not just on the beach either. You think Elissa's the first student who got a special lesson from him after class? Did you think you were, Elissa?"

Morris put his hand on Bryce's chest and pushed him back a little. "Calm down, mister."

"Oh, Ms. Jaffe," Bryce said, "it's such a sad story. One your readers would really want to hear. A beautiful girl, smart enough, but not—shall we say?—academically inclined, in danger of failing her classes, and along comes John Nash, the eminent professor, and all he asks in return for some grade improvement is a bit of extracurricular apple polishing.

"Only this time the adventure goes too far, and a little Nash starts growing as a result. The eminent conservative is now faced with an unwanted pregnancy. Fortunately for him, everyone thinks the kid's mine. Including me.

"I pay for an abortion. I hold her hand before and after. I make her tea and fix her goddamn pillows. And it's only afterwards, when Nash is in his cups and not thinking too carefully about whether he should really share his every private thought with this particular young acolyte, that I find out whose fetus it was that I paid to have scraped into a basin."

Elissa pulled free of Geoff's arms then and, in three steps, was at Morris's side, shaking furiously. Without breaking stride, she smashed Bryce under the chin with a tremendous uppercut. Morris pulled her away.

Bryce's head snapped back with the blow, and he was slow to right it.

"Come on," Morris said, waving his men back toward the main building. "Get him out of here."

It was close to six in the evening, a week later, and the beach was nearly empty. Geoff and I faced each other across a picnic table that was bare except for an unfinished bottle of beer in front of me and a finished bottle in front of Geoff.

"It feels like everything is coming apart," he said. "Nash killed, Elissa arrested, Lionel Bryce's nephew in jail…"

"Well, it's over now. Elissa's back." We could see her on her inflatable raft, bobbing near the shore. "As for Bryce, he brought it on himself."

"I'm still glad Lionel didn't live to see it." He pulled my beer over to his side of the table and drank down what was left.

"What I still don't understand," I said, "is why Elissa allowed herself to be expelled from Albesar, to be publicly humiliated, when she could have turned the tables on Nash at any time by telling the world what he'd done."

Geoff shrugged, looked out at the water, and pointed with his beer bottle. "I've known her since she was a baby. But I can't say I've ever understood her."

A few minutes later, he left, carrying the bottles in one hand and his towel in the other. I watched his retreating figure. Maybe it was the approaching sunset, or something about his posture, but the sight of this naked man dwindling in the distance no longer seemed ridiculous to me. It had a certain dignity.

I walked to the water's edge where Elissa was paddling with one hand, making her raft turn in a slow circle. I sat in the sand an arm's length away. She was facing away from the shore and couldn't have seen me, but when I sat down, she spoke.

"I heard what you were saying," she said. "About what I could have done, and not understanding why I didn't do it." She kept turning, slowly, slowly, and eventually she was facing me. "Do you really not understand, or were you just saying that to Geoff?"

"No," I said, "I really don't."

"Did you ever think about what you'd do in my position? You're a student who's flunking, he's a famous and esteemed professor, at Albesar no less. You can tell the world you let him sleep with you to get a better grade, but that won't get you readmitted to the school."

"You were out anyway," I said. "It would at least have punished him for what he did."

"Sure, it would have punished him," she said, "but what else? It would have destroyed Ronald. He didn't know the child wasn't his."

"But he did," I said.

"But I didn't know that. I thought he didn't."

I didn't want to keep pushing, or at least part of me didn't, but the part of me that makes me a reporter and a detective couldn't hold back. "I still don't understand. Why was it worth it to bear this burden just to protect Ronald? He'd left you."

I could see the wet tracks of tears on her cheeks. "He would have come back. If it was his child and I'd lost Albesar because of it, he'd have come back. Eventually. I know he would."

I left her on her raft, still turning in her slow circles, staring straight up into the sky.

Charles Ardai is the founder and editor of Hard Case Crime as well as an acclaimed author. His five novels include the Shamus Award-winning *SONGS OF INNOCENCE*, which the Washington Post called "an instant classic." In addition to the Shamus, Ardai has received the Edgar Allan Poe and Ellery Queen Awards. He was a writer and producer for six years on the TV series *HAVEN*, inspired by Stephen King's first Hard Case Crime novel, *THE COLORADO KID*. King has called him "a true renaissance man" and "a master of the short story." Ardai lives in New York.

THE FIVE THIEVES OF BOMBAY BEACH

By Rob Roberge

Why hat brings me here to this this postapocalyptic blistering hellscape of sand and ballistic heat and toxic water and the smell of millions of tilapia skeletons that crunch under your feet as the stink of sulfur fills the air and trips your gag reflex the minute you step out of your car? To a place whipping up newly exposed, dried scabs of wind-carried pesticides and particles of heavy metals and nitrates from decades of agricultural runoff? Why here in a hundred- and- twenty- degree desert in August? Why Bombay Beach?

I'd found out I had a father. This was back in Chicago. This was five years ago by my mother's deathbed. Found out that she hadn't fucked some stranger to end up with me in her life. That there was a man she knew. A man she was *with*. A man who knew about me. It revised my whole life. Took a red pen to sentences I thought were done. Knocked me off my axis. Divided my life, I felt in the moment she told me, into *then* and *now*. One of those things, like love, like death, where something primal and inarticulate makes you *know* life will never be the same.

My mother said they were maybe going to marry before she wised up. Though she had no idea what had happened to him after my birth. That he "had issues" and it was best I didn't know the man. Not knowing him was one thing. Not knowing he existed? Another. She gave me his name. Walt Reed.

Two weeks after that, I still had my father's name and I had a dead mother. My focus shifted to him so quickly that I don't know if I've ever really mourned my mother. Maybe I'd have time to feel guilty about that when I finally found my father. It's like I couldn't miss her until I found him.

My birth certificate did not have a father's name on it. The father space was blank, except that someone wrote "Negro." My mother was listed "Caucasian." And me? Seven and one half pounds of, apparently, "Mulatto."

Facts here and there. Born in Newark, New Jersey, June 12, 1944. The rest was all like constellations. You find a dot here and there. Another few. You get enough of them, you connect them into an image. A picture. Something that makes sense.

I know how to make stories out of scraps. I make documentary films you see on PBS and at festivals. When you're telling the story, really the footage is material. The arrangement is the story.

Tracking my father took five years. I can't count the times I wanted to stop. On a tape loop in my head, I asked and asked, *Why do this to yourself?* I never knew he existed. So why the need to find him?

Still, info trickled in. My fingers blued from forty-year-old ditto paper. My eyes blurred from slurs of retina-scathing light from the microfiche.

My father was a sick man. Diagnosed manic-depressive a couple times. Schizophrenic others. Schizoaffective disorder at Belleview. I researched all of them, though I really had no way of knowing which, if any, was a correct diagnosis. The only thing all the reports had in common was that he didn't take his meds, whatever they were. No matter the doctor or hospital, he did not take his meds.

I couldn't slow the turbine of anger that my mother had kept him a secret. Kept me from my own life. Why? I worked it from every angle I could think of. Maybe I was wrong. Maybe she thought he was dangerous. It seemed like I would have heard of the man, then. Violence can be a fingerprint on the street. It's what identifies you. But men can be safe as all hell out in the world, and monsters to women and children in their living room. Maybe she was trying to *protect* me. I tried to feel her. I tried to miss her. I know I loved her. I tried to feel that. I knew I would again. I hoped I would. But all I had was this mystery of Walt Reed. This stranger who'd become the most important person in my life.

The evidence that always put my stomach in a zero-gravity machine? Near the box or line for "Family," where my father (or some intake nurse or doctor) had to fill out his paperwork, every single time, the "Family" entry is blank, or crossed out with an X. In every psychiatric intake form I could find, every booking on his rap sheet, every form on the medical paperwork, the military paperwork, the VA shit —but there was nothing violent on any of the records, which let me breathe a desperate breath I didn't know I'd been holding.

Family: _____ Family: X

Did my father really *think* he had no family? Was being that alone a choice? Did he even make what we think of as choices? Did he not want to be found? What could possibly have happened?

I hated myself for clinging to this one hope: That my father said he had no family, said it repeatedly without ever changing it because he loved me—he knew I existed, he *must* have—and he didn't want to be seen the way he was. People stay away from people they love when they think it's best. Sick people don't want to be seen. People leave when they think the world is better off without them. Typical clinical depression. Typical suicidal position to find yourself in, if you really think that. I'm like that sometimes, and I'm not broke and I function. Still. It's there. I'd found the source.

I'll never know the reason for that absence next to "Family," but he *had* a reason. He must have. I'm choosing to live with my fragile version. He was keeping me, in his mind, safe. That there was a memory of me inside of him. There was love. There was—damn, I hope there was—regret. I don't think I'm right for a second if I focus on it too long, so I don't.

The thing about research is that it's not chronological or organized. It doesn't start with his birth and end with his death. You pick up a document and it's 1967. A picture from 1954. A handwritten note from a girlfriend, date unknown.

Evidence jumps in time. New info resonates with old info. So what did I get?

Institutions in the sixties, the fifties. Youth "camp" in his teens. Psych wards by twenty-one. Pools of puke and shit and slobber, and men and women bound helplessly to themselves as they rolled in it all.

There is one picture I have of Walt Reed. A booking photo from 1969, when he was twenty-five years old. He looks like me, fifteen years ago. Or, I look like him, thirty-five years ago. I look at it all the time. I'm in there. I can see me.

I imagine him at every age I've been. And, whether it's a fact or not, I choose to believe you could not mistake we were blood.

The National Archives in Washington, DC burned in 1973. Good luck finding those records. Still, I checked the death and assault database of every prison and hospital I knew he'd been to. Nothing.

My father showed up again in Los Angeles in 1975, living downtown at the SRO Cecil Hotel.

His paper trail died for another year or so, and then the last evidence I could find brought me here. The last place anyone saw my father. 1977. His last mailing address: 1561½ B Avenue, Bombay Beach, CA.

I looked it up.

Salton Sea was really a lake formed when a canal from the Colorado River busted entirely, and the Colorado filled the Salton Basin. An accident.

Fifty years later, it was called California's Riviera. Filled with people skiing in the Salton Sea. Fishing, boat racing, and more. Sinatra and the Rat Pack hung at the North Shore Yacht Club. You'd see Sonny Bono. The Beach Boys. That ended when the Salton Sea all but died because of pesticides and heavy metals from fertilizer and the agricultural runoff. The last nail in the coffin? The floods that took out the larger east side of Bombay Beach in 1977. Left it underwater forever. Six thousand people used to be there in the early sixties. It got more visitors than Yosemite. Last census had the population at 285 people. Two-thirds over sixty-five.

Town full of old people. Someone knew my father. If I couldn't find him, I had nowhere left to go.

I headed to the Bombay Beach VFW to find Merle Hopper. Retired Army. On the phone when I first called, he blew hot and cold until I mentioned my father served in Vietnam Changed everything. He was talking to me out of fraternal obligation to my military father. Nothing to do with me. But he said he'd talk. Gave me one thing to do, at least, when I got there.

My energy sinkholed when I stepped out of my car. Sweat pooled and attacked my eyes. The heat put gravity on steroids. Merle waved me over from a picnic table outside of the VFW. On the steps, my legs felt heavy.

He said, "Duane, I'm guessing?"

I smiled. "Duane I'm confirming." Held the smile. I had to be *Friendly* New Guy if I was going to get anyone to talk.

He said, "Get you a drink?"

It was just after noon. The sun pinned me. I thought I could have burned up. Exploded. Like god was a sadistic kid with a magnifying glass. A drink didn't sound bad. And, you know, when in Rome. "Great," I said, "You mind if we head inside, though?" I made it to the top stair. "This weather's an adult dose."

He stood, and I thought we were going inside, and relief washed over me at just the thought of cold air.

He said, "Inside's worse. Humidity's over fifty percent. Swamp cooler don't work if it's over thirty. Just takes this same shit air and blows it in your face." He headed toward the entrance. "Besides, it's broken. You're not missing anything. It wouldn't be working if it was working." He pointed to the table. "Relax. Have a smoke. I'll grab some drinks."

By the time we were on our third PBR chased with Jack Daniels, I knew that Merle got home from the war and didn't recognize his life—the ground shifted under his feet, right was wrong, down was up, two plus two never would add to four again as long as he lived. His wife tossed him.

"Can't blame her," he said. "Though I do wish she could have seen what I saw for a week. Get some idea. I mean, hell, I didn't *want* her to see it. Or understand it. But I did, in a way, you follow?"

I nodded.

"She got the house. Kids. I got the trailer in Bombay Beach where we used to stay in season."

"Back when everything was good?"

"Not good for me. Look where the fuck I ended up."

"I meant, you know. Sinatra. The boats. The skis."

"Boy oh boy, have I been hearing about the good old days forever here. Shit, I've been here long enough, they talk about when *I* got here like they was good times. Maybe 1960 was the cat's fucking pj's. By '90, it seemed the last place on earth before the slabs with plumbing. Shithole."

I'd slowed my pace on the third beer, and it turned warm in a frighteningly short amount of time. "Was it already like this?"

"Nah. It was better. It was still the worst place on earth." He laughed. "But it was better than now. We had families." He pointed at me, seemingly happy. "Black families."

Hearing this place had a legit Black population shocked me, and I said so.

Merle said, "Early nineties, happened right after Rodney King, people leaving the city came here because it used to be safe." He gestured again toward me. "Lot of Black people."

I took a sip of my beer, and it was as hot as coffee.

Merle said, "But the nineties were a long time ago."

No good place to start, so I just did. "That kind of ties in with this missing person I'm trying to find."

"How so?"

"You ever hear anyone talk about a Black guy named Walt Reed? Would have been here before you."

"Don't know much about anything before my time. Except, of course, that this place was heaven on earth itself." He lit another smoke, put it in the ashtray. None of the ones in there were even half-smoked. "You say Reed?"

"Reed, yeah. Walter. Walt."

He looked deep in thought for a moment. Took a deep breath and then puffed his cheeks as he let it out slowly. "Not familiar, no."

"Folks would probably remember him as crazy. Really strange guy?"

"Really strange guy doesn't narrow it down much around here. But, no. Never heard the name."

"I'm hoping to ask around and see if anyone knows anything about him. Any way you could help me? Get a foot in the door with people?"

Merle shrugged. "If this person you're looking for was before my time? I keep to my business, and I expect the same. I ain't exactly a social butterfly. You want me, you find me here. You want stories, go to the Inn."

"You can't help me with the people?"

Merle laughed. "I could only hurt you with them." He took off his glasses and wiped his forehead. "No offense." Put his glasses on. "Duane is it?"

I nodded.

"You want to hear stories about how life was perfect in 1960? You'll hear plenty. Start poking in people's lives, and memories that don't include water skis and fish and boats?" He shook his head. "The stories tend to dry up."

I'd rented a trailer in town. I cranked the AC and crashed facedown on the bed. I must have slept for five or six hours, but it was still light and incredibly hot when I went out.

The Inn was the Ski Inn, where the locals and the tourists—what was left of both—drank. Locals clustered at the bar. Three old guys seemed to care what was on TV. Around the corner of the bar from them, some guy they called Turtle played video poker.

I leaned on the bar, looking around. The bartender, a smiling woman named Nancy, said, "What can I get for you there, hon?"

I was a little unsteady from my morning with Merle. Worried no one was going to give me five words. I needed Nancy's kindness more than she'd ever know. "Maybe a soda water with lime?"

She leaned over so I could hear her better. "And what do you want to drink?"

"I've already had an early start," I told her. "Trying to pace myself."

She winked at me. "A smart man." She looked over the bar and shook her head. "And a smart man is a lonely man around here." A bell rang when she closed the till. She loudly said, "When you want a real drink, first one's on me, sweetie."

I thanked her and raised and lowered my soda water. She put my change on the bar, and I left it there. Senior citizens gathered at the tables, at the bar. The booths in back. The place had a crazy vibe. Dollar bills from all over the world were glued on every flat surface. The bar, the tables, the panels of the ceiling fan. What looked like a bunch of cans of soup for sale were labeled Fish Assholes. There were pickled eggs, and this was the kind of town where someone might actually eat one of those rancid floaters. Somehow it wasn't shocking that the place had stayed in business after the world had all but ended in town. Tourists were easy to spot. Younger clothes. Sunglasses from l.a.Eyeworks, not Walmart. I cringed when I realized I had more in common with them than the locals. I was in button flies and a black dress shirt. I smiled, remembering my ex-wife, Melinda, who used to make fun of me for wearing black everywhere. Once in the Florida Keys, I was melting into myself, and I begged her to stop and have a drink somewhere cool. She said, "It's not my fault you think Johnny Cash is comfortable at the equator." I could blame our ending on me going crazy trying to find my father, but that seemed easy. If I could really understand what brought us down, maybe I could have understood how to hold us up.

Four old white people went out for a smoke. I could see them through the front window. I nursed my water. If Merle was telling the truth, the town had Black folk once, but they'd clearly moved on. A leather-skinned guy came up next to me with his can in an orange beer cozy, looking me up and down.

Time to fit in. Or be friendly knowing you don't fit in. I introduced myself.

He wore what he'd probably been wearing since the sixties. Beach shorts. T-shirt. Boat shoes. No socks. The guy held his beer up in a toast of sorts. "Buster." He finished his Coors Light and slid it out of the cozy.

I put a twenty down on the bar. "Let me buy you a drink, Buster."

"I can afford my own beer." Gruff. Defensive. He looked over at me with menace. My body wobbled. I *really* didn't think these people were going to tell me anything, did I? I pulled away from Buster, hands up, and sat back in my stool, keeping my eyes on him.

Buster broke out in deep laughter. So did Nancy. So did four women by the jukebox. Everybody from town. All the tourists just stayed together and looked around, wondering what was so funny.

Buster said, "You should have seen your face!"

In ten seconds I went from the verge of pissing my pants to realizing that I'd gotten that foot in the door. Laugh when you're punked. You're either in on it or you aren't. I put myself into it.

Buster put his arm around me. "Where's that beer, Duane?"

Buster smelled of beer and salt and patted me on the back a couple more times before letting go, and I liked him more than our time together could ever justify. Just a feeling. "I thought you didn't want that beer."

"I said I could afford my own beer. Doesn't mean you can't buy 'em all night!"

I paid for two beers and two shots. Buster and I laughed and we knocked the shots back and now we were friends. It seemed like he would have let me crash on his couch.

He said, "Tell me the truth here, Duane. You aren't one of those LA hipsters come out here to study all the weirdos in the weird, little town, are you?"

"No."

"Knew it. Still. What's your angle?"

"I'm a journalist." I took a sip. "Not writing about the town. Doing a piece on some missing people. Here. Other places."

He looked at me. And kept looking at me sidewise as he drank his beer. "Missing people?"

"Nothing as interesting as it sounds." I didn't want to go into any details. You nail people with a bunch of questions when you first meet, you may as well have cut out their tongues. "Long story. Boring."

"Nice to see a man who hates his job." He laughed and pushed me in the chest. Being Buster's pal could end you in an ER.

"How long you been here, Buster?"

"Been staying here over half the year since the fifties. In season, you know? But full-time? Sixty-five." He burped. "Got divorced. She got everything except." He paused. "Bombay Beach."

Divorce. House. Shithole. I wonder how many of these guys followed that path. I ordered us two more drinks. I wanted to ask Buster about my father. But I had to remind myself to slow play it.

I said, "So you've seen pretty much everything go down around here? Good times to bad?"

"There's a bunch of us. Here from the beginning. Not like we could live anywhere else now."

"Was it like people say?"

"People are lying turds." He laughed. "What do they say?"

"The good days here. The Sea. The tourists. The California Riviera. You know."

"If anyone tells you it was heaven, they're understating it." And here I got one of what turned out to be many stories about the heyday. The parties on the beach. The drunken boat races. The time Peter Lawford fucked Miss Salton Sea and Miss Runner-up in the same damn banquet room at the yacht club. "Both sixteen," Buster said. "Not a big deal back then. Not a secret. The Beach Boys were there. I got high with Sonny Bono. Sinatra himself had a guy almost kill a guy for him before he changed his mind. The five bars in town, the best steaks in the world, fish bigger than duffel bags, and so on."

"Guess you've seen pretty much everything, then?"

"Seen it all. The good. The bad. The piles of shit. Even in the good days, we had some troubles. But by the seventies, you're talking drugs, graffiti from kids from god knows where. Abandoned buildings and squatters. The five thieves."

"You had five burglars? In, like, sixty years?" I was thinking this guy had no idea what real crime was.

"Five *thieves.* All at the same time. Same five scumbags and their families stole everything. Your shit disappeared, about six, seven of us would take care of it. Eight when Thorny was in town with the railroad. Clem, Loco, Pierre—this guy who came down from Montreal in the winters. In the winters he was one of us. My kid, Rhett." He paused. "Great kid. You would have liked him, Duane." Buster cleared his throat. "We'd just go to one of the five houses and beat their thieving asses till they talked."

"What about the cops?"

"Cops don't come here. Haven't in decades."

Holy fuck. "What if it wasn't one of the thieves?"

"It was always them."

"What if it wasn't them *that time*?"

Buster shrugged. "Bunch of thieving beaners, half of 'em. The rest just scumbag speed freaks. If they didn't do *that* something, they had done something else worth a beating."

I didn't know how far I could push without losing traction with Buster. "Lot of people frown on that word, Buster."

"Which one?"

I smiled. *Be careful.* "I'm guessing you know."

He looked at me, and I saw a simmering anger that slowly faded to annoyance. Still looking into my eyes, he said,

"I will use whatever words I want."

I held two fingers up for another round. Neither of us needed it, but I had to stay the Friendly Stranger.

Nancy put two beers in front of us. By now, I had a tab.

Buster looked away from me and said, "There are a lot of words I have *chosen* not to use, if you follow." He looked straight ahead at the bar. Turned to me and gave me a huge smile. "You're a good kid, Duane. Not a pussy."

"So, the thieves." I hated myself for letting "beaner" go by. "Okay. The ones you're talking about. Who else did this vigilante justice?"

"Security. Protection. Not vigilantes." He took a drink. "Guy we called the Kraut, but no one really knew where the fuck he was from. Some reason, all he stole was radios."

I laughed. "Not exactly the perfect crime. I mean, if someone lost a radio."

Buster said, "Yeah. Not much in the Kraut's head." Buster looked up. "Ham radios, too, the Kraut. Not just listening-type radios."

"Still. Did he ever get away with it?"

"No one got away with nothing. And, yeah, the Kraut was way too stupid to get away with anything. Wasn't as stupid as Stupid Kenny, though—there was a smart Kenny in town, but he was just Kenny, but Stupid Kenny was—hell, *is* like a five-year-old kid. Surprised he doesn't shit his pants."

Nancy brought our drinks and said to Buster, "Five-year-olds don't shit their pants, genius." She put the empties on her tray.

Buster's face clouded for a second. The noise from the bar filled the gap where we'd stopped talking. He stayed like that for an uncomfortably long time.

Buster looked at his beer but didn't take a drink. He cleared his throat and looked at me again and seemed like he'd snapped out of whatever it was. "Still. I'm kinda shocked Stupid Kenny even knows how to use the can." He shook his head in what looked like empathy. "It's sad as all hell. Poor bastard. Sometimes it was hard to beat the shit out of Stupid Kenny."

I could not believe what I was hearing. Beating the

shit out of Brown people, sure. Savage. But hardly a shock. Whether they stole any shit or not, probably. "You beat him? This Kenny?"

"Not Kenny, Kenny. Stupid Kenny."

"You beat the shit out of a guy who was basically a child, mentally?"

"He stole. A dog can learn not to shit on a floor. Doesn't take an Einstein." Buster looked at me and softened. "I'm not the bad guy, kid. Clem, maybe. Hell, I promise I always made sure we beat Stupid Kenny less. No kicking when he dropped. No one ever got seconds." He finished his beer, then added the one Nancy had just brought into his briefly empty cozy. "It's in the past. Kenny's okay." He paused. "What can I say? Those were different days."

I couldn't talk. I offered Buster a smoke.

"Nah," he said. "I've got leukemia."

That moment went by like every moment anyone tells you they have cancer. And the next moment. What do you say? There are no correct words. You may as well chew gravel. "Damn, Buster. I'm really sorry."

He laughed. "I've had it for fifty years. Maybe I *should* start smoking!"

"Leukemia?"

He nodded.

"That's not something people have for fifty years, Buster."

Buster called Nancy over. Said, "Nancy, sweetheart, do I have cancer?"

"Forever, darlin', forever."

He looked at me and smiled at her confirmation. "They gave me six weeks to live fifty years ago," Buster said. "Now, once, sometimes twice a year, I go up to Eisenhower Hospital —sometimes even the Mayo Clinic—and they have groups of doctors poke around at me and try to figure out why I'm not dead."

I said, "You're shitting me."

Buster said, "I am not. I mean, tons of doctors."

"That's crazy," I said.

"I'm not talking just any doctors." He put his beer on

the bar and leaned into me like he had a great secret. "Smart doctors. Orientals."

I was at the VFW when the guy Buster called Stupid Kenny came in to order a six-pack to go. While he was waiting, I walked up, but as soon as I got close, he jumped away like I'd snuck up on him. I slowly put my hand out and introduced myself. He looked away.

The bartender Kristy handed the bagged six-pack to Kenny, who brought a fistful of balled singles and loose change out of a grimy Levi's pocket. I dropped a twenty on the bar and split the change between Kristy and Kenny.

Kenny looked at me, shaky as a morning drunk. "What do you want?"

"Do you mind if I ask you a couple of questions. It's Kenny, right?"

He nodded.

I led him to my booth by the front window. Merle sat outside at the picnic table on the porch, looking back at me every once in a while.

"Kenny. Do you remember—I'm going to ask you about a long time ago."

"Okay."

"This would have been in the seventies."

He downed half his pint. "*Love Boat!*"

"Okay. Do you remember a Black guy named Walt from back then?"

No answer. But it looked like he was trying.

"Here for maybe a year around the floods," I said.

Kenny downed the rest of his beer. "He talked to himself. Lots." He looked up. "Is that who you mean?"

Adrenaline shot through me like when you're in a car accident. And after, I felt weightless, dizzy, confused. "That's who I mean, yes."

"Talked to himself, yup."

"Can you tell me anything about him? Anything."

"I think people thought he has stupid." He paused. "Like people think I'm stupid but not the same as people think I'm stupid."

I paused. Breathing. "He left town, right?"

Kenny shook his head. "Everyone said he drown in the Sea."

I thought about it. The whole east side of the town was underwater to this day. It got ten times the water the west side did. My father lived on Avenue B. West side.

"Did anyone else die?"

"Dogs and cats floating in town the next day. Chickens. Clem's pigs. You take a step, a dead dog hits you in the thigh. In the chest some places. Birds. Cats. All floating."

"And the dead guy. Where was he?"

"He couldn't breathe underwater. Just like the animals. That's what they told me in the morning. He talked to himself and he couldn't breathe underwater."

"The morning?"

"The next morning. I remember because I cried because I had Tim-Tim, my cat, and he was on the water too."

"Kenny. If I buy you some more beer, will you keep what you told me a secret?"

He smiled. "I like secrets."

"So, no one gets to know about what we talked about, right?"

"Dogs and cats float." He smiles. "Just us!"

I bought him another six-pack and left it at the table with him.

The next day I saw Buster at the Inn.

"Hey there," he said, beer and coffee in front of him on the bar. "How's my young Woodward doing? Or are you Bernstein?" He punched me in the arm.

It hurt, but I laughed. "That missing person thing, Buster."

"Yeah. What's up?"

"The guy I'm looking for was named Walt Reed."

Buster put his coffee down. He looked in the mirror behind the bar. Straight ahead, like he was looking past anything in front of him. Through the wall. "Not ringing a bell."

"I hear he died in the flood. Seventy-seven."

Buster paused a long time. The ice machine released

a new load, and the fresh cubes cascaded down their metal slide into the cubes already below.

"Black guy. Probably crazy. Really strange."

Buster looked a little scared, a little confused. "Yeah. I never knew the name, but yeah. That guy was here one minute and gone the next. No one knew him much. But, yeah. That flood." He shook his head. "That killed this town, more or less. Ruined everything. And that guy—I never knew his name. Gone, though. That much I know."

Never knew his name? I left that there for a while.

People saw Buster liked me. The town opened up.

After nearly every single one of them told me I should do a movie about their lives, they started to talk.

The floodgates opened. They all knew Walt Reed. The strange Black guy who kept to himself, who ate out of the VFW and Ski Inn garbage. Who people mostly ignored. Everyone told me they really didn't know him. Every one of them said he had only been in town a few weeks. I didn't remind any of them he was here long enough to have a mailing address. Still, no one seemed to know much, and everyone said that he was killed in the 1977 flood.

That was it. My answer. My fistful of air. How many years had I lost? For *this*? No one knew a thing about him. A guy I didn't know died here. I walked back to my trailer. I left the AC off. I wanted to suffer. I wanted to hurt myself. I pressed a knife hard into my palm and pushed as slowly as I could. Just steady, slow pressure. I needed to see myself open. I needed to see the second I bled.

Later, I was transcribing the interviews to see if I could have missed anything.

RUTH ANN JORDAN: "And then one minute he was there, and the next he was away…"

JANE YATES: "He was there one minute and gone the next…"

MILFORD HADEN: "Here one minute and then disappeared…blink and miss it…"

FRED SHEPPERD: "You know, you blink, you miss it…"

There were more. All more or less the same. I needed to see Buster. And I didn't know yet what I'd be walking into. I had no idea what I would do. I felt like I should've felt angry. But feeling like you should feel something and actually feeling it are as far from each other as Wyoming and Pluto. Maybe someone else would have wanted to hurt Buster. Maybe I would have once. A year ago? A week ago? Now? I just wanted it over, whatever *over* meant. If a man loses his ghost, what in the world is left?

I went to the Inn, told Buster we had to talk. That I needed his help. That I'd be by the shore and could he swing by whenever he was out?

"Problem?"

I hesitated. "More that it's personal."

He looked in my eyes sadly. Nodded. "Let's go." He got off his stool, slapped me on the back, and gently squeezed my shoulder, and we were in his truck and on the way.

We parked in the sand lot over the berm—built after the floods to protect what little was left. We walked down to the shore without talking. I lit a smoke. It didn't even make a dent in the foul, rotten-egg-and-dead-fish, sulfur smell. We stopped. The water was maybe twenty feet away.

"Hey, kid. I hope those folks were some help."

"I got a lot, Buster." I patted his back. "Thanks."

"I'm sorry there isn't more to know. Hell, I saw him the day of the flood. Maybe east side of town." He shrugged. "After that? Never saw the guy again. He was…"

"He was here one minute, gone the next, wasn't he?" I said.

Buster looked away, and I realized I wasn't angry at all. What was in me didn't have a name. But I wasn't anyone I'd ever been prior to that moment. No anger. I felt no fear. Nothing in the world felt like it could help or hurt.

"That's right," Buster said.

I shifted my weight. Sand crunched.

Buster said, "Anybody tell you different, Duane?"

I paused. Thought about just telling him I knew. "No."

"Well there you go, then."

"Nobody told me a single thing different, Buster."

"Like I say, there you go."

Birds squawked in the distance. A couple on a 4x4 rumbled by and waved as they passed. Buster waved, smiled. Quietly, and with sarcasm and hatred under his breath, he said, "Good-bye, you pieces of LA shit. I hope you all fucking drown." He waved more enthusiastically and screamed, "Come again!"

I said, "Pretty much everybody saw the same thing. Heard the same thing." I checked my front jeans pocket for my phone. My right for the keys. A nervous habit. "Said the exact same thing, which was kind of strange."

Buster finished his beer. Took it out of its cozy, took a cold one out of his pocket. It went into the cozy. The empty into his pocket. He pointed to the beach. "I don't litter here. Damnedest thing, right? I'll throw a McDonald's bag out onto the freeway. Don't litter at home. A million dead fish. Poison water." He took a deep breath and let it out. Looked out at the water over toward the tragic, flickering lights in Salton City.

I said, "It wasn't you, was it?"

He didn't move. A light wind ruffled his T-shirt by his belt.

"I'm talking about Reed," I say. "It wasn't you."

"I know who you're talking about." He nodded slowly. Turned. His eyes looked exhausted as he looked at me. "Father?"

I nod.

"Fathers." He let out a quiet, sad laugh. "Your father didn't drown, but you know that." He nodded. "Guy called Sparkplug. Crazy fucker. Liked beating people." He cleared his throat. "Some things happen too fast to stop."

"You telling me you tried?"

"Telling you it wouldn't have made a difference."

"And he beat Reed?"

He shook his head. "No beating."

The light of the setting sun spread an angelic beauty of light on Buster's face. My arms. The sand and the dull, crushed bones. Stunning light on the water. On the mountains. When you're shooting, they call this the golden hour. Best time of the day. It's perfect. It's incredibly brief.

I said, "You were there, weren't you?"

Buster said, "I was."

"What the fuck were you doing?"

"It was a different time. I protected my town."

I just stared at him. Buster didn't seem to *have* fear. If there was a time in his life when you could have made him fear death, it seemed to have passed. A man who would let you strangle him, it looked like. He didn't seem like a man who'd done what he'd done.

I said, "What did Reed do that people needed protection from?"

"It's a lifetime ago." He shook his head. "Someone comes in the Inn late one night, too late for anyone to have any sense, and says there's someone breaking into Marci and Red's place."

I didn't say anything. It was still over a hundred degrees. The hottest I'd ever been outside in the dark. I waited for more from Buster.

"Sparkplug thought he was one of the five thieves. Shot him."

What isn't said is that my father was even more disposable than the thieves. Shoot the Black man. Now I was angry. But it wasn't at Buster. There was something about him that seemed like he gave a shit about me.

Buster said, "Turned out, he wasn't doing nothing but looking through garbage in the alley."

I was still angry. But I was unexpectedly flooded with relief that they didn't beat him to death. That stranger. That poor bastard, whether I'll ever feel like he was mine or not. Maybe he died fast. Maybe he had no idea he died. Maybe the lights just went out if it was fast enough. "Where did you put him?" I asked. "The Sea?"

"Sea's got more salt that a hundred oceans. Anything tossed in floats."

I imagined Kenny walking through town, seeing his dead cat floating outside his trailer. Living a life where he was called Stupid Kenny and would be called Stupid Kenny till he took his last breath. All the man would ever be.

I said, "Where is Reed?"

"Body drop. Out in the Mojave. North of the Colorado. Put him in another desert."

"Where?"

Buster shook his head. "God himself couldn't put the tail on that donkey, kid. You know how many bodies are in the desert? Stack the bodies toe to toe, I bet you could get to the moon."

I let out a quiet sigh.

"Not what you wanted?"

"I have no idea what I wanted. But, no. Something other than this."

"It'll be okay, kid." He stopped. Took a boat shoe off, dumped out sand, and put it back on. "Really."

I wondered why I didn't, somehow couldn't, hate him when I hated most everything he represented. What he'd done. He was helping me. I needed him, and he'd come through. But still, I wondered if I was betraying my father more than he ever could have betrayed me.

Buster said, "Trust me. You live long enough, and over the years, everything becomes something else."

I looked out at the water. This accident. This beauty. This poison. And there I was. This life that brought me to stand next to this man who saw my father killed. Who saw some stranger with half my DNA killed.

Buster looked at the dying sea. "A mistake. Had its day. God blinked, and a century passed." He bummed a smoke. Surprised, I lit his. Then another of mine. The smoke mixed with the smell of sulfur and bone and salt and sand in the humid air.

We walked a long time without talking. Ended up on an old pier that was so far from the receded water that you couldn't see where it met the shore of bones. Birds walked the shoreline.

What didn't I say to Buster?

In the dried basin of this lake, of Death Valley, of other places most brutally hostile to life in any form, the tardigrade (a phylum of eight-legged segmented micro-animals) enter a dormant state known as cryptobiosis. Dormant for time humans cannot fathom. It was thought to be an extinct species for centuries. For millions of years, they live their death-like lives in mud-caked basins. I'm talking millennium after millennium after millennium, until time is the smallest dot possible on the horizon. Until time is air and there's no way to see where it starts or where it goes. They're just there. If there's enough rain at the right time, they come to life. When the water evaporates, they're back in stasis. They live. They die. They live. They do whatever it is they do and have been doing for millions of years. And they will. Again and again and again and again and again.

Imperceptibly this water in front of me would disappear. The sky to our right burned atomic bomb purple and pink and darkened at the corners of brilliantly backlit clouds. After another moment, we turned around and started the long walk to Buster's truck, the broken bones beneath our feet, broken bones in our wake, broken bones in front of us. The shore of bones as far as you could see. All you could hear as we walked.

Rob Roberge's most recent book, the memoir *Liar* (Crown, 2016), was named a Spring 2016 Barnes and Noble "Discover Great New Writers" pick. It was singled out in The New Yorker, which wrote, "...both the smallest and the biggest pieces of his memoir fascinate," and was chosen as one of the best non-fiction books of 2016 by both Powell's Bookstore and *Entropy Magazine*. Roberge is the author of four books of fiction, most recently the novel *The Cost of Living* (OV Books, 2013), about which Cheryl Strayed said "is both drop dead gorgeous and mind-bendingly smart." He is Assistant Professor and Core Faculty at UC Riverside's Palm Desert MFA in Writing Program. His short fiction and essays have been widely published and anthologized, and he wrote and directed the short film *This Regrettable Event*.

LIGHTHOUSE SCENE FOR MILES

Liner notes for a jazz record
by Fred Madison
1953-1954

By Michael Scott Moore

Strange as it may seem today, Miles Davis's career looked to be over in 1953. His early records, notably 1949's Birth of the Cool, had brought him a measure of fame, but a heroin habit had spoiled his control to the point where critics in the early '50s were writing in terms of his downfall. At twenty-seven, Miles had reached an age when most jazz musicians either killed themselves or got married, and cognoscenti were prepared for either disaster. Young disciples of Cool like Shorty Rogers, Conte Candoli, and Chet Baker had placed higher than Miles in the DownBeat readers' poll for Best Trumpet of '53, and it looked as if their flat-footed idiom —West Coast jazz—would be the sum of Davis's influence.

Personally, too, Miles was a wreck. One late-spring night, Max Roach found him on a Manhattan sidewalk outside Birdland, high on horse, wearing some old, dirty clothes.

"Looking good, Miles," Roach said, and slipped a pair of hundred-dollar bills into his breast pocket.

The story goes that Roach's charity offended Davis. "Max and me were just like brothers, right?" Miles said later. "That shit embarrassed me so bad that instead of taking the money and going and shooting up like I normally would, I called my father and told him that I was coming home to try to get it together again." So he bought a bus ticket home to St. Louis (or actually Millstadt, which is in Illinois) and spent the summer on his father's well-appointed ranch. Doc Davis raised horses, cows, and prize hogs on two hundred acres of farmland remote enough from New York to give Miles a chance to clean up.

In September, on their way to California, Max Roach and Charles Mingus visited Miles on the farm. The Lighthouse Café outside Los Angeles had offered Max a drumming gig; Mingus was going home to South Central. They figured Miles could use a vacation. Miles had nothing else to do, so with his father's blessing, he took off with Mingus and Max for the coast.

The story of his bottoming-out in California—his self-destruction, his wandering, his sessions at the Lighthouse—not to mention his return to form a few years later with a new kind of music—has never been properly told, and these notes for *Miles to Go: The Unreleased Tracks (Vol. 32)* will have to serve as a stopgap until some future historian does the job. His time in California did more than prefigure a major transformation of jazz. It also set a precedent for lost or strung out players who wanted to renew their careers. The bebop movement in particular, which Davis had helped propagate, was still in its romantic adolescence, and until Miles survived his saison d'enfer on the coast, it wasn't yet okay for a jazz musician to swing back, so to speak, from the wages of sin.

To set the scene: In 1953 the Bomb was young, the economy booming. Eisenhower held the highest office of any man on a golf course and Ginsberg hadn't yet written *Howl*. Kerouac was still on the road—just like Miles and his friends—but in the era before the civil rights movement, a certain sense of liberation would have been lacking for the three musicians. "Back in those days, Mingus was death on white people," Miles recalled in an interview. "Couldn't stand nothing white." In wide stretches of the country, this feeling was mutual. "Somewhere out in the middle of nowhere, in Oklahoma I think, we had eaten up all the chicken that my father's cook had made for us, so we stopped to get something to eat. We told Mingus to go and get the food because he was real light-skinned and they might think he was a foreigner."

But Mingus—the genius of "Wednesday Night Prayer Meeting" and "Hog Callin' Blues"—was still *persona non grata* in Middle America. He came running out to the car with his blood raging.

"Them white motherfuckers won't let us eat in there," he said. "I'm gonna blow up their fucking place!"

"Mingus, just sit down and shut your fucking mouth for once," said Miles. "If you say another word, I'm gonna break a bottle over your head, because we're going to end up going to jail over your loud mouth."

Mingus shut his mouth, and they made it to California without further incident.

The beach town where the Lighthouse still stands is now a Los Angeles suburb, but before Eisenhower's freeways, there was a fair amount of farmland between the city and the sea. The bar belonged to a small-town habitat with the same white and mainly Midwestern population that had earned Los Angeles itself the mocking sobriquet, "Omaha on the Beach."

Billy Jarvis tended bar at the Lighthouse almost every afternoon. He was a burly, crop-haired older brother to the regular patrons, a curt kid who kept a close eye on the goings-on. After three years in the service and a stint in Korea, a job in a California jazz joint must have struck the right note of R&R. But Jarvis later told friends that he took the job because of what's now known as combat stress—he became easily enraged. Watching the bar gave him the occasional excuse to knock some heads together.

After dropping Mingus off in LA, Miles and Max drove

about an hour southwest, on country roads, to Howard Rumsey's place near the club. Rumsey was Max's boss. He organized music at the Lighthouse and played bass for the All-Stars (the house band). Max was clean; he had a job and things to do. But Miles was unemployed.

Just how much of a wilderness period this was for Miles can't be overstated. His rise to the front rank of trumpet players in the late '40s had been phenomenal. From an introverted, young sideman in Charlie Parker's quintet, Miles had matured into an aloof, New York bandleader, an angrily cool individual "artfully turned out in British tweeds," as one writer would later put it. But his newfound mastery proved hard to maintain. No sooner had he come into his own as a player than the New York jazz scene began to dissolve. When footloose ex-soldiers from Europe and the South Pacific got married, the audience for Manhattan's lively nightclub scene retreated to the suburbs. By then, more than a few great players were lost to heroin. "I got hooked after I came back from the Paris Jazz Festival in 1949," said Miles. "I got bored and was around cats that were hung. So I wound up with a habit that took me over four years to break."

A contract with Prestige ran out in '52. The label couldn't keep track of him. "In those days a lot of guys used to disappear from the scene for months," said Bob Weinstock, who worked for Prestige at the time. The reason, usually, was dope.

Audiences, fellow musicians, and eventually even critics came to notice Miles's loss of control. It amounted to a failure of confidence. During this period, Joe Gordon's reputation as a trumpet player was strong, and although Joe would never pose a serious threat to Miles's dominance, talk spread about his aggressive style. In 1952, the story goes, Joe sat in with Miles and Charlie Parker at Birdland. "Miles heard Joe play, and then walked off the stand," recalled Cecil Taylor, who was present. "Bird ran up to Miles and grabbed him by the arms and said, 'Man, you're Miles Davis.' And Miles sort of came back and stood around shuffling his feet."

In California, that fall and winter of '53, Miles played

very little in public. Once in a while he sat in with the All-Stars, but most of his days were spent scoring for heroin or drinking at the Lighthouse bar. One day a friend in LA wanted to deliver a box of jewelry to a dancer at a Hollywood club. Miles went with him. Another dancer, Frances Taylor, came out to accept it.

Fate can develop stray events the way a good musician develops a few stray notes. "She was so fine, she almost took my breath away," Miles recalled. He gave her his phone number, but they didn't meet again until Max's girlfriend arranged a blind date between Frances and Miles. "It was a co-incidence that I met her like that that first time," said Miles later. "But after Max got us together, I knew something was meant to happen between us and so did she."

Then, on Max's birthday, in early '54, Miles had a violent run-in with Billy Jarvis. It started with a bit of tomfoolery with a buck knife. "I had been taking judo lessons while I was home in East St. Louis, and so I had this knife and I was going to show Max how I could take it from someone about to stab me," Miles recalled. "When he does it, I take the knife from him and throw him over my shoulder, right? So Max says, 'Man, Miles, that's something.' I put the knife back in my pocket and forget about it."

They held a birthday party for Max at the bar. For an hour or so, they drank and talked. When Max had to play a set, Miles made a joke.

"It's your birthday," he said, "so you pay."

Max refused and got up to play. Billy Jarvis overheard the exchange.

"He's paying," Miles told him, jerking his head toward the bandstand. "I don't have any money."

"He left you with the bill," Jarvis answered.

"I told you I can't pay it," and it was entirely possible that Miles had no money. So Jarvis took a pen from behind his ear and wrote up the tab on a piece of paper with his meaty hand. He laid it on the bar and left. Miles let the paper soak up beer. He forgot about Jarvis and watched the band. The bartender returned a few minutes later.

"Come on, man, I want my money."

"Just relax," said Miles. "I'm not going anywhere. You'll get your money as soon as they're done." He laughed in Jarvis's face. "It's Max's birthday."

Sources are unclear about what happened next. There must have been an exchange of insults. The situation escalated, and Jarvis got angry. "I'm gonna kick your ass, 'cause you're a black motherfucker," he said in a voice so loud he caused the band to falter. Members of the audience turned to look. The horns and piano kept playing, but Max had gotten up from his drum kit and was striding to the bar. Miles widened his eyes at Jarvis.

"How come you had to say that, man?" Max asked him, pulling out his wallet. "He ain't doin' nothing." He left more than enough cash to cover the bill and strode back onstage, swearing, still shaking his head. The bartender wasn't appeased. It must have burned his pride to watch a colored man settle an argument by laying down more money than he, Jarvis, earned in an afternoon. He whispered, "When I get off, I'm gonna kick your ass."

Miles remembered his buck knife.

"You don't have to wait that long. You can get off work right now."

He'd also observed—a trick from judo class—that Jarvis was left-handed. So, when Jarvis came lurching out with a wild left hook, Miles knew which way to move. He smacked Jarvis on the head and pulled him over the bar. Glasses shattered. Jarvis got to his feet again and punched Miles in the stomach, but Miles caught his arm and swung him into the audience. Instead of seats, the Lighthouse had church pews; Jarvis rammed his head against one of them and made half a dozen patrons spill their drinks. People stood and shouted. Onstage, Baker had slipped into an elegant solo on "In the Mood."

The band let him play through. "Max was up on stage with this shocked grin on his face," Miles said later. "People were screaming and running for cover." Some of Jarvis's friends tackled Miles and pinned him to the floor. Someone else called the police. But the band kept playing. "The whole time, Max didn't even get off the stage."

A bouncer broke up the fight, and when the police arrived, things looked bad for Miles. Although Jarvis had thrown the first punch, he wasn't strung out. More importantly, he wasn't black. A situation involving a black man at the Lighthouse equaled a situation *caused* by a black man at the Lighthouse, and the logical solution was for Miles Davis, the future of jazz, to get hauled off in a paddy wagon.

"The police take me down to the station, and I tell them that the guy had called me a 'black motherfucking nigger'—which he did—and threw the first punch," Miles recalled. "Then I remember that I got this knife. I got scared as a motherfucker because if they find this, I know my ass is going to jail."

But the police never searched him, and Miles thought to mention his uncle, William Pickens, who had a high position in the NAACP. "They just let me go," he said. Max arrived, still smiling, to drive him home. The story goes that in Max's apartment, Miles stretched on a couch to sleep off what was left of his heroin, looking rumpled and broke as ever. Max reached into Miles's coat pocket with another two hundred dollars and repeated what he'd said in New York.

"Looking good, Miles."

"But I was fucked up and Max knew it," Miles recounted later. "I looked in the mirror and said, 'Goddamn it, come on.'"

So he returned, again, to Millstadt. He retreated to an apartment in a guesthouse on his father's ranch, locked the door, and stretched out in bed, intending to kick his habit cold turkey.

"The feeling is indescribable," he said later. "All of your joints get sore and stiff, but you can't touch them because if you do, you'll scream. So nobody can give you a massage. It's the kind of hurt I later experienced after an operation, when I had hip replacement. It's a raw kind of feeling that you can't stop. You feel like you could die and if somebody could guarantee that you would die in two seconds, then you would take it. You would take the gift of death over this torture of life. At one point I even started to jump out the window—the apartment was on the second floor—so I could knock myself unconscious and get some sleep. But I thought that with my luck, I would just break my motherfucking leg and be laying out there suffering."

Two figures loomed over Miles's future at this point. The boxer Sugar Ray Robinson served as a role model for his determination to quit. Robinson cut a flamboyant figure outside the ring, wearing a velvet cape and broad-brimmed hat, but when he trained, Miles noticed, "He disciplined himself...I said, 'If that mother can win all those fights, I can sure break this motherfuckin' habit.'"

The other figure on his mind was Frances, the beautiful dancer he'd met in Hollywood, who would become his muse, his lover, his victim, and his wife. It wasn't always a happy or peaceful union, but she would preside over Miles's consciousness for the rest of '54, while he worked on new ideas with undiscovered players in Detroit, kicking off the hard bop movement with a return to the blues, and going on to record such now-classic sessions as *Walkin'*, *'Round About Midnight*, *Kind of Blue*, several indelible appearances at Newport, and, of course, "Fran-Dance," named for Mrs. Frances Taylor Davis.

First, though:

"I laid down and stared at the ceiling [of the guesthouse at Millstadt] for twelve days and cursed everybody I didn't like. It was like a bad case of flu, only worse. I lay in a cold sweat. My nose and eyes ran. I threw up everything I tried to eat. My pores opened up and I smelled like chicken soup," he told Marc Crawford in 1961. "Then it was over."

Michael Scott Moore is a journalist and a novelist, author of a comic novel about L.A., Too Much of Nothing, set in the fictional town of Calaveras Beach. His travel book about surfing, *Sweetness and Blood*, was named a best book of 2010 by The Economist. He's won Fulbright, Logan, and Pulitzer Center grants for his nonfiction; MacDowell and Wallace Foundation fellowships for his fiction.

He grew up in California, but worked for several years as an editor and writer at *Spiegel Online International* in Berlin. Mr.

Moore was kidnapped in early 2012 on a reporting trip to Somalia and held hostage by pirates for 32 months. *The Desert and the Sea,* a memoir about that ordeal, is out now from HarperCollins. He runs a website at www.radiofreemike.net

THE CROSSING

By Oliver Brennan

R obbie had been dead for three hours when he started talking to me. I'd been driving north for almost two. Burying him in Mexico hadn't crossed my mind.

He was in the back of the truck, under the surfboards and sleeping bags. I was working through my last pack of smokes, rolling to a stop at a military checkpoint somewhere between Colima and Jalisco—the Michoacán Cartel had been showing teeth lately—trying not to think about what life would be like in a Mexican prison if they found the body.

The guard waved me up. He looked too young to be responsible for a machine gun.

It's time.

A dead whisper is how I'd describe it to someone, someday. I leaked some piss. I can't be sure if it was before or after saying, "What the fuck?"

I turned to look in the back, make sure he wasn't sitting up, face pressed against the glass that separated us.

Muuuussiic.

Robbie's favorite Slayer tape—*South of Heaven*—raged from the one working speaker. The tape deck mounted into the dash was older than the truck, so the volume didn't work. I turned it off. My brain hummed. The road crunched under the thinning tread of the truck tires before I stopped completely.

The guard tapped his finger near the trigger of his rifle, put his hand on the roof, and said, "*Buenos días, señor, ¿tiene alguna fruta hoy?*"

"Fucking fruit?" I laughed, too loud probably. He jumped back a step, then started in with me, laughing. A rim of silver capped his front four teeth. "*De ninguna manera,*" I said. "*Odio la fruta, siempre lo he hecho.*" I didn't hate fruit, but adding to the lie felt right, like it was a good time for embellishment.

He held eyes on me long enough to let me know he was boss, I think, before waving me through.

Get to Thad. He'll know.

It was a good call. Thad was the Candyman in Sayulita, a gringo surf town with a decent wave. He'd helped us before, and knew how to get things across the border—a body though?

I turned on the music and tried not to cry.

Ice.

I swung to a stop at a roadside tienda. The truck groaned from the heat and being pushed too hard. A carton of smokes and ice were the priority. What I wanted but couldn't have, ever again, was to sit on the beach with Robbie at our spot outside the town of Manzanillo. A sandy cove with a pumping point break that we'd declared, after splitting a bag of mushrooms, was our favorite because it reminded us of being stranded on an island.

The wave broke off a rock at the north end. It worked on most swells, but on a northwest swell, it was world-class. About an hour after high tide, when the ocean felt like it was trying to suck you out to oblivion, the peak of the wave would pitch over and barrel into a liquid tube. On those days, when my confidence was up, I'd put my hands behind my back and, deep into the bottom turn, close my eyes and let instinct take over. I'd try to keep them closed until I could hear, almost feel, the echo chamber of being covered by the water as it crested over my head, and I wouldn't open them until I knew I was covered, deep in the barrel. When I finally would open them, it was do or die. That's when I'd get low, heavy on the front foot, point my hands toward the closing light ahead, and hit the gas. A purgatory of perfection.

"We never got crowds there," I said, not sure how long I'd been talking to him out loud.

I don't need to go back.

I cherried another smoke against a fresh one and said, "What?"

I'm going south, Red. Can't you smell it?

I couldn't smell much else but cigarettes and the road, a burning trash pile now and then. "No," I said.

If you get to Thad, we'll make it.

"You're dead. There is no 'we.'"

I got out of the truck and puked into a trash heap buzzing with flies. Put my hand on the hood for support but pulled it back fast before the hot metal burned me. I shook my head to get the sound out. Dust settled on the vomit. The flies too.

Ice.

I nodded, said, "Yeah." I spit, wiped my mouth with my arm, then wiped my arm on my board shorts. I stood over the garbage pile covered in my puke and lit a new smoke. I hoped to hear a bird, something beautiful and alive that was supposed to sing, instead of the hum in my ears.

The ice machine was rusted-out at the bottom corners. The sun scraped at my exposed neck.

"This is it," I said, and flicked my smoke toward the trash pile—I wondered what would happen, how big the flames would get, if it caught fire.

I stuck my head inside the ice machine because I couldn't see a thing except darkness and bits of light punching through the rusted metal. I grabbed two bags that were as far back as ice could get in a middle-of-nowhere place like this—paradise.

It's not enough.

"It's all they got," I said, and carried the bags inside even though I didn't have to.

Inside the tienda, a fan with rainbow tassels spun so fast it rattled. A girl, maybe fourteen, flipped through pages of a magazine with pictures of other girls that looked like her, in age at least, wearing gowns. If I had to guess, her quinceañera was on the horizon. The gown she stopped at, kept her eyes on instead of me, was purple with green lace.

I piled chips, soda, bottled water, and two Mars bars on the counter; the ice was next to my feet. "*Buenos*," I said.

She touched at something on the picture, like maybe she could get a bit of the texture from the page, and said, "*Buenos*." Eyes locked to the magazine, she leaned over to the register, hit a key, and the cash drawer popped open. Not much in there, but I could have taken everything.

Focus, Red.

I nodded, not crazy enough to answer, to think this girl would be hearing him too.

"*Quarenta*," she said.

I fumbled out fifty pesos. She gave me ten back in small coins. I put them in the Velcro pocket of my board shorts. The weight made them sag, probably flashed my butt crack on the way out the door.

I put the ice on Robbie's stomach to keep the soft organs cool.

"It'll have to do for now," I said.

Sayulita. Thad.

Dust deviled up behind me. I lit a cigarette. Slayer pumped "Read Between the Lines" out of the crackling speaker, a much better song when you can hear the guitar riffs.

"You were naked when we found you," I said.

Never got to surf Scorpion Bay.

"I thought about that," I said, old cigarette cherry to cherry with a new one, puffing until the smoke felt right. "Things we talked about. The ones that held on, you know?"

Never surfed Chile.

"Your shorts, the yellow ones, were around your ankles. Your hands and feet, they were twisted inward like you were playing at something."

Broken.

"Hans, that Norwegian slab hunter who rides for Quiksilver? He pulled up your shorts, I think."

You cried hard.

I pinched the base of my skull. Squeezed. The cig-arette smoldered between my cracked lips. The road disap-peared, and I felt the fine, black sand of Pascuales. It was hot under my feet, under my hands and knees. The warm ocean followed. It lapped at Robbie like it was trying to pull him back out, kill him again. The back half of the surfboard was still attached to his ankle with a bright orange leash. It pushed and pulled with the pulse of pounding surf. People gathered. His yellow shorts around his feet looked matted and old. The pale white of his ass pointed up at the too-bright sky. It was a puzzle my fried brain couldn't put back together. Robbie was too strong to die. I was the weak one.

"You watched out for me," I said.

Mind the road.

"I think God fucked up," I said.

Robbie's laugh sounded like a trillion shards of glass, slivered and shifting against a scorched earth.

We were close.

I didn't remember making the left into Sayulita, or before that, driving through Puerto Vallarta. The questions running loose through the folds of my vagabond brain had taken over. They played near that vast reservoir I had seen once before on a mushroom trip: Am I actually here?

I hit the brakes fast and skidded to a stop hard enough to put me sideways at the sign, not into it: Bienveni-dos a Sayulita. Two dogs fought in its shadow. Maybe I was lucky.

The road into town, once you crossed the bridge over shit creek—a tributary that dumps raw sewage into the lineup when the rains come—was lined with groms. Young surfers trying to be big. They stared as I rolled through their gauntlet of judgement. A tall one spit then laughed too loud.

"Fuckin' groms," I said.

Thad.

"We haven't seen him since…"

The reservoir inside me roiled, churned, and pulled my

past to the surface: Killing Elton Hoosk and burying him like we did was the karmic chain linking me to forever do bad things. Before Mexico, before Elton, before Robbie died, my life might not have been easy, but it had been simple. I had known what I wanted.

He was sad for us, Red.

"Don't say that. You don't know that."

Thad's place was a block from the beach and tall enough to see when the wave was working—even the north end. It had a thatched roof, a moat full of putrid mud, and a drawbridge. After the moat and the bridge, an eight-foot wall of cut palm trees, some with holes cut wide enough for the barrel of a gun to slide through. Thad was fucking nuts, but his heart meant well.

The place shouted paranoia. He had enough reason for it though. In his line of work, being paranoid was part of the formula that kept him breathing. A wooden sign, blue with white letters, faded and cracked, hung crooked over the double wooden gate. It read: Surf Shop of Sayulita.

We're close.

"I'm so tired," I said.

The gate opened a crack.

"*Cerrado*," Thad said. He probably thought I was some gringo surfer looking for wax or a new leash.

"Thad?" I put a hand against the fraying stalks of the palm tree wall to keep myself vertical.

The gate opened a bit more, enough to see the stubble that covered his face and head, a constant shadow of black, ten-grade sandpaper. He blinked hard as if trying to get the previous night out of his eyes. "Red?"

I nodded.

He smiled—front two bottom teeth missing—and opened the gate wide.

"Get in here," he said, pulling me close and hugging me too hard. His smell was distinct, but I couldn't put a finger on it. He looked past me. "Where's Robbie?" Thad, pushing close to forty years old, still looked cut from stone. His skin was crocodile thick. His tattoos, knuckle to shoulder on both arms, were so faded I couldn't tell if they looked like a mistake, intentional or not. The scar across his chest ran from above the collarbone to the bottom of his rib cage. It was a keloid, an off-color beige, and a reminder of his trade. I wanted to run my fingers along it like a map, ask if he had screamed or kept his mouth shut while they were cutting.

"Dead," I said.

Thad lurched his head forward like a rooster and said, "What?"

"He's in the truck," I said.

"In the fuckin' truck?" Thad ran out of the compound.

I followed, saying, "In the back, under the boards."

Why he didn't look there first made me think that getting Robbie across the border might work after all.

Thad climbed in back and rustled around. "Fuck." He fell backwards off the tailgate, saying it over and over —"fuckfuckfuck"—landed on his ass and pinched his nose. "Christ, he stinks."

Under different circumstances, I'd have been laughing at him for freaking out so hard. I leaned in to take a whiff. He was right. Robbie had taken a turn.

Remember.

Robbie's voice was getting worse, maybe decomposing with his body; the "how" of that wasn't a pool I was going to swim in.

"Ice," I said. "Like, a lot."

Thad popped up, brushed himself off, latched onto my shoulder, and said, "Why?"

"He's got to get across."

His hand went heavy and tight on my shoulder, an anvil of muscle, tendon, and bone leading me back inside the compound. He locked the gate behind us and flopped onto an old couch sitting by a glass counter that needed to be cleaned. "Fuck, Red. I gotta mellow out here." He opened a wooden box of pre-rolled joints and popped one between his lips, hit match after match until one lit, and got the joint to glow. "You're too mellow, man. Waaaay too mellow," he said. Smoke leaked from his mouth and nose. He held the joint out for me.

Goddamned right I took it.

I closed my eyes and inhaled. The sweet stink of quality weed coated my insides and filled me with good intentions.

I woke up looking across a wooden floor. A spider crawled in front of my face. Flip-flops scuttled across my line of sight.

A voice: it sounded far off. "You passed out, dude."

Thad lifted me to the couch. Cigarette scum coated the back of my throat and teeth. I spit on the floor.

"Don't spit on my floor. Fuck."

"Sorry," I said, and spit again—this time behind the couch. "Ice."

"Here," he said, and pulled out a white bag shaped like a surfboard about eight feet long, maybe nine. He unzipped it, laid it open on the floor like a sleeping bag half-ready for two, said, "Sand goes first. It'll catch the rot and water when the ice melts. Put a towel over that. Then roll out the Cling Wrap, keep it connected to the roll, though, because then—" He looked at me, shook his head, got a glass of water, downed it, and started in again. "Robbie. Get ice under his arms, between the legs, around his core to keep the important parts that go south first nice and cool. Coffee after that. For the smell. Finish off with the Cling Wrap. Use the entire roll, more if we have to. He'll be a tight package. Hopefully the border dogs aren't trained to sniff for coffee nowadays." He flipped over a thick plastic sheet inside of the bag that was meant to separate two surfboards. "Fold this over, tape it down, and put a board on top of him."

He squatted, bare feet splayed out like a fisherman from the far east, hopped toward me a bit, and said, "I haven't been north, up to the border, for, like, ever. Just so you know, I'm winging it here."

"Me too," I said.

"You're a crazy fucker, Red. Getting across the border, not ending up in some kind of ass-fuck situation? Mexi–prison? Well, I think this is your best shot besides not doing it at all."

"Where're we going to get that much coffee?" I never

thought about that, coffee. And what kind? Dark, medium, mild?

"Don't worry about it. Take this." He wrestled with the handles of a wheelbarrow behind a curtain. "Go get some sand. I'll get all the ice in this fucking town."

I don't like the border much.

"I'm just trying to get you home," I said.

What's home, Red?

"Are you talking to the body out in that fucking truck?" Thad turned and waved his slab of a hand at me while walking away.

I pushed the old wheelbarrow toward the beach. It sank into the sand when I dropped the front wheel off a broken concrete step.

"No shovel," I said, and used my hands.

You don't have to do this.

"I'm doing it," I said.

Where?

"Where what?"

I don't know home anymore.

"Your voice. It's like a goddamned rake in my head," I said.

Take me to Oregon. That place my mom talked about sometimes. Burn me.

"It's cold there."

My throat. A lozenge. It hurts.

"Robbie, you're dead."

"Cat shit or dog shit." Thad grumbled and sifted through the sand in the barrow.

"Probably." I lit a cigarette. "Maybe it doesn't matter."

"Smoke this. Not that." He handed me another joint. It was sticky. Smoke floated around my eyes, and I closed them. The smell I'd been ignoring—rotting flesh—made them flit back open.

Robbie stood in front of me. His eyes, caved into the sockets of his skull, looked black instead of that traffic-stopping blue he'd carried with both pride and humility. The sharp parts of his bones looked like they could rip through his skin. His hands shook, and his head was cocked like a curious pit bull. His teeth looked good though.

Get it done, Red.

"Where's the coffee?" I asked.

"Back there." Thad pulled sticks and anything that could rip through the Cling Wrap, ruin everything, out of the sand. He took a pull off the joint, set it on the floor next to him, and said, "If he falls apart when we move him, I'll shit my shorts."

"I'll do it," I said.

Thad looked up quick, like I'd scared him. "What?"

"All of this," I said. "You got everything we needed. It's all I asked for."

"Negative. We do this together." He stood and moved toward me. I took a step back. "Think about it," he said.

"What?" I needed to move. Get back to the truck. Take care of Robbie.

"The border," he said.

I nodded.

"For what? Are you going to put him in the ground up north? You think all of it won't come crashing down?" The joint on the floor stopped smoldering, its final cloud of smoke barely a wisp in the canyon of silence between us.

"It's what's right, burying him with family," I said.

Listen to yourself.

Robbie, there again, in front of me, water dripping from his hands and eyes, reached out. I jumped back far enough to knock my head on a support post.

Thad flinched. "Fuck, Red." He got closer, maybe to see if I was okay.

"I didn't kill him," I said.

"Don't say those words again unless it's to a lawyer, and not a public defender, one that costs money. And you'll have one if this goes anywhere but where it's supposed to go, because I'm your first phone call," Thad said.

He's us, Red.

The tears wouldn't stop once they started, so I gave them a voice, fell to my knees and put my hands over my face; shame had nothing to do with it.

Thad started in with me. Dead Robbie too.

The setting sun glared red, gold, pink. Purple breaking in from somewhere. "Storm's coming," I said from behind the wheel, all cried out.

Thad, his hand on the cab of the truck like that guard a million years ago, looked up. "Yeah. A Southy. San Pancho will be going off."

"The river punched through the beach already?"

He nodded, said, "I think this is the year for me to get back in the water." Then said, "This place, it's been a part of us for a while now." Thad glanced past me through the back window at the stack of boards and camping gear covering our dead friend. "Maybe always has." He patted the top of the cab. "You'll figure it out before shit gets bad." He walked off. Flip-flops kicking up dust.

Signs flashed at me. Border. US Border. Nogales. Border. Nogales. Border 10 km. Check vehicles. I downshifted to pull over. The engine whined. My stomach twisted like a snake eating itself.

"Will they check us, you think?"

Maybe.

"Prison?"

Don't get caught.

"Bad," I said, and opened the door to get out and stretch my back. A truck hummed past. Flies buzzed. I smelled shit. Piss. Gas. Coolant.

I popped open the truck canopy to see what Border Patrol would see if they checked. The stench was like a sledgehammer. I spun and hurled the water I'd just managed to get down, wiped my mouth, covered my nose with my shirt, and looked inside again. Surfboards for days. Stacked to the brim. A chore for anyone looking.

Perfect for a guard with something to prove.

"Fifty-fifty chance?"

Eighty-twenty if the dice fall your way.

"Fuck."

I closed the back of the truck but left it unlocked—

less suspicious if they could open it themselves.

Fuck.

"If I get busted here, do I go to Mexican prison? Do I go to American prison? If I'm an American and you're an American, where do I go if they find you and think I killed you?"

Out of my element.

His voice rolled hard through my skull.

Border prison can't be fun.

"I heard somewhere that when you die, your hair, it keeps growing. Nails, too, I think."

I can feel it.

"Doubt that," I said.

I looked down the road behind us. Desert on both sides. Filth on both sides. Diesel rigs pushing forward. A thick layer of twisting heat—gas and illusion. My stomach churned. I tried to piss next to the truck but was dry. My mouth puckered for a smoke. I needed to cool the adrenaline.

I leaned against the cab of the truck and watched as an armadillo was crushed and flipped by an orange big rig. Lit my smoke. Waited for the armadillo to twitch, but it didn't.

"Don't talk to me when we get there. I need to be on it." I couldn't hear him: breathing, rasping, wheezing, nothing but my ringing ears.

"Robbie?"

Nothing.

"Rob?"

Must be asleep or something.

The back of the line was loose, not packed in enough to trap anyone with second thoughts. Cars jockeyed for position. A camper scraped against a truck. The guy who climbed out of his truck, waving his arms and screaming, wore a white cowboy hat and a belt buckle full of rhinestones.

"Robbie?" My voice, a loud whisper. "Fuck." I thought about the sea: soup-hot in August, salt stinging after a long surf session, cool enough in February to make you shiver. Water temp is how we'd read the seasons, track time if we felt like time meant something that day, month, or year.

Border Patrol flanked the cars as the line moved forward.

Tightening.

Razor wire on either side. Fifteen feet high, give or take.

Dogs.

Poles with mirrors attached to the bottom so they could look under your car. All cars. Suspicious cars.

Try not to be suspicious.

"Where'd you go?"

Tired is all.

"I'm scared," I said.

Me too.

They stopped the old couple in the camper. The caballero was still waving his arms. He pointed at the bumper hanging off his truck.

The officers laughed. The old guy's dime would never put the bumper back on that new truck.

The dogs watched.

Two Border Patrol officers started my way. Checking cars. Using the mirror. The dogs. What could they smell? What were they trained to find? Dead bodies? Coke or weed? Heroin? Why the hell would you try to get across with that shit? Why would I?

I wanted out of the line. Back to the water's edge. The sea. Watch dolphins feed and surf. Ride point breaks until my arms fell off. I wanted Robbie out of this damned truck. I wanted him gone.

Dogs barked. Pulled their leashes taut.

I turned the wheel to the right and gassed it forward. Slammed it into reverse. Gassed it. Two more and I had it.

I cranked the wheel, gassed it again. Stopped short of hitting a brown Volkswagen Bug.

The officers ran at me.

Reverse. Gas.

Border Patrol closing in. Emergency in their eyes. Yelling back to a booth. Waving.

Forward, and a hard crank to the right.

Out. Gone. Border Patrol puppets clambering in my rearview, strung along by those dogs. One guy fell. I lit a smoke and laughed.

Good move.

"Fuck." I exhaled. Baja point breaks flooded my mind.

Mind surfing.

I could barely understand him.

"What's that?" A glance in the cracked rearview mirror showed nothing but road, rock, dirt, and heat.

Nothing.

I leaned my head back and closed my eyes. Felt the road hum against the dying tires. Took a final drag and flicked the half-smoked Lucky Strike out the window. "Baja. Yeah. Wild enough. I'll burn you there."

Robbie coughed, I think. It reminded me of my grandfather hacking up lung batter the size of actual cookies —brown and black—before he died.

I'd like that. Stay here. Burn me here.

A coyote slinked along a barbed wire fence. The sun spit red, gold, and green—drained its last life of the day in front of us.

I hit the eject button on the tape deck. Threw Robbie's favorite Slayer tape out the window. It bounced a couple of times and spun to the side of the road.

Dust clouded in the distance ahead. Headlights. Two cars coming my way, side by side, broke the horizon.

Oliver Brennan holds an MFA in Creative Writing and Writing for The Performing Arts from the UCR Low Residency MFA program. He writes horror and crime for the screen as well as crime fiction. Since 2017, he's been the short story editor for *Close To The Bone* Publishing and *Near to The Knuckle*. From 2019-20, he edited for *Kelp Journal*. In 2018, he consulted as online editor for Out of The Gutter Online. From 2018-19 he was a copy editor for The Coachella Review. His short stories can be seen at West Wind Review, Out of The Gutter Online, Near To The Knuckle. He's currently working on his first novel.

BAD MOON RISING

By David M. Olsen

The Elkhorn Yacht Club and Harbor was completely dark when Moon DeMarco returned from surfing the breaker side of the marina. The thick planks of the dock clacked under each step. Layers of fog drifted around her like smoke. Knee-high lamps lit the dock surface, leaving darkness on either side.

Almost to her boat, *Moon Beam*, a 35-foot Ranger, she anticipated the pure joy of peeling out of her frozen wetsuit and the sting of hot water on her skin. But when she got to her slip, she stopped dead. Her pulse thudded in her ears. The braided-steel lifeline that ran around the cockpit was unlatched. She always latched it. She edged slightly closer, scanning the boat. Then she saw it. A man sitting alone in the dark, legs crossed, on her ship.

"You trying to get dumped in the canyon, mother-fucker?" Moon said, a slight waver in her voice. She'd always thought it would be a neat trick to hide evidence in the Monterey Canyon. Sink anything five miles into an ocean canyon, and it would be impossible to find. Especially with all the marine life to devour it.

"I don't know why you did it, but you stole the catalytic converter off my friend's car earlier," the man said.

Moon flicked on a keychain flashlight and shone it at his face. She sighed. It was Cody; he and two other Palo Alto twentysomethings had chartered her boat for a three-hour bay cruise earlier. A bro trip down the coast. "Get the fuck off my dock. All sales are final."

Moon was the handywoman at the yacht club since she got cut off from her family's considerable fortune and needed a place to lay low. Her side hustle was chartering sailing trips around the Monterey Bay. She mostly booked tourists who wanted to see the array of wildlife the bay had to offer. Whales, orcas, sunfish, seals, and sea otters. She had a humble website, no social media, and a flip phone. All under her alias, Moon Summers. It was lucrative in the on-season. In the off-season, and whenever it was too hard to pass up, she had another hustle. Catalytic converters.

"What do you get for those things? A few hundred bucks? It's costing three grand to replace." The man pulled his hood back. His lips were thin, his nose long and sharp, and his dark hairline was receding. She remembered his name, Cody Singh. She'd pegged them all as rich children of tech millionaires.

"You should get the fuck off my boat while you still can."

Cody scoffed, stood, and took a step toward her. Moon gripped another item on her keyring, a metal cat face with spiked ears that doubled as brass knuckles.

"Come any closer and you *will* fucking regret it." Moon sized him up. He was taller; she was only five-five, one-thirty. But, at twenty-eight, she was at her peak physical condition. Toned with loaded shoulder muscle from surfing almost every day. And running this ship. Cody had a sunken chest, delicate hands, and appeared gaunt. He looked like the kind of Silicon Valley kid who came of age jerking off to internet porn and feeling like a tough guy from endless hours talking shit into his Call of Duty headset. She could take him. But even if she couldn't, all she had to do was yell. Antonio would tear this asshole apart.

"I get that there's some rhodium in there. That model of Mustang had about a thousand bucks, maybe? But seriously. It's so, I don't know, passé to steal car parts. So, *redneck*."

"You've broken onto my boat to what, insult me for being too blue-collar of a thief? Anything else before I have you buried at sea?"

"You don't want to do that. Look, I don't give a shit about Bjorn's fucking car. He can afford ten. I'm here because while I tried to figure out how you hustled us earlier—which I did— I had an idea. One that might be a little more lucrative than used car parts." He scoffed, or laughed, or had an asthma attack. Moon couldn't tell for sure.

"For the last time, we're done here," Moon said.

"I mean, I could call the cops and tell them about your operation? Or you could just hear me out. If you don't like it, I'll leave."

Moon hesitated at the threat. She wanted to avoid cops at all costs. Lawrence Shepherd, the manager of the yacht club, had done her a favor hiring her. It wasn't easy getting hired with a felony on your record, even if you used to be rich. If she lost her job, she lost her boat and her slip. Everything she'd built out here on her own. But she also wouldn't be bullied or blackmailed by this tech industry washout.

Moon stepped onto her ship and stood toe-to-toe with Cody. Lifting her closed fist so that Cody could clearly see the purple, brushed aluminum cat ears shimmering in the dim light.

"There is no way we work together, ever. Do you understand me? Now get the *fuck* off my ship."

Cody held up his hands, and Moon backed him up until he stepped off *Moon Beam* and onto the dock. He didn't leave. Instead, he crouched so they were eye level again, staying out of reach.

"Look, Moon. I am very good at what I do, and right now I'm just trying to help you make a quick fifty grand and never bother you again. I could also call the cops and tell them how you're stealing the converters. All I had to do was pull up the blueprints to this wharf from the digital archives to find the retired water reclamation lines under the parking lot. What did you do, create a slide-away door in your special little parking spot there? It doesn't matter. The cops find that, you and whatever grease stain you're working with are fucking goners."

Moon stood speechless. This prick, in a matter of hours, had blown up her entire operation with Antonio. An operation they had delicately laid out for months. Swapping the cat converters for cheap metal tubes to cover up the sound. Her parking space for Moon Beam Charters had even been canopied on both sides by Cheryl Knight's makeshift flower beds. Moon felt her leg muscles start to jump with adrenaline and anger. She wanted to claw this guy's eyes out.

"You do what you need to do," Moon said. "But I promise you, I'll find you." She turned and started to unlock the hatch door to her cabin.

"All right, have it your way, Jessica *Moon* DeMarco, right? Seems like if you're hiding out here, you're probably hiding from someone. Maybe they'll pay fifty grand to find out." He turned to walk away.

Moon stopped and thought about how fast she could get to the .22 pistol her mother had given her on her fifteenth birthday. This prick was too smart to be so dumb. He knew her real name. She breathed. Maybe she'd go along with his deal and make some money. Or maybe she'd find a way to bury him at sea. All she knew was that she'd have to hear him out. If he gave her name and location to the right people, someone would come for her.

"All right, Cody. I'll give you five minutes to pitch your deal. For your sake, I better like the pitch. Now, step into my office." Moon smiled feeling like the grim reaper. "Let's talk below deck." She opened the hatch doors. Cody hesitated but stepped back onto the boat. "And don't ever. Ever. *Ever*. Step foot on my boat again without permission."

Cody nodded and ducked, then descended the ladder into the belly of Moon's ship.

"So wait, the guy wants you to sail him and these influencers out on the bay, and he's going to hack their shit?" An-

138 | THE SILVER WAVES OF SUMMER

tonio said. He wasn't looking at Moon; he was watching the black swells coming out of the dark gray fog settled over the Monterey Bay. This was their Sunday morning ritual, their church. Six a.m., no matter the weather, no matter the surf, they paddled out. One-foot waves, or fifty-foot waves.

"Yeah. He says if I let him set up Wi-Fi and a signal blocker, he can hack these two influencers' phones and steal their accounts."

"And he's going to line up the influencers?" Antonio said.

"Yeah. Some guy called Fable at the Table. Runs an Instagram and YouTube empire."

"Never heard of him."

"Me neither. But 1.2 billion viewers have," Moon said.

"And this doesn't come back on you? It sounds like a setup."

"He'll be on board, posing as a passenger and handling all the tech shit." A wave swelled toward them, reflecting the red streak of morning sunlight peeking over the coastal range behind them. "Says he can time it out so they are long gone when he takes over their accounts and demands the ransom."

"A hundred thousand to get their Instagram back. Sounds like some bullshit."

"I guess they make twenty thousand a post. Plus, he can reroute their YouTube revenue if they don't. That's in the seven-figure range."

"Christ. Sounds dicey. This isn't really your domain. Or mine." He turned toward Moon and studied her face. "You're going to do it, aren't you?"

"He has some dirt on me. He knows about the converters."

Antonio's eyes turned steely, his smile too wide, and Moon felt a chill. "You mean dirt on *us*," he said. "Where does this motherfucker live?"

Moon had met Antonio here at the marina. He was the boat lift operator, and he'd hauled her boat out to bottom paint it when she'd bought it. They became friends, even though she wanted more. He seemed to have an easy way with women, and she just wasn't on his radar. Still, they'd hatched the plan to steal the catalytic converters for some extra cash. They thought they'd never get caught.

"The car he drove had a Los Gatos license plate frame. A gray and white '53 Corvette. Hard to miss. You still have a guy who can run license plates?"

"Hell yes, I do. High school buddy, Sammy G. Works at the DMV in Watsonville," Antonio said.

"I bet this tech kid has a daddy who collects cars. Hell, I bet he lives with daddy."

"This little bitch blackmailing us. Probably thinks he's smarter than us. Better than us. What, because he can write code? The world was better off before all those bastards starting linking everything up. You know they put a fucking microchip in a pig's brain?"

Disliking big tech was something they bonded over. Antonio was good with cars and computers, but they both hated the Silicon Valley for what it did to the people there. The homelessness, the dichotomy between the rich and poor. The capitalization on the private lives of everyone. She'd felt close to him during their planning phase, and she'd told him about her past, not her real name, but about getting involved with some major drug dealers back on Oahu in college. He knew that she'd turned informant too. He also knew that the guys she'd help put away were out now, and that they would send someone to kill her if they knew where she was. He never asked what her real name was. That was the beauty of Antonio, and this place. Everybody was here for reason and didn't ask questions. One day, she had told Antonio that he was beautiful. He'd handled her so delicately. All he said was, "You're lovely, Moon." And kissed her hand, then got back to work. His voice had said two things. If you keep at it, you'll ruin what we have. And, you're sweet. But Moon didn't feel sweet.

"He's smart. We're smarter," Moon said. "But he knows my real name."

Antonio's smile and eyes softened, and he refocused on the horizon. "If he told you that, then I guess you have to go through with it. I'll get to work on my end."

"I guess I will," Moon said, watching the horizon.

"We'll see who's stupid when he drives back over in that '53. Make sure he parks in the special spot, over by the ramp." Antonio laughed. "The VIP spot."

Moon smiled, then laughed. A solid ten-foot wave swelled up, and Moon turned to paddle, but Antonio was already on it. "Party wave," he said. So Moon paddled to catch up. They caught it, side-by-side, and she made slow curves behind his aggressive lip cuts until the wave gave out and they fell together into the whitewash.

Moon slipped through the back door of the yacht club and into the washroom. The yacht club was a humble, blue-clapboard building at the edge of the marina that could use a fresh coat of paint. Some members used it for special occasions, but it was mostly liveaboards who came in for laundry, showers, bathrooms, and self-serve liquor. Moon locked her surfboard in a broom closet Lawrence had turned into a surf locker for her and grabbed her keys. She tiptoed, still dripping seawater from her wetsuit, into the bar and took two bottles of Lagunitas IPA from the cooler. She quietly made her way to the washroom, then stepped outside hoping for freedom. Instead, she felt Lawrence's presence. She turned.

"I restock those IPAs every other day, and I never see a single dues-paying member drinking them," Lawrence said.

Moon grinned and slightly cocked her head. She liked watching Lawrence's face soften when she acted innocent. He was in his mid-sixties and, Moon was pretty sure, had managed the Elkhorn Yacht Club and Harbor since he was born. He was short, wide, and had a halo of gray hair surrounding a bald, peeling scalp. She'd never seen him in anything but a Hawaiian shirt, shorts, and faded Top-Siders.

"I was just going back to the boat to get my wallet. The surf was huge."

The heavy waves boomed on the other side of the rock jetty. "There's a goddamn small-craft advisory," Lawrence said, his bushy eyebrows expressive.

"That's the best time. I'm usually the only one out."

"Please don't drown out there. I don't want to explain it

to the police."

"I've surfed Pipeline."

He nodded and changed topics. "I saw Antonio coming back from Watsonville earlier. Please tell me, for the love of Christ, that you two are not up to anything?"

"I made you a promise. I'm clean now." Moon said, though it was clear he knew something was going on behind his back.

"I hope not. By the way, you can use the shower at the club." He gestured to her dripping wetsuit. "But the beers are for members."

"I've got hot water onboard, and I'll pay you back for these. I promise."

He nodded. "I still need you to replace the cleat on slip F-38."

"I'll get to it first thing tomorrow," Moon said, back-pedaling along the small strip of crabgrass between the yacht club and the curb that dropped into the brackish marina water. She turned.

"I know you won't let me down," Lawrence called after her. "I put my neck out for you."

Moon sighed, he always slid in his little knife of guilt. The old man had taken a chance, sure. He knew she came from a good family in Pebble Beach; he also knew she'd been cut off after the felony incident. She owed Lawrence big, and stealing the converters under his nose made her feel like shit.

On the way back to her ship, Moon stopped at slip F-11 and rapped lightly on the galley glass. Cheryl Knight's tangle of gray hair bobbed up the steps a second later, her bulging, green eyes stared at Moon like a startled animal.

"Lagunitas IPA," Moon said, and held up a bottle of beer. Moon had met Cheryl at a homeless shelter in Santa Cruz and learned a lot about the older woman in small doses. She used to surf, for one. And had traveled half the world. But Cheryl didn't surf anymore or talk much. She also hissed at people she didn't like. Cheryl was the unofficial gardener for the yacht club and had helped Moon with the special catalytic converter space with her makeshift flower beds along the walkways and around the dumpster. Cheryl nodded at

Moon and did a sort of meow. She took the beer and went below deck.

Moon made another stop at F-21, Antonio's Norsemen 440. She knocked and he parted yellowed curtains. He smiled and pointed to his cell phone; his dark eyes flashed in the dim light. He was always on that thing chatting with someone, probably a girl. He had a confidence in life that Moon wished she had. She left the beer on the rear deck, and he mouthed "thank you." Moon nodded and tried to hide her disappointment, heading back to her ship. *Moon Beam.*

Fifteen minutes after their charter was supposed to depart, the influencers texted that they were lost. Moon called them and told them to look for the Elkhorn Yacht Club boat, a small, wooden sailboat at the entrance. Told them to come park at Moon Beam Charters. The VIP spot was already taken by a '53 Corvette with Los Gatos plates.

A few minutes later, a pearl white Mercedes E-Class with white rims and a surfboard rack pulled in, bumping Cardi B, windows cracked. Moon came out the back of the club, and when she approached, the passengers cut the music. Loud bickering immediately followed. Moon stood in front of the car, ignored.

"This isn't a fishing charter, dipshit."

"It doesn't mean we *can't* fish."

"Leave the fucking fishing pole, moron."

"I'm bringing the fuck—"

Moon cleared her throat. "You gentlemen need a hand with your gear?"

"Hey there...hi. Are you Moon, uh, from Moon Beam Charters?" the driver said. The door lifted like a Tesla wing; he stepped out. He was at least six feet, broad chested, and had sharp, Nordic features with tufts of bleached blonde sticking out of a trucker hat embroidered with a fat, gold anchor and a gold leaf pattern. He also had on a ridiculous Captain Morgan-looking sailor outfit, ruffled shirt and red crushed velvet overcoat.

"And you are?" Moon said.

"Mariah Fable. *At* your table." He grinned and cocked

his head and held a pose. Moon assumed he must have practiced that same pose at least a thousand times with a selfie stick.

"I'm Moon. I'll be your captain for the next few hours. Do you have anything you need to bring aboard?" Moon used her non-regional dialect voice like this was a Disney ride.

"Just my backpack—"

"And fishing gear," the passenger said, his door ascending. He was smaller, with a round face and shaggy hair pulled into a green knit beanie.

"Sorry. That's Logan, he helps produce my shit. And he's annoying as fuck."

Logan pulled two fishing rods and a tackle box from the back seat. These guys had a vibe about them like nobody ever told them no. Moon took an even breath and nodded to the tangle of lines and fishing hooks Logan still wrestled with.

"Logan, buddy," she said. "Do you have a fishing license? Salmon tags? Crab permit?"

"Don't you provide that shit?" Logan said, his eyes narrowing.

"I provide sailing. I booked an influencer so that they could promote some nautical-themed sparkling water or something."

Logan's face dropped. "I promised this company in Key West I would do a post with these."

"No fishing gear," Moon said. "Fish and Game will have your ass. What else do you need?"

Mariah answered, "We have an ice chest too. It's in the trunk with the sparkling lemonade—"

Logan threw his arms up. "Wait. What the fuck, man? You said we could fish? Why the hell do we need a license? It's not like there are cops out there." Logan wasn't letting it go, but he seemed to decide that directing his frustration on Mariah was better than directing it at Moon. But she caught his angst and clutched the cat ears in her pocket.

"There's a Coast Guard cutter right there, and four Fish and Game boats in the South Harbor there. They will board us and check our catch. If we have fish or get caught fishing, the fine is in the thousands, and I lose my captain's license." Moon couldn't wait for this trip to be over so she didn't have to deal with these morons. Taking a hundred K from them was starting to sound well deserved.

"Fuck, man. Fine." Logan slunk down and put the rods back.

Moon followed Mariah to the back and watched him pop the trunk. Inside sat a silver YETI 110. Moon opened the lid. On the ice were three bottles of Veuve, a bottle of Cognac, a dozen beers, and a case of Sea Spray Sparkling Lemonade.

"You guys plan on drinking all that in three hours?" Moon asked.

"We'll sure as hell try," Mariah said, stepping beside Moon. "And don't worry, we share."

"I don't drink," Moon said.

They shrugged and stood behind Moon with their arms crossed, waiting. Moon leaned over and heaved the ice chest from the trunk and set it on the dirt. She took a dolly from the yacht club, slid the ice chest on, and wheeled it over the uneven marina planks to her boat. Mariah and Logan followed, pausing to take selfies and short videos near parking lot signs, the yacht club deck, a random fishing trawler—a seal that barked and flopped off the dock to get the hell away.

At her ship, Moon dragged the ice chest onto the rear deck. Mariah and Logan followed, finding new angles to take more photos of themselves. Moon lifted an eyebrow. Add alcohol to these two space cadets, and she was certain she was going to lose both overboard.

"Is this Moon Dream Charters?" Cody asked, approaching the rear deck.

"Keep it moving, cheese nuts," Mariah said. "This is our ship."

"You must be Fabian," Moon said, using Cody's previously chosen alias. "Climb aboard, we're about ready for departure."

"Hey, I thought we chartered this boat," Logan said. His whine was grating.

"I charged you the shared charter rate," Moon said,

clipping the lifeline back in. "There are life jackets under the seats. Everyone needs to have one on. It could get bumpy out there, so stay fucking seated, especially if you're drunk. If you fall overboard, there's a good chance you'll have hypothermia before I can get you back on the boat. Alcohol increases your chances of hypothermia. If you drown, well, that's why you signed the waiver when you booked."

"Man. You must be a real hit on the old-millennial dating scene," Mariah said. Logan laughed, his little camera already rolling.

"Tinder profile: Remain seated. Alcohol leads to hypothermia," Logan said. They laughed.

"Always wear a life jacket, for your protection against getting wet," Mariah said. They laughed again. "*Nobody* should get wet."

Moon ignored this. She pulled the covers off the sails and started the Volvo diesel engine. It rumbled the fiberglass and teak beneath their feet. The influencers stopped recording long enough to crack open a bottle of orange juice each. Dumping three-quarters of it overboard, they filled the bottles back up with Remy Martin XO and champagne.

Moon fought a dry heave but savored the momentary silence. She untied from the dock and pushed off with her foot, then reversed the rest of the way and turned the ship seaward. She changed gears, and the boat pushed forward, gliding over the calm, dark green waters of the forebay, a spread of land on the starboard side, where the freshwater from the Elkhorn Slough mixed in with the open ocean.

The forebay was uncovered by the low tide and held hundreds of resting pelicans. As the *Moon Beam* passed, one pelican clamored awkwardly forward, bounced a few times, spread its massive wings, and took flight low along the smooth waters. A moment later, Moon rounded the corner and angled between two rock jetties toward the open sea. At the center of the opening, where the tides interlaced, five-foot swells formed, white-capped.

The influencers were laughing about something again. Moon steered toward the largest of swells. She hit the first one, and the front pitched up, dangled for a beat, then slammed into the next. The boat shook hard like it might come apart. A soft foghorn blared, and they pitched again. The influencers were dead quiet, their drinks on the floor, their hands tightly clutching life jackets and railing. Moon smiled to herself. Worked every time.

A few minutes later, the boat planed through smooth bay waters. The influencers slid back into their seats and chugged their drinks. Then, like they hadn't just shat themselves, started back with the multishot poses, trying to get the right chin-to-sun-to-sky ratio.

Cody nodded to Moon, which meant the signal blocker was about to launch. She nodded back. Cody tapped at his phone screen, and within sixty seconds, Mariah and Logan were holding their phones toward the sky, looking for bars. Moon tried to hide her smile. It was like the air they breathe was cut off.

"Whoa, whoa. Your contract never mentioned anything about dead zones," Mariah said, squinting at his phone.

Moon shrugged. "The whale population is cutting back on social media."

"She's got jokes. First the fishing, now this? Does she even care about her online ratings?" Logan said.

"Relax, Bill Dance, just sign into the Wi-Fi," Moon said.

Logan muttered something about who the hell Bill Dance was and tapped at his screen. Moon locked the steering in place at five knots, angled into the small, two-foot seas. The boat rocked gently while Moon cranked the mainsail up and unhooked the boom. It luffed for a second before it filled with wind, and the whole ship keeled over several degrees. The influencers scrambled for purchase again. Moon didn't hide her smile this time. Captain Morgan looked ridiculous.

"It's all part of the package," Moon said. Cody laughed.

Moon moved to the other side of the ship and cranked up the jib halyard. It luffed until she winched it tight, and the hull got closer to the water with each crank. A spray of ocean rushed over the starboard deck.

"Christ. Are we going to flip this thing?" Mariah asked.

Moon cranked the jib another half turn just to see the influencers lean toward the sky like they were about to roll straight into the sea. Moon caught Cody's frown and fell off the extreme tack until the ship righted itself. Mariah and Logan both sighed and got their bearings. Moments later, they were chugging beers and glued to their disconnected phone screens.

"What did you say the Wi-Fi code was?" Mariah said.

"Moonsails01. All lower case, one word."

Moon wondered what would happen if these kids figured out that she played a role in this scam. She watched Cody; he looked tired and oily, and like he would turn on her in a second. Not that it mattered. Moon learned back in Oahu, you always hedge your bets. She had believed in her boyfriend at the time, she loved him. Jackson Cash. Not his real name, in fact, nothing about him was real. And he'd betrayed her, left her for dead. And so, when she went down, she informed. She vowed never to put that much faith in another human again. Always have a plan B. And C.

"That's not working," Logan said.

"Actually, I'm in," Cody said.

The influencers messed with their phones a little longer before Mariah got frustrated. "Dammit. I should have known it would be a goddamn dead zone." Mariah shot a dirty look in Moon's direction. "My followers can't go three hours without at least a story update. *Fuck.*"

"Should have brought the fucking fishing poles, man," Logan said.

"It looks like you just have to reset your phone's network settings and login into the VPN directly with the router's proxy settings. I mean, if you have an Apple phone," Cody said.

"What the hell is he talking about?" Mariah said.

"I have a ship to steer," Moon said. "Let Geek Squad help you. You guys want to head toward Capitola or Monterey?"

"We're here for the backdrop. Keep us close-ish to the shore and make it pretty," Logan said.

"Actually, can we get a shot of a whale? The sparkling lemonade company would fucking love that shit," Mariah said.

"Maybe we can get a seal to drink some. Holy shit, can

we like, pour some into a seals mouth?" Logan asked.

"Keep that toxic shit on the boat," Moon said. They were getting louder, which meant the alcohol was kicking in.

"I need to post a story," Mariah said, throwing a can of beer overboard in a mock tantrum.

Moon narrows her eyes at Mariah. "If you throw anything else into the ocean, I will kick you overboard," Moon said, venom in her voice.

A moment passed, and Mariah realized she was serious and turned away. "Logan, get us online." Mariah handed Logan his phone and watched the horizon. "And this network better be secure."

Cody took the phones from Logan, frowning at the screens while he worked. His little plan was working. A moment later, Cody handed both phones back, and the influencers went back to gathering footage and posting stories. It was done. Now all Moon had to do was survive the next two and a half hours without killing anyone.

"Can I piss overboard? I always wanted to do that," Logan said, standing at the back, unzipping. Moon steered toward a four-foot swell.

"Go for it," she said.

A high fog rolled in and covered the sun a half hour before they got back to the harbor. Mariah slept on his back along the rear seat after puking three times. Logan had recorded it all, probably for extra clicks or views or whatever made money come in the door. They'd been wasted the entire time, nearly fell out of the boat a dozen times, and took about a thousand photos drinking the Sea Spray Sparkling Lemonade, even though they retched every time they tried it. Moon tried it and nearly puked too. She pulled into her slip and tied the boat off.

"You okay to drive?" Moon asked Logan as he helped a comatose Mariah to the dock.

Logan gave a quick nod. "We're staying just down the road. Carmel. We good."

Watching Logan sway with the unsteady dock while trying to keep Mariah steady was the only enjoyable thing the two influencers had provided Moon all day. When they started their car, Moon half expected the Mercedes to blare to life with that guttural roar of a car with no exhaust. But it sounded smooth. Although Moon knew Antonio would be tempted with a high-end car like that, he did what he was supposed to do. Moon smiled. She could always count on him.

"Should we finish this?" Cody said.

"Let's go below," Moon said.

The next phase of the plan was simple enough, though Moon didn't know much about it. She watched while Cody flipped open his laptop, logged into his app that tracked every keystroke the influencers had made on their phones since he logged them in. Within an hour Cody closed his laptop and looked at Moon with a satisfied grin.

"Well. I've got everything we need. I set the software to boot them off their platform in exactly forty-eight hours. According to the story update Mariah made before puking and partially falling off the ship earlier, they'll be at The Standard rooftop for a pool party at that time."

Moon grinned. "Cut him off right when he's about to post shirtless with lemon-vomit water and C-list celebrities? I love it."

"You have a mean streak, Moon." When he said her name, an uneasiness passed between them; Moon could sense it. He knew who she was and had threatened her.

"When do I get my money?"

"Right. Assuming they pay the hundred K, I'll transfer you fifty K twenty-four hours later. I estimate three days. Maybe four."

"I want cash. Remember?"

Cody stood and tucked his laptop into a padded backpack. "I have no idea how to get that kind of cash. Can't I just wire transfer it?"

"I don't have a bank account. I barely have a cell phone."

"Right. You're not as well hidden as you might think."

"Thanks for your fucking input. I require cash."

"Look. I still have to break their access, extort them

for a hundred K, and give them access back. All you had to do was steer the fucking ship. Now you want small, unmarked bills?"

"You couldn't have done it without the ship, *Cody.*"

"You can't do shit without what I've got here in my bag."

"You're welcome for that. Now you're going to bring me cash. In four days."

"How the fuck am I going to turn that around? I can't exactly walk into Wells Fargo and ask for fifty large without raising questions." Cody stood and opened the hatch. "In fact, I don't think your little tour—smashing through the biggest swells you could find to scare the pretty boys—was worth half. I'm thinking more like twenty, or even ten." He climbed up to the cockpit.

"You have four days. Now get the fuck off my boat."

"I'm gone." He stepped off the boat, straining the ropes. He took a few steps with his head down. "Maybe I'll bring you ten."

"Hey, Cody. You're going to need these." Moon jangled her own car keys.

"I have my keys, thank you." He turned and started walking down the dock, head down, then slammed into Antonio's broad chest. Antonio was tall, lean, and scared the literal piss out of Cody. Smiling, Antonio whispered something, and Cody slowly turned around and looked up at the boat lift holding his Corvette fifty feet in the air directly over the muddy marina waters. He whimpered, lost his footing on the planks, and fell on his ass.

"Put it down. Goddamnit, it. Please."

Antonio helped Cody up and escorted him to Moon's boat. She stepped up next to him on the dock and slid the keys to her '71 Dodge Tradesman into his shirt pocket. "Antonio helped me rebuild the engine a couple years back, so she's running pretty well. Please don't scratch her though."

"Please. Christ. That car is worth two hundred thousand. Easy."

"Is it your dad's? Doesn't matter. You have four days to bring me fifty K, and you get it back."

"What are you going to do, sell it? It's one of a kind."

"No. We'll just hit the release on the boat lift, the straps will drop away, and the car will plunge to the bottom of the ocean. Gone. Forever."

"Look, okay. I'll give you half, but I have to transfer it."

"In cash."

"Fuck. Are you serious? That's not my car, it's my— You don't know who you're fucking with. The people I work for won't allow this."

"Four days. Cash."

"Fine. I'll try to figure it out. Christ, you're fucking nuts."

Moon stood with Antonio and watched Cody walk carefully down the dock. He stepped over the aluminum bridge and neared the dumpsters.

"Wait for it," Antonio said.

When Cody got close to the flower beds, Cheryl jumped up and hissed. Cody let out a high-pitched scream. Antonio laughed, and Moon smiled. She felt a slight triumph, but Cody's comment nagged at her. Who the hell was his employer? She didn't like it.

The back door of the yacht club opened. It was Lawrence. He shook his head and glanced up at the Corvette suspended over the harbor. "I've never seen a Corvette sail before. Not sure how it got up there, but I hope it's down by the time I get back from Santa Cruz. And please, no trouble. Huh?"

They sat on the front deck of *Moon Beam* while Cody pulled away in Moon's van. A few minutes later, Lawrence pulled away in his late 80s Cutlass. Moon let out a sigh of relief.

"Better get the 'vette down I guess," Antonio said.

"There's still time. I'll steal you a couple of beers."

He smiled, and Moon followed him down the dock, toward the club, wishing she could somehow watch Mariah's reaction in real time when his entire world got ripped away.

Four days later, on Wednesday, Cody chugged into the

yacht club parking lot. He didn't say anything. He left the keys in the van while Moon and Antonio inspected the bag of cash. It checked out, so they led Cody to his car, which was covered with a tarp behind a stand of kayaks. He pulled away and sped off in the direction of Santa Cruz.

Moon got back to her boat and again noticed there was something off. The braided-steel lifeline was unhooked again. Someone had been on her boat. Again. She opened the door and stepped into the ship. Sitting on her table was a note. She opened it.

Jessica Moon DeMarco. Those of us at the Civilian Cyber Army think it's time for you to have a few social media accounts with your current location. The boys from Oahu have been, I understand, released. Godspeed and good luck.
–Cody

Moon balled the note in her fist. She went up the dock and knocked on Antonio's boat. He opened his hatch and motioned for him to come aboard. She followed him below deck and sat beside him at his table. His laptop was already opened with a GPS locator blinking.

"Do we get to have some fun?" Antonio said.

"He works with the Civilian Cyber Army? He left a note in my cabin. He's going to get me fucking killed."

"Not if we cut his brakes first." Antonio, while he had access to the Corvette, had taken the liberty of rigging it with a GPS tracker and a weakened brake line that could be severed remotely with a single keystroke. It was their plan C.

"This Mariah guy must have been a target. I bet their plan is to make us take the fall for it too."

Antonio did some quick Google searches. "Civilian Cyber Army is headed by Sergey Trinity, and that looks just like your guy. Says here they're basically hackers for hire. Has a penchant for flashy cars. Kind of high profile for criminals." The picture in Wikipedia was a dated picture of Cody Singh. "The car was registered to Cody Singh. So, they're at least thorough."

"Probably already registered to another name." Moon

said. "I wonder who wanted to fuck with Mariah?"

"Who knows. Rival YouTube star? Crazed fan? Bill Gates? We doing this?"

"I think it's the only option. He's going to get me killed."

"What if his people come for you? For us?"

"Well, I'd rather have nerdy hackers than ex-military. How about you?"

"The guys you turned in were ex-military? Shit, well, hackers it is." Antonio said.

"Wait until he's going over the 17 pass, on the downhill side. That'll make sure it's a big enough drop."

"I like your style." Moon gathered closer to Antonio's screen.

"Guess we're not as dumb as we look, are we?" Moon said.

"Ready?" Antonio said, and smiled. Moon nodded. They hit the Enter key together.

David M. Olsen is a writer, photographer, filmmaker, and poet. He attended Stanford's OWC program in novel writing and holds an MFA in Creative Writing and Writing for the Performing Arts from the University of California, Riverside - Palm Desert. He is at work on a collection of linked short stories, a novel, and a chapbook. David is a former fiction editor at *The Coachella Review* and is currently the Editor-in-Chief at *Kelp Journal*. His work has appeared in *Catamaran Literary Reader*, *The Rumpus*, *The Coachella Review*, *Close to the Bone*, *Scheherazade*, and elsewhere. He resides on California's central coast where he surfs regularly.

SUNDAYS ARE FOR ROBBERIES

By Samantha Tkac

I heaved a satchel full of items that felt like they were mine and fled down the front stairs two at a time because Sunday mornings were for robberies, and my sister was the driver.

The satchel fell down my back, and its strap peeled my shirt up over my breasts as I ran across the prickly lawn. My tits were out, and the world didn't pause like I hoped it would. The teenage boys across the street picked the hangnails off of their shredded boogie boards and didn't notice Brett running after me. He was quicker than he looked despite his bowlegged gait.

Items fell out of my bag and onto the sand. Brett snatched up a crucifix pressed with triangular fragments of amethyst.

"This is mine, this is mine," he said. He stacked the items beneath the doughy arm that I'd used as a pillow an hour prior. Luckily, the wind chime with aquamarine stones didn't tumble. I planned on hanging it up outside of the condo I hoped to rent and soon. I was saving up the best I could.

Last night I called Brett from the bar, and he picked me up on his Harley. At first he wanted to fuck me, and then he wanted something sex-adjacent: my sundress over my head and my face slammed against the seventies-era paneling in his living room. Like a snapshot, I remember the exact view of the sea glass picture frame from where my face landed. The moonlight sparked beads of amber within the blue stones. I thought of sunsets on the Atlantic. When my head made contact with the wall a second time, I wasn't reminded of anything—I saw fire, pure and real.

I met Brett at the farmers' market in the southernmost town of the Barriers. He had pulled off his motorcycle helmet and approached the fruit stand next to ours. He pressed crescent moons into Linda's navel oranges with black-rimmed thumbnails and hummed loudly enough for her to look up from the pages of her Sudoku.

After indenting the peels and leaving Linda in a tizzy, he closed in on our stand, carrying with him an orbit of whiskey breath the length of his arm. He knocked into my carousel of bracelets, and I instinctively adjusted the wooden sign on the table. It read, "You break, you buy," with a little purple heart so that people wouldn't think I was being a bitch about it. The bracelets teetered on the tips of their metal branches while he ran his hand over his sun-spoiled scalp. He watched them sway without an attempt to save them from falling.

He looked hard at Nadia. She was a year older but looked younger than me. With pinched features and skinny arms stitched across her chest, she gave off the impression of an angsty teen forced to be wherever she was. She could rope lovers in if she wanted, but people were a little hesitant to approach her. So, they usually fell onto me. Brett ended up buying a bracelet made of conch fragments painted Tinker Bell green. His one-dollar bills felt like thrift store velveteen, like the skirt I'd bought Nadia for Christmas and that she'd tossed in the back of our Jeep; we had no occasion to wear it, not yet.

I slammed the passenger door and pressed the lock button until my knuckle joint ached. I loved these moments when everything felt heightened, when every brain cell sizzled. Nadia's vibrating side-eyed wickedness pulled me in, and I felt the flutter of laughter in my chest as she ripped the gear stick into drive.

I was finally with her, tucked in beside her. Brett threw himself against the car and thwacked the passenger side window. I licked the glass, the only thing separating his hand from my neck. His palm screeched down the length of the car as we tore away. Then Brett was a body in the rearview, shimmering in a plume of sand and dust.

I felt a little bad. Brett was nice enough. He liked looking at me during sex. His index cocked like a trigger on my chin, he pulled me back to him when I tried to disappear into the mountain of decorative pillows, and bored into me with eyes the same color as the useless gray seashells I chucked back into the ocean. I only made necklaces out of seashells that glistened pink.

Brett's hand had left sweat marks on the glass. I rolled down the window to erase every last trace.

Nadia and I sped up Highway 14. The road led all the way up and down the Barriers. From the pebble-crusted shoreline down south to the unpaved town of Vacova where the wild mustangs roamed, the Barriers were a slender string of finger-shaped islands that stretched up the coastline, acting as a barrier between the Carolinas and the Atlantic. We didn't need to take any turns to get where we wanted to go.

I wanted to tell Nadia the origin story of the welt on my lip, but when she accelerated to fifty, I stayed quiet. Besides, I checked Brett's wall for dents afterward when he was busy making coffee. I hadn't left a mark.

The way Nadia drove was a good indicator of her mood. I mimicked her pissed-offness, staring straight down the eye of the highway and hoped I was giving off the impression of someone who knew something. Nadia smacked me on the knee. She knew I didn't know shit.

"I need shaving cream, the soap isn't cutting it anymore," she said. Suspicion slithered through my chest. We never shaved unless we cared, and I thought we'd agreed not to. I noticed for the first time that she wore a sweatshirt. It was swampy outside.

"Aren't you hot?" I said. She shrugged. "And who the hell do we need to shave for?"

"*I* want to," she said. She tightened her grip on the wheel. "Besides, women shave, Shiv." She may as well have said, "Fuck off," but her tone didn't stop me.

"We don't have to be like everyone," I said, knowing that if she shaved, I would follow suit. That's how it was. If she didn't finish a bite of her burger, I didn't finish mine. We didn't have a scale and I'm glad we didn't. I liked to pretend we weighed the same.

The next song was Britney. As if by obligation, we screamed the lyrics until our voices split.

Nadia's hands were on the move. She was always searching for something—grasping against the seat fabric for a lighter, gesturing for a beer, tapping my wrist for a hairband—with one eye on the road.

"My purse," Nadia said. She motioned to her plump faux Gucci in the back seat that I'd taken off of a bejeweled and unsuspecting woman last weekend at Hidden Sailor. Just the purse. I wasn't interested in taking money.

I pulled out a spliff that had been rolled with nimble fingers and was definitely not a product of our handiwork.

She made a fist, meaning "hand me a beer." I dug through her bag in search of a warm cylinder. Beneath a nest of candy wrappers, I fingered a button bag filled with coke. The sharp corners, the soft clumps—I knew what it was before I pulled it out.

"From who?" I said. When she didn't respond, I figured she'd nicked it off the guy she'd spent the night with.

Nadia and I weren't homeless. But after Mom shattered a bottle of Chardonnay against my collarbone in June, we chose to move out of her condo on the west side of the island. Our basement room had overlooked a particularly brackish part of the sound where the oysters thrived. They clicked and spat when low tide forced them into the evening air. I was an oceanside girl. I preferred the sound of crashing waves to any chirping oyster when it came time to sleep. Nadia and I crashed on the beach when it was warm enough. We slept in our Jeep when it rained. If the temperature dipped down to where our entwined bodies wouldn't stop the shivering, we mingled with the tourists and eyed for Eddie Bauer polos I made sure Nadia found a bed, and then I went my own way.

We had little money to spend, but every dollar we spent wisely. Most of it went toward supplying material for the jewelry I made and sold at the market. While Nadia turned cones upside down at Dairy Queen, I strung together fractured parts of shells with a drill bit and wire in the back seat of the Jeep with a flashlight between my teeth. I knew how to make my paint last a long time. Add a little seawater, and my forest green turned to pear. Add more, and it would fade into an olive pastel. In the end, I'd have a sage glaze that shimmered like the midmorning sea. Something about the salt water made the paint sparkle and last. I felt there was nothing my beautiful Atlantic couldn't do for me.

After grabbing shaving cream at CVS, we pulled into the McDonald's next to the Circle K because it had a full-length mirror and outlets. We propped our legs into right angles against the tile wall and dragged razors up our shins. Nadia went farther up her dress, hunched over, digging the blade against bristled folds.

"The guy I was with last night is throwing a party," Nadia said.

"You're being thorough," I said. The sound of the metal grating against her flesh sounded like seething, like someone hissing through their teeth.

"He's nice." She watched my face. In an instant, her shin bubbled with bloody notches. "He's nice, Shiv." The notches drooled.

"So what, is this a date?" I said. I tucked away a spike of envy. I moved to the mirror and maneuvered my breasts so that my nipples sat on the ledge of the shirt's elastic fabric. "And isn't he a little young?"

"Shiv, he's four years older than you," she said. She splashed water from the sink onto her legs. The floor swamped with hair-flecked mountains of pink cream.

"So what did you guys do last night, watch a fucking movie?" I tried to laugh but could only muster a scoff.

"He lives at his parents' house up north." She patted down her legs with brown paper towels from the dispenser. "He has an acre of beach, I swear to God." She smeared Vaseline across her eyelids. "You'll like him."

Nadia drove north. The view of the sea skated across the dunes. In the middle of the island, we sat in traffic among SUVs like skyscrapers, their rooftops piled with luggage. I caught glimpses of the sea in rectangular blocks between towering pink-and-blue mansions, but that's only because I knew when to look.

We bore witness to the last exodus of the Barriers. We were headed into the second weekend of September, and shoulder season was well underway. That meant early closing times and no more Eddie Bauer polos.

As much as I liked the empty beaches during the fall and winter, I worried about the dwindling market income, the cold beach, and the lack of starving flesh. Money and warm bodies were summer luxuries.

Vacova didn't have any paved roads. The properties were only accessible by driving on the shoreline. We ambled over the ramp and eased our Jeep onto the beach. I removed the Jeep's soft top and stretched out above the roll bars. We flew by the sea castles with their towers and balconies. They sat far apart from one another, sad-eyed in their hibernation.

With the salt on my tongue and my hair an angry scribble against the competing winds, I felt the end-of-summer sadness ebb away. I looked down at my beautiful sister as she revved to forty, an impossibly fast speed when driving on sand. She grinned up at me, flushed from the engine-power high.

I flopped back down in my seat and smiled back, forgetting about my split lip. My welt yawned open, wide as a toothpick. I yowled, and Nadia notched up Ariana Grande and rolled down the windows. She hated when I made a fuss.

"Stick your head out the window," she said. I did. I inhaled the beach and felt better.

With a free hand, Nadia snapped open the Bud Light and handed it over. The foam flowed onto my bare knees, and I felt buzzed before I had the chance to swallow.

We pulled up on the unmarked shoulder of Eric's property. It was an oceanfront shingle-style mansion named Lemuria. We waited for the song to finish, our shoulders switching in unison and our throats taut as we inspected our necks for wiry hairs in the vanity mirrors. When the song ended, Nadia ripped out the key.

I never felt prepared for the cut of the engine. No longer were we creatures moving through space, the gusts of sea air flowing through the open windows and making my lungs feel fresh and enormous. I felt panic in the silence. I scrambled away from it, falling out of the door and into the evening. I sucked in the Atlantic.

The glow off the measureless horizon tinged our cheeks red as we walked hand-in-hand through the sand and around back to the party. I found Eric right away. I hoped I wouldn't, but I felt the same way I felt when I saw him at Hidden Sailor the night prior. He was dreadfully attractive. But, he seemed safe—and nice. And therefore, he was Nadia's. When I caught them in a kiss after coming back from the bar's restroom, I didn't realize I had fled in the opposite direction until I was on the far edge of the parking lot, my big toe scraping against fissured concrete. I reminded myself that Nadia needed a safe place to sleep and that's all that mattered. I dug out the receipt for the bracelet that Brett had scribbled his number on, and I was shivering on the back of his bike thirty minutes later.

Eric stood with his back to the sea. Smoke leaked from his mouth and shaded his gorgeous face for a blessed moment in time. His eyes drifted to the pink-marbled ocean and then focused on me. He tucked his vape into the pocket of his linen shirt and moved in.

"What happened to your lip?" he said. I wanted to tell him that Nadia and I didn't talk about wounds, because things heal and disappear, so what was the point?

I wonder how long I stared at his stupid face, my finger pressed against my weeping lip, without saying anything. His expression twisted into a concentrated look of concern that I felt he must have practiced over and over in a bathroom mirror; it was a look so perfectly *sincere*. I hated him passionately. It was the kind of hate that clumps in your chest and flicks at your clit until you have to do something about it.

I stormed into the house and hated everything more. "Lemuria" boasted floor-to-ceiling windows with a panoramic view of the sea, and the table looked like real wood, and there were no lamps made out of cheap plastic. It had been a long time since I'd been inside of a beach house that had style, even if it was a snobby-rich kind of style. Most of the places I ended up in had a sparse, inhabitable feel because of the slapdash rental turnarounds. The walls I stared at from the old mattresses were often glaring pink, the bedside lamps in the shapes of turtles, dolphins. And the names of the houses were reflective of the kind of thought that was voiced once, casually, as an offhand joke. "Hey, what about Rock 'n' Reel?" And then, when it came time to put pen to paper and name the damn place, nobody could think of a better idea, and that stupid pun became a neon sign in the owner's brain. I felt sorry for the owners, and the houses. And even the renters. I was sure they were all beyond themselves with self-loathing.

I looked at every pretty thing in Eric's home and envisioned it in pieces. The tables held candleholders, ashtrays and vases, all of which were made of some sort of stone or glass. I wanted them shattered. And drilled. And strung with wire. I wanted to make a necklace that I could nestle against my throat.

I found the master suite. Nadia's clothes were strewn about as if it were her own bedroom. I found the bathroom and hiked up my dress, planted my foot on the white marble counter and thought, How long has this been going on?

As I masturbated, I imagined Eric suspended in the dark sea. I glided toward him from the depths as he sunk beneath the surface. Our limbs tangled and our hands clasped. Our nostrils streamed bubbles that combined into a single tendril. I hovered inches from his neck. His tendons flexed and his Adam's apple bobbed. I imagined him breaking through the surface, screaming with every ounce of energy he had, trying to get my sister's attention.

"Nadia, come here—Nadia!"

He dipped under the surface again and gave me that look, like I was his last hope. I came with a lung-burning gasp.

Why was I crying? It felt not unlike vomiting: hot and throaty and with some convincing.

Someone rapped on the door. I stood pigeon-toed and damp and didn't answer.

"This place is nice, right?"

When I opened up the bathroom door to my sister, I saw that she was happy. Her eyes communicated no intricate desires. On her, happiness looked like a tide pool, so shallow and clear you could see a starfish breathe.

I bit my tongue as we walked back outside. I felt like if I said a word, I'd lose everything I knew in one breath.

Most people trickled out by midnight, but Nadia wanted to stay. Nadia was a master at pinpointing that point in the night when people either needed a thrill or their bed. There were seven of us left. We were drunk and sitting in sand-crusted swimsuit bottoms when Nadia straddled Eric and pinched the button bag out from her swim top.

She took off her sweatshirt, and I finally got a look at her arms. In the moonlight, I could see circular bruises that tracked down. With her press-on acrylics, she straightened the powder into a neat line that started at Eric's wrist and trailed up his forearm.

Then she was a vixen in a flutter of drippy lashes, twisting a fifty up her nose that someone said they wanted back. I took my turn with the dollar. I bent over Eric's arm and noticed his erection through his swimsuit. With his free hand, he tucked a strand of hair behind my ear. His lips found my forehead, his teeth like warm stones against my skin. I glanced at Nadia. She was on her back and pointing at the constellations.

Afterward, I moved into the ocean, hoping the white-noise roar of the sea would deafen the fun happening behind me. Each snot-webbed snort was followed by an eruption of laughter. I waded waist-deep, meditating on the thermic grasp of the ocean on my genitals. I hoped that the frozen feeling wouldn't fade, that it would clamp down forever. But my body adjusted. I felt saturated through and through.

I wanted my face against a wall, something. Nadia screamed my name, half laughing, like, *what the fuck are you doing?*

I moved to the shoreline and clawed at the pebble clusters. The shell of Nadia's big toe moved into my eyeline.

I wanted her to ask me about my lip. Or maybe I didn't. But I wanted a reason to be mad at her, and her not asking, I decided, was going to be my reason.

"Brett was nice too," I lied. She hugged me, and my anger dissipated the moment her head met my shoulder. She was my star, and I was clasped in her orbit. She knew it.

The ocean frothed against our identical ankles and melted into the sand. Nadia took me by the hand, and we waded back in, together.

We floated belly-up with one leg secured against the seabed. We held hands so we didn't get swept away like Mom had taught us. The ghost crabs dashed across the shoreline. Their little beads of movement were so quick and intentional.

"Hey, Na'?"

"Hey, Shi'?"

"What happened to your arm?" I said.

Her hand went slack in mine.

"What happened to your face?" she said. Then, quickly, "Do you like him? Eric?"

We moved to a pillowy dune, and I fell asleep in the crook of her stomach. When I woke up at 2:00 a.m., I was alone. I lifted my head and was drawn to Eric's beach house, the only light for half a mile. I saw movement in the window of the master bedroom. Bodies moved together, apart, together. I heard a yip of pain or pleasure, and I couldn't tell the difference. I walked in the other direction. Nadia said she liked him; I reminded myself of that. She said he was nice.

All of the seashells looked gray under the moonlight. I tossed them back into the ocean. When I returned to my spot, the light in Eric's window was off.

On Monday night, I ended up with an Andrew in a musty cottage along a barren stretch of the sound. He tied my wrists to his son's bedposts with red fishing wire. My teeth ground against the fibers of the *Finding Nemo* comforter. He propped me into an obtuse angle and tunneled into my apex. I didn't say no when he went *there* and *there,* hoping each time that gulping the pain would make a bubble of memory I could escape into when I wanted Eric the most.

It was Tuesday morning, and Eric was in the passenger seat when Nadia came to pick me up. I showed off the red rings on my wrists on the center console. I wanted him to flash me that look of concern one more time. Just for me. When nobody said anything, I told them about being bound, how garish the decor was, how he'd finished all over my back and wiped it up with his son's T-shirt. I talked loudly, inspecting the crotch of Eric's pants from my back seat angle. I avoided Nadia's glare in the rearview.

Back at Eric's, it was just the three of us. We took mushrooms that Eric casually pulled out of his cupboard next to the cereal. When the mushrooms spiked our brains, we scuttled with the crabs on the beach. We lay pin straight on our stomachs, perpendicular to the shoreline. We faced the ocean like we were prepared to shoot across the surface.

I was in the middle. I reached for Nadia's hand, but her fingers skittered away. To my left, Eric's hand found mine. His pinky curled around my index finger. He rolled his head

to the side and looked at me, but then I realized he was focused on the bruise on my mouth. He parted his lips as if to
say something but didn't. I wanted him to kiss me. I didn't
want to feel any pain.

Nadia and Eric snuck off into the darkness. I heard
them fucking and didn't move away. The sounds she made
were hard to decipher. There was a fine-lined difference
between the expression of pain and pleasure, a sick reality
of human nature. In pain, a creature wanted physical alle-
viation. In pleasure, a creature was clasped in a nerve-fritz-
ing high, struck by how marvelous a thing it was to have a
body. These opposing feelings inhabited the same screeching
sound my sister made. I faced their general direction, blinded
by darkness. In the end, I waded into the Atlantic. I tucked
myself safely into my underwater cocoon.

On Wednesday I stayed with a painter named Marcy
who had bought a green pebble necklace at the market. I
hadn't used my drill bit, because the pebble had a hole right
in the middle that I'd strung the wire through. Her head was
a bobbing triangle of red curls as she gushed.

"You *must* tell me how you come up with this stuff!"

Marcy's collie, Winston, buried his head in the couch
cushions during that night's thunderstorm. I watched the
lightning jab the sea and rested my cheek against Winston's
neck, hoping that my touch would lessen his shudder and
wondering what Nadia was doing. I thought about Eric with
Nadia, and felt rotten.

Marcy went down on me for an hour but no luck.
Afterward, she sniffled above a mixing bowl, her elbow
propped like an arrow to the door. She mumbled about the
late hour and the weather and how to get me home. I called
Nadia, but it went straight to voicemail.

On Thursday I woke up on Marcy's couch with no
wounds inflicted. So, I took a knife from her kitchen and
pierced the cap of my forehead. I dragged it down an inch. I
spent the morning hugging Winston against my knees and

waiting for Nadia while Marcy sighed loudly from her desk, clacking away at her keyboard. Nadia decided to show up at ten. Before I left, I slipped Marcy's pink stone ashtray into my purse and didn't even make a run for it.

Eric was in the driver's seat. A hook to the groin when he turned to me. Last night, with Marcy's tongue flicking against me, I pretended it was his tongue. But it was useless. I wanted Eric. And this wanting felt bigger than me. When I took Marcy's hand and tried to get her fingers to latch around my throat, it didn't feel right. When her fingers fell and caressed my breast, it felt worse.

I slammed the back door of the Jeep for a touch of drama. Nadia scrolled through music in the passenger seat. She let each song play for five seconds and clicked into the next one. She wore an enormous UNC sweatshirt that stopped right above her scabbed knees.

I lifted my chin to catch the sun on my lips. Eric turned all the way around.

"Are you okay?" he said. His words felt like a death sentence in the best way. Nadia snapped her head up.

"She gets off to it," she said. "Ignore her."

On Friday night, I wanted Eric to touch me so desperately that I pulled one of his friends into the bathroom and lost all motivation two minutes in. Slack-jawed with my teeth pressing down, I looked up at him drearily. His face held no concentrated expression of sincerity—only black-eyed lust, which was fading fast. He detached my head.

I staggered back down to the beach and burned through a bottle of Tito's.

I went skinny-dipping, alone at first, and then other bodies slipped across my skin. And then it was Eric's mouth on my shoulder. Nadia sat on the shoreline, knees tucked into her chest. Her big toe poked out of the fabric of her worn-out Vans like a white flag. Eric watched Nadia watch him as he spoke.

"Tell me what happened to you," he said. I didn't know where to begin.

Eric held me by the shoulders. The swells lifted our

feet off the ocean floor and touched us back down, toes first. We were full of the helpless grace that I only felt when I was neck-deep.

"For example," he said, "tell me what happened to your lip."

"I hit a wall," I said.

"Tell me what happened before you hit the wall," he said. The look of concern I ached for transformed into a look of fascination. A flame clicked on in his inner eye, hungry and urgent, brighter than the moon's glint in his pupil. I hadn't noticed that look before. And now I did. I noticed.

"Did you like it?" he said.

I dipped my mouth beneath the surface. A cool breeze cut across my exposed forehead. He looked down at me and then to the beach. He was assessing the risk, how far away Nadia was, what he could and couldn't get away with as he eased his palm onto my skull. I felt the hungry pressure forming there. He wanted to push me under and against him.

Instead, I catapulted off of the ocean floor and powered down on his shoulders. He sank with a delicious ease. When he resurfaced, he was laughing, spitting and coughing up water. I forced him under again.

Nadia's crouching silhouette unfurled and stretched as tall as the sky. She waved her arms, fingertips brushing the stars.

"Shiv, *stop.*"

Saturday night was five drinks at Hidden Sailor, and then it was a husband and wife in their SUV and me in their back seat. Then it was being asked if I wanted any wine, dear? A gimlet, perhaps? And then it was a coffee table pushed aside and a quiet tangle of bodies on a nylon carpet.

Afterward, I felt a warmness in my stomach as I poured myself a syrupy glass of Pinot Noir. There was a messiness to this room—books strewn about, unwashed glasses in the sink—that lent a cozy, lived-in feeling to the space. I wondered if this couple would be my Eric. I wondered if there was a room in which I could throw my clothes about and make mine. I wanted to watch a movie or hear a funny story when I noticed the wife staring at me. She stood in the foyer, draped in a blanket, her hand on the handle of the front door. The husband sat on the couch, his skinny legs a glaring white, his penis—which had connected us twenty minutes prior—buried in dimpling folds. I felt the urge to vomit, or to snatch up his penis and throw it out the window. His head fell into his hands. The couple appeared dazed and caught in the aftermath of a grisly crime.

Around 10:00 p.m., Nadia picked me up. She swung by and didn't come to a complete stop. She ambled along the gravel shoulder at five miles per hour, and I dove into the back seat. I sobbed and wrenched my fingers through my ocean-knotted hair. She notched up the radio to drown my noise. I reached toward the driver's seat, seeking comfort. My knuckles grazed against her heavy cotton sleeve.

I expected us to pull into some empty parking lot and call it a night. But we were headed north, once again, to Eric's house.

"So what, we live there now?" I said. I wanted her to tell me about a terrible breakup. I wanted devastating details that would bond our souls like ions.

"*I* live there," she said. I punched the back seat.

"He'll leave," I said. "The beach will be lonely as hell soon."

"He's not here for a little sun and sea air, Shiv," Nadia said. "He lives here now."

It could have been a smooth ride. There was only one road that Nadia had to stick to. But I was at the mercy of gravity that night. Nadia made every turn possible. She screeched in and out of neighborhood inlets and made ragged three-point turns in fast food parking lots. With my neck tensed and arms barred, I grit my teeth through that burned rubber smell she knew I hated.

"It doesn't have to be lonely for me," she said, twisting the wheel.

"Take off your sweatshirt," I said, "if he's so great." We were back on the highway and shooting north. A car turned the corner up ahead, coming straight for us.

"Don't you dare," she said. Her lips curled into a snarl. She veered into the opposite lane. "You hypocrite."

I held my breath. We were about five hundred feet away from collision before I stretched from the back seat and yanked the wheel to the right. I absorbed the sound of the blaring horn from the passing vehicle. I let that sound marinate with my rage.

"That's what I thought," she said. She pulled the sleeves of her sweatshirt over her wrists. "You can sleep at Eric's. There's a guest bedroom."

When we got to "Lemuria," I went straight to the bathroom off the kitchen. I splashed handfuls of water onto my face until every trace of concealer covering Brett's yellowing bruise was gone. I pinched the welt. Spots prickled the corners of my vision. I dug my thumbnail into the center. My face turned ugly in a second.

I kicked around the shore and kept my distance from Nadia and Eric. Around midnight, he gripped Nadia's arm and pulled her up the beach and into the house. I didn't wander away and pick at shells. I followed. I waited in the kitchen while he dragged her up the stairs by the bottom of her sweatshirt. I waited until I heard the bedroom door click shut.

I eased open the drawer next to the sink. All the silverware had thick, coral-pink handles. I took out a carving fork. The long snake-tooth spears flashed at me.

I didn't let the sound of the Atlantic wash through the walls and abate my fear. I chose to tune in and listen to what was happening as I padded up the stairs. I heard Nadia. Whether she was in pain or pleasure, I'll never know. I sheathed the carving fork into the waistband of my joggers.

I knocked on the door. The silence that followed reminded me of an engine being cut off. I told myself not to panic as I waited for Eric to answer. The door creaked open.

"You," Eric said. He looked pleased. He glistened like

he was fresh out of the ocean. Nadia couldn't see me from where he stood. But I could see her. Through the large vanity mirror, I saw her on her side, gagged by a band and her arms bound behind her. This didn't mean anything bad; I knew that. I was looking in on a subgenre on Pornhub.

But I didn't know the context.

I couldn't be sure.

"Come with me," I said before Eric could pose the same question. I had the feeling he was leaning in that direction by the way he was letting the door fall open. I didn't want Nadia to see me.

I nodded toward the guest bedroom. He looked back at Nadia and said, "I'll be right back," as if he were running to the door for a pizza delivery.

Right at the point when Eric's pounding lost its thrill and I found myself waiting for him to finish, I took out the carving fork from beneath the pillow.

I thought about how my nights never turned out as I expected, but this one would—I would make sure of it— as I plunged the fork into the tender valley above his pelvic muscle. It took two and a half stabs to make the metal tines disappear.

The pink handle jutting from his stomach looked more natural to me than the husband's flaccid penis had—that shriveled thing, like a stack of innards on his lap! No, no, no— I didn't like when things changed too fast; hard to soft, fast to slow. I didn't like *silence*.

I didn't let Eric soften before we parted ways. I made sure of that too.

I shut the guest room door and didn't need to decipher his screaming to know that he was, indeed, in pain.

Nadia threw herself against the balcony railing as I shoveled sand on the beach below. She made sounds that rose and fell in time with the thundering exhales of the ocean. I couldn't make sense of her words. I wouldn't. Still, I watched her as I worked. Even while flailing and gesturing, she was beautiful to me. Like the sea, there was no stillness in her.

There never would be.

As I nestled Eric's body into the belly of the earth, I hoped Nadia realized that his transition would be kind and slow. When he reached the water's mouth, he would be fed in pieces—not all of a sudden, not all at once. I filled in the hole and looked up at Nadia. She gripped the iron railing, and I could feel all of her energy directed toward me. It was a glorious Sunday morning, and my sister was mine. Nadia twisted away and disappeared into the house. She knew as well as I did when it was time to run.

Samantha Tkac hails from Northern Virginia and holds an MFA from Butler University. She has worked all kinds of jobs, but her favorite was when she worked as a journalist and wrote about mental health reform for correctional facilities and schools. Despite the nature of her fiction, her dad is always her first reader. Her fiction has appeared in *The William and Mary Review, Writers Resist, The Squawk Back, Drunk Monkeys, Cathexis Northwest Press*, and elsewhere. She is currently working on her first novel.

WASTELAND

By Alex Webb Wilson

Water

He watched the dogs ahead of him, trotting with their spines flat as if they were stalking something. Whenever he tried to touch one, the animals would pull back beyond his reach, blending with the desert. They faded to shadows if he looked at them directly, becoming indistinct from the rocks and arroyos.

He never stopped walking, so he could only glance at them quickly and then look back at the ground to select his footing. Now he checked the North Star, and the dogs remained in stride with him in his peripheral vision. For a moment, as he adjusted his course, aligning himself east, where the road would be somewhere ahead of him, he thought the dogs might have become people.

He rubbed his eyes with his cracked fingers and thought of how long he had been walking. He could not be sure, three nights possibly—the road should be close now, he told himself, and licked his lips, certain only of his thirst.

Oil

He was driving a section of the plain that stretched beside the ocean when he tore the oil pan. A bait ball had formed near shore, seagulls and terns diving on sardines that a school of dorado had pushed to the surface. The sun was low over the water, and he blinked in the glare, then switched the Tacoma into four-wheel drive, doing nearly forty miles an hour.

He should have been reading the land ahead of him. Instead, he reached back for his surf casting rod and began to change out the filament. He accelerated in the track, steering with his knees, and calculated how long it would take to strip the line and reach the water through a draw a mile in the distance. The bait shifted north in the afternoon light, and he set the rod aside and cut through a saddle.

He had never been to that particular corner of the peninsula. He had spent so much of his life fishing along its coast with his father, crossing into Mexico from their bungalow in San Diego, that it felt as if he had seen all of it. He had slept so many nights on the ground or in the camper shell of his father's F-150 with the smell of cigarettes and fish and rubber, that it had never occurred to him that he might discover an unfamiliar section of the coast, or what it would be like to experience it in isolation.

If someone had asked him, he would have said he liked the idea of finding this place, where he wouldn't see his father behind every yucca, his fingers tying jigs in the firelight, his back bent toward a fish on the line in knee-deep water. After he had turned off the highway, however, and had crossed the wasteland in one long run a week earlier, he had realized he missed his father more in those hours than he had in the eight months since the funeral. Watching the dust plume in his brake lights, he also saw he had missed a fork somewhere west of El Crucero.

Now he looked aside from the birds as bits of silex began to rattle against the undercarriage. He was nearly even with the draw as he crossed a salient of volcanic rock in the truck and the plain fell away toward the ocean. He downshifted but did not apply the brakes in the scree to avoid losing traction.

The boulder that tore the oil pan sat in a blind hollow of rock just ahead of him. The cab vibrated with the rasp of metal on stone as he struck it with the Tacoma. He rolled to a stop and left the engine running and lay beside the truck and pressed his body flat to check the damage.

The bed of volcanic rock was sharp on his palms, and oil ran onto the ground near the front axle. The skid plate below the oil pan was nearly ripped away, and he could see bright hints of the pan itself through the torn metal, like bone in a deep laceration.

He climbed back into the truck and rolled forward to the edge of the salient and came to a stop on a patch of level earth near the draw that led to the ocean. In the short distance he had driven, the thermometer on the dashboard had crept into the red, and now he shut off the engine.

He walked around the truck, listening to the pooling of the oil, and the wind, and the silence around him.

Blood

We had this cable, he heard his father say. It was rigged to tow a device outfitted with lights and cameras and a new type of sonar for mapping the bottom. The submarine I was assigned to had been retrofitted to tap the telecom wires the Russians had laid in the Bering Sea, and this device was supposed to find them. It was designed to correct its own depth along a winch that was mounted under the boat in a modified torpedo tube. The opening faced the screws, and you'd hear the reel working in, and then you'd hear the hydraulics paying the reel out, and at the time, no one really knew what we were doing.

We had CIA agents and techs onboard who knew the equipment, and they bunked with the officers. It's not too often you see someone from the company up close, but on a sub, up close is the only way you see anyone. I only ran into them when I rotated through the con, and they were in the con, too, with the captain.

I don't remember the exact month—it was just as Vietnam was heating up, and I was maybe two years out of dive school. I dove with a lieutenant who knew the gear, a guy by the name of Rich Ayers. It was going to be our job to dive on the Russian wires and affix the bugging hardware once we found the telecom instillations. That's what the device and the winch and the cable were for. We had to pinpoint the locations first, though, so we were towing this thing along behind the submarine.

The last time out, we had been on a similar operation in the Sea of Okhotsk, and we'd been able to haul a whole bunch of crab off the bottom. We worked for days at depth, sleeping in a saturation chamber outside the sub, and there were king crabs all over the telecom wires. On the last day, before decompressing, we dove just to go bug picking, and we fed the whole crew that night, and the captain brought out some drinks for us to have with dinner. We were excited to see about the crab again, even though it seemed like something that would never happen twice, and it didn't.

Water

He had been walking for two nights when he first became certain he would run out of water. There was nothing exact that he had calculated to determine this—he simply intuited it from the weight of the four jugs strung across his shoulders.

The first evening, after he had left the truck, the load had seemed too dense and shifting for him to bear the entire distance. Now the jugs were light enough that they had become almost comfortable to carry. He stopped walking and took a careful sip from one and thought of how most of the water had disappeared inside of his body and evaporated from his skin into the desert.

The cardon and the plain of baked rock, with its piñon and creosote trees, still appeared clearly to him in the moonlight. He had not seen the dogs yet or his father. The landscape still only wavered in the convection of daylight, and he was still certain that he was walking east, alone, and that if he picked three points on the land for orientation, after checking the stars, he would eventually reach the forward edge of the triangle, where the road would be waiting.

His landmarks were large and plain enough to remain visible under the moon, and he had already arrived at several that evening. He drank again in rotation between the four jugs to keep the balance of the weight level, then sat on the ground, which was cold through the fabric of his pants, and pulled off his sneaker. The sole had come unglued from the heel panel, and he opened his backpack and pushed aside three more liters of water.

Inside the bag, he also carried jerky and sunglasses, filament and light clothing, along with a knife and a roll of duct tape, all of which he had gauged for their weight and purpose. He was sweating and breathing quickly, but a chill had spread along his back and rib cage as soon as he had stopped moving. His feet throbbed, and something settled deep into his legs in their stillness.

He leaned over to draw the duct tape around the sole of his sneaker, and the too-light water jugs shifted on the line around his neck, tightening against the raw skin under his collar. It was cold enough in the dark that he could see his breath, and he checked the Seiko on his wrist and saw that it would be dawn in an hour.

He felt himself sitting in his father's lap and turning its bezel with his small fingers, watching the second hand pass around the dial. Later, he understood that his father had always worn the watch because it represented a part of his life —the five years attached to a submarine out of Pearl Harbor, not the contract work he did for the Navy—which he used to define himself.

He thought of the photos he had seen once of his father in dive school, thin and young and bearded. He compared those images with how his father had looked before he became sick, his face and hands darkened from thirty years of welding at the shipyards in Chula Vista. In his mind, he saw the pale band along his father's wrist where the dive watch had covered his skin, then thought of the boulder and the dead Tacoma.

He sat drinking beer in the passenger seat of his father's F-150, off-road, south of Ensenada. His father had held the wheel with two hands, evenly spaced, and did not like to speak while driving to maintain his concentration. Lavender and *nudata* were in bloom on the hills, which meant his birthday had just passed and soon it would be Easter.

His father never allowed him to drink at home in San Diego, but he was legal in Mexico and they were alone together, cutting across an empty basin.

"Always be aware of what you're doing," his father said, "when you operate a vehicle."

He tried now to remember if he had been holding a Tecate between his knees when he tore the oil pan on the Tacoma. He looked back to the west and heard the silex rattling against the undercarriage and saw the terns in the sky before he struck the boulder. He told himself that he had not opened a beer since crossing the wasteland on the way in; he had been listening to the radio and trying not to think of the funeral.

"I was looking at all the life," he sang softly now. "There were plants and birds and rocks and things."

When he stood up, he felt dizzy. The duct tape was tight around the arch of his sneaker, and his foot was hot because, with the tape wound around it, the sneaker had less breathability. He took another sip of water and tightened the caps on all four jugs and realigned his checkpoints. The sky had not yet begun to lighten in the east, but he could see a range of mountains in the pale silver light and a stand of ocotillo, which he guessed he could reach in about an hour.

He was alone under the late moon, and a light wind had come up, smelling of dust and juniper and dead vegetation. He began to walk again, estimating the dimension of shade he might find on the plain and how long he could continue without more water.

Blood

I used to tell you stories, and you would sit and you'd look at me. I never had anyone look at me like that—my own parents barely looked at me, and I thought about that when you were little. I wanted to make sure you knew I was looking back at you, and I felt like I'd look at you and sometimes I'd see myself, and sometimes I'd see my father, and sometimes I'd see your mother.

I'd make you something to eat, and we'd clean whatever we caught, and you'd listen. I remember the night you were born; when you came out, you pissed right on the nurse who was holding you. They hadn't even cut the umbilical cord. You didn't want her grabbing you like that; you were cold, and you were pissed off after all that pushing and compression, and you screamed and pissed all over her.

"Good luck with this one," she said, and handed you to your mother. Then your mother handed you to me, and we just sat there looking at each other, and I told you all about who you were and how you ended up here.

If you don't want to hear about it, I can tell you something else. Maybe I can tell you the story about the dogs we fed that summer. You probably don't remember them—I think you were five. It was right after your mother left, and we'd get up early, and we'd go eat burritos and head down to the pier and cast a little. The water was warm that year, and there was a guy who caught a white sea bass out past the last piling. The fish was seventy-two pounds, which was a record, I think, until the next El Niño.

Anyway, the dogs, they were just puppies—I don't know if you remember. I don't know what happened to their mother either. They were skinny, and they were living behind the market on Palm Avenue. There was a patch of chaparral, and they were back in there, and you wanted to take them all home with us, and I remember trying to explain to you that they were lucky we were just feeding them.

If you don't want to hear about it, like I said, I'll just tell you about the cable and the shark and the time I went overboard. We never talked much about what it was like, about how it was for us, and for you growing up, so maybe you just want to hear this other thing. When you were a kid, it was one of your favorite stories.

We were still outbound from the islands, and we were still testing the device and running diagnostics on the winch and the listening and the video gear. I mean we dragged this piece of machinery all over the Pacific, and I remember it feeling like we were babysitting. On most patrols, especially before the boat had been converted, we ran fast and quiet, and we hardly ever surfaced. Now we had this thing attached to us, and everything was different.

So the way this goes, as they're reeling the thing in to recover it one morning, the whole mechanism jams, and the lights come on in the bunkroom where I was sleeping. I could tell right away that we'd stopped the engines, and it seemed like we'd blown the tubes and we were coming shallow.

Anything that can break at sea will break, and that's exactly what happened. The cable was supposed to be made of one continuous strand of wire with electrical conduit woven inside it. I guess the rumor went that the contractor who'd produced it had welded more than one section of wire to another to save on material and labor. According to the CIA techs, the contractor claimed that wasn't the case, but they had lied and the welds broke, obviously.

So now we try to reel it in, but there are these huge steel threads unwound and jammed in the winch, and we have to surface and speak with the captain. He comes up to periscope depth. "It's perfectly calm," he says. "It's a perfect day to dive on this thing." Which means we go over the side, me and this lieutenant, Ayers.

So we gear up, and the boat surfaces, and we jump in, and we get underwater, and we can see the cable is hanging straight down, perfectly vertical from its modified torpedo tube, which is a problem. I'm looking at Ayers and he's looking at me, and now there's this mess we have to deal with. We can't see the device at the end, because it's thousands of feet at depth, probably dangling like a yo-yo.

I'm trying to problem solve and just hanging there in the water and looking at the cable. Pretty soon though, the lieutenant grabs my elbow and starts swimming back to the boat, headed for the modified torpedo tube. He's kind of hauling ass, but my first thought was that he wanted to take a look at the other end of the problem, so I followed him, and the two of us jam in there with our tanks, and there's the winch, all tangled with stainless steel wire.

So now we're on top of each other in this tight space, and as our exhalations from the regulators bubble up, it begins to create a few inches of air in the compartment. I can see his eyes through his face mask, and they're like dinner plates, and I'm thinking to myself that he's worked up because we've got a hell of a job here. It's obvious we're going to have to cut away all this wire or maybe even blow the cable, and then try to recover the device, because the boat isn't seaworthy and we need to do something.

After maybe a minute, I can cock my head back in the airspace and take off my face mask and talk with my lips almost touching the steel overhead.

"What do you think?" I say, and he spits out his regulator and looks back down toward the end of the compartment. "Lieutenant," I say, "I think we need acetylene torches."

"Shut up for a second," he says, and I remember being kind of taken aback, because he'd always been pretty formal, like a naval officer. Then I see a shadow pass outside, in one sweep, maybe fifteen feet long, and I realize it's not the wire that's making his eyes huge.

I mean at this point we've kind of forgotten completely about the wire, much less the multimillion-dollar device dangling in the dark somewhere at the end of it.

"Did you see that fucking shark out there?" he says. "It came in for a look, maybe ten feet behind us as soon as it noticed the silhouette of the boat on the surface."

Now the only thing we're both thinking about is the fish in the water and how far we need to swim to get to the deck ladder and up onboard again.

Oil

He waited for the engine to cool, then took his tools from the cab and lay with a flashlight beneath the Tacoma. A line of ants was moving across the ground at the edge of the pooling oil, and he turned up the collar of his shirt and rolled down his sleeves to keep them from becoming a distraction. The sun had set by the time he had removed the skid plate, and he was very thirsty but not hungry. He sat on the tailgate and watched the horizon darken and drank a bottle of water from the cooler.

Fear was something he had not felt on the peninsula since those initial trips with his father. When he was a child, death had always seemed present the moment they crossed the border. He didn't understand what that meant then or why it affected him. He only knew the change came with the thin, dead dogs beside the road in Tijuana, the fish pumping blood across his father's hands beside the campfire. In this foreign place, it came from the papier-mâché shrines alongside the road in the hanging passes, where there were no guardrails or shoulders, the faces of the dead smiling from pictures inlaid in votives.

When the cartel wars had begun along the border, he was much older, but the effect was similar. The bodies strung from overpasses served as a reminder that the presence of death was immediate and often on display in this place, and that its nearness made his own life, and the untouched persistence of that life, more vibrant.

His fear of it by then had dissipated, however, and death had become something for other creatures. He seemed to move through the landscape, walled off from it in the cab of his father's F-150, or within the circle of their campfires at night, like a tourist.

Its nearness was an attraction only because it was just beyond the glass and the flames, and even after his father died—consumed by the lymphoma—he'd believed there was something foreign about the experience. Death lay in the bed, yet it was also distant, because he was twenty-six, and did not smoke, and did not believe that, for now at least, it could penetrate the skin of his immediate existence.

Now he watched the ants moving near the oil. He raised his flashlight, and they became more animated in the beam for a moment. The column had turned wide around the pool, but some of the insects were closer to its edge, pausing to inspect those trapped in the slick beneath the Tacoma.

Occasionally, one would pull another free from the dark blue liquid, and they would both comb away the lubrication before continuing. More often an ant would reach into the slick, and the surface tension would break, and they both would become engulfed, moving their legs quickly, then more slowly, trying to swim until there was stillness.

He took a final sip from the water and put the empty bottle back into the cooler. He brushed the colony away in the dust and lay under the truck with his tools again and began loosening the bolts that held the oil pan to the under-carriage. The rent from the boulder was several inches wide, running the length of the pan, and in the illumination from the flashlight, he could see clearly into the reservoir. It took him nearly ten minutes to unratchet the first bolt, which had been bent by the impact.

He had five extra liters of oil with his spare belts and hoses in the camper shell, and perhaps enough water for five days in the cooler. He did not have an extra oil pan, but maybe, he thought, he could peen the tear from the inside, then patch it with a scrap from the skid plate, or even some tinfoil. If he could save the leftover oil in the reservoir and add the five extra liters, he might be able to drive back across the wasteland without the engine seizing.

He stood and went to the tailgate and set out the tools he needed.

Blood

So I tell Ayers that I'm going to take a look. More airspace had developed and we're bobbing upright now, so I ditch my gear under the boat and he holds onto it, and I take a breath and turn in the tube and swim back down to the end of the chamber. I put my hands on either side of the opening, about five feet across, and I'm upside down, staring toward the stern.

I poke my head out, and you have to understand that when you go from an atmosphere inside the sub, with pipes and noise and all that compression, and then you jump into the ocean with three hundred feet of visibility, where there's no bottom, that experience alone is tremendous. You spend all this time inside of a machine without daylight, surrounded by noise and the smell of oil and other humans, then you're outside in the middle of nothing, in all that light and space, and it's like seeing everything in the world with new eyes or something.

So I look toward the stern, and I'm holding onto the edge of the tube, and I look to my left, and as I'm starting to swing my head back to the right, the fish comes past within about three feet of my face mask. It was an oceanic whitetip, which is the same species that ate all the fighter pilots who were shot down in the Pacific during the Second World War and also the guys on the *Indianapolis*.

At the time, with its dead eye and flat skin, to me, it just looked like another piece of machinery. So I recoiled up into the tube and swam backwards, and its body blocked the light coming in through the opening. A whitetip won't bump you or anything—it just comes in and nails you, and they get pretty big, ten feet average, but this was a lot bigger.

So I surface into the airspace, and Ayers is there with his dive knife, waiting for me to give him something, anything, to help us make a decision.

"Lieutenant," I say, "do sharks come into caves?"

He would repeat that to me afterward—do sharks come into caves—then we'd pull our legs up, like we were back in the tube, and laugh about it.

Water

He lay under the ocotillo, moving every hour to follow the shade as the sun climbed away from the mountains. The temperature equalized just after dawn, and he was no longer too hot or too cold, but soon the light seemed directly overhead and became blinding. The ground under the stand was littered with spines from the plants, and he had to carefully brush each patch of shadow before he could reposition his body.

He rested his head on the backpack and slept until he felt the glare on his legs and stirred again. It was not even ten, and the caliche was already dead and brilliant. He rolled down his sleeves, then took another shirt from the backpack and wound it around his head so that the tails hung over his neck, and the collar, which he turned out, formed a brim across his forehead.

He consolidated the remaining water into two jugs and distributed the weight evenly, roughly a gallon between them. Then he held the two empty containers over his mouth, catching the drops that fell from the rims.

When he woke in the early afternoon, his hands had become so dry that his fingertips were split. He repositioned himself again, but the angle of the sun left very little shadow.

He adjusted the shirt on his head, wrapping the sleeves around the lower half of his face, and sat upright, as far as he could wedge himself under the cacti without touching its branches.

Spines from the ocotillo had lodged in the seams and patterns of his skin. He squeezed the flesh at the base of his thumb until the largest one came free, coated in a milky liquid. He carefully picked away the first one, then quit.

He drank a mouthful of water, which was hot and tasted like plastic. He opened the pouch of beef jerky from the pack, and it took him a very long time to eat it. The curing salts burned in his mouth, and his tongue seemed huge and rough and difficult to manage.

By two, the empty valley beyond the ocotillo had become so bright and shimmering it appeared to be featureless. He watched his non-shadow under the branches and felt as if he should be sweating, but his skin was chalked across his chest and cold along his neck and shoulders. He sat for a while, lightly touching his cheeks, then reached into his collar as if testing for a fever.

It occurred to him that he was cold because he had heat exhaustion, and that the only solution was to drink more water. He opened one of the jugs and took three careful sips and repeated the process with the other. His mouth became slick and warm for a moment, and he took a fourth sip of the hot water from each jug and sat covering his head with his elbows.

He pulled his legs in close and angled them against his body and closed his eyes, which also felt too large, and rested his head on his knees. There was nowhere else to move, no other feature on the caliche, the branches of the ocotillo now offering only three strips of shadow.

In his dream he imagined he might have seen the dogs for the first time, coalescing from the desert. He recognized them as the strays he had fed with his father in the empty lot in San Ysidro. Only now the animals were adults in his vision and as thin and desiccated as the ocotillo. It was still hot and brilliant when he dreamt, and he was often confused while tightening the jugs or reading the watch, tasks which he found that, even fully awake, had become increasingly difficult.

At dusk he left the ocotillo and began picking way points to the east. In the next valley, he dropped down into a forest of cardon and was forced to backtrack in the purple light, uncertain of his orientation until he came to the far side and returned to the caliche.

He focused closely on re-taping the sole of his sneaker sometime near midnight and found himself sitting after a moment, watching the mountains in the starlight. Then he began to speak, looking back down at the tape in his hands, and found that if he repeated an instruction, as if he were re-laying an order from his father, he could complete it.

He had been walking again for perhaps an hour when the dogs appeared silently beside him. They seemed to be an extension of his body, which was why they did not frighten him even with their backs flattened and their teeth shining. He continued east, barely aware of them, falling into a presence where there was only the rhythm of movement.

Sometime late in the night, he came across what appeared to be tread marks from his Tacoma. The tracks wove across the wasteland to avoid arroyos and small pieces of scrub, and he found that he could follow them approximately in a single direction, east, toward a saddle at the edge of the mountains. The fork he had missed in the truck would be somewhere on the other side of the range, he told himself, then the road beyond it, and his father's voice reminded him to watch for the split as soon as he exited the saddle and that if he could join the track, which led eventually to the highway, his route would be more defined as it crossed the next set of flatlands.

He was shivering and held his arms across his chest and close to his body. He stopped in the treads and listened for the sound of another vehicle and was almost surprised by the silence that had been perpetual since he had left the ocean. He could see his breath again, soft clouds of condensation. The dogs stalked out ahead of him, then paused, the largest in the pack looking back as if waiting for him to continue. He lowered his head and began to walk again, and they spread around him without creating a sound or leaving any sign in the dust, trotting east, toward the saddle.

Blood

So now we have to look at this job, and we're both scared, and we've both seen the fish. I mean we have to swim air tools down there now to cut away the cable or repair it somehow, and maybe bring down the torches. We have to surface and swim the length of the boat and then climb this steel ladder to the deck, which is in itself a challenge.

You need to take your flippers off before you get onto the ladder, and you need to take your face mask off, and then you hook everything over your arm, and hopefully there's a deck handler leaning over the top to grab the back of your tanks, to haul you up by the harness. Initially, the first two or three rungs on the ladder—trying to get organized with your gear with the submarine rolling in the swell, and you rolling around next to it—can take forever. If there's someone ahead of you on the ladder, you just want them to get up over the gunwale, especially when you're in the water with something like a fifteen-foot whitetip.

So we leave the tube, and Ayers is looking behind us, and we surface and get to the ladder, and he tells me to go first. He knew I was thinking about the shark, we both were, but he said, no, you go. So I climbed out, and he just waited, and I bet that was a really long three minutes.

Then he finally came onboard, too, and we reported to the captain, and like I figured, we had to bring all these air tools out of the boat, plus the torches, and post two guys with rifles on shark watch and spend something like eight hours —it was at least eight hours, maybe longer—cutting away all that cable.

They say working underwater is like working in orbit. You need to have something to hold onto, and you work your way from one place to another, hand over hand, but working in vacuum, you don't have the buffeting of working underwater. A submarine doesn't float particularly well by the nature of its design, so you have to watch that it doesn't settle or roll and smash you. Working in orbit, you also don't have to deal with whitetips or some other fucking thing that wants to eat you.

So we cut all that stuff back and spliced it and got out of the water, and we were able to winch in the cable, but we didn't recover the device, because it had hit the bottom and been shorn off its mounting. Anyway, we had to go back to Pearl after that to reequip, and all the cable had to be stripped off onto the dock by hand to be investigated.

I wasn't involved in that job though—I guess I'd done so much work on it already that they decided to give me the day off, which I remember clearly, because all I wanted to do was be dry and sit on my ass in the dark and watch television.

Oil

He laid the pan on the tailgate and ran his fingers into the tear and removed the gasket and aimed the flashlight into the reservoir. The gash came alive with backlight, a smiling and jagged aperture. He wiped his hands and stood back and cocked his head and looked at it from another angle. Then he used a funnel from the tool kit to pour the remaining oil into a jug, checking it under the beam, leaning forward to watch the flakes of metal shimmering and spinning in the lubricant.

He searched through his cooking supplies and transferred the oil again, this time separating it through a coffee filter. As it drained, he considered whether it was even possible to peen the tear, or if he should, instead, cut away a piece of the skid plate and try to bolt it to the inside of the reservoir. He went and checked the toolbox and found that he did not have metal shears or even a hacksaw. He held the oil back up against the flashlight, where it was now mostly clear.

When the overhead bulb in the camper shell flickered, he went to the cab and switched off the lights, then pulled himself into the driver's seat. It was almost black on the plain because the moon had not yet risen. He could smell the oil on his hands and his own sweat and the ocean somewhere to the west. Closer, he could smell the dust and the dry wood scent of the chaparral just beyond the window.

He turned the keys again and checked the charge on

the battery, then turned them back off and made sure all the gauges were unlit and removed them from the ignition. In his mind, he saw the pool of oil in the dirt, the small metal flakes shining in the filter, and the five extra liters in the camper shell.

He did not know yet how to patch the tear once he had peened it closed, and decided he could only deal with that aspect of the repair when he came to it.

"I can only deal with it when I can deal with it," he said, and heard his father's echo.

He shut off the flashlight and closed his eyes and saw the garage of their bungalow in San Diego, his father lying on the warm asphalt. He saw the old F-150 and the pack of Marlboros set aside on the running board, which his father would not smoke while working under the truck, close to anything flammable. Then he saw how little difference there was between the garage and the rest of their home.

Each item had a place, he remembered, and everything was returned to that place when not in use, which created order, but a gallon of Gojo sat in the kitchen, orange scented with large grit, and the closets were filled with fishing tackle.

He made his bed every day, but his sheets were filled with sand because he never hosed off his feet after surf casting at the end of Seacoast Avenue. A black-and-white photo hung on the wall in his father's room, visible only when the door was closed: a group of men sitting cross-legged on the deck of the sub, his father among them, wearing his dive watch and holding a rifle.

Two chairs sat facing the television in the living room; otherwise, it was unadorned by pictures or even a small table. The curtains in the bedrooms consisted of sheets tacked across the eastern windows, and the dead grass in the yard was clipped short, which caused it to burn further. In the bathroom, a roll of Bounty sat beside the sink instead of hand towels.

His girlfriends' houses smelled like laundry and food and their mothers, who treated him like his father had approached the stray dogs that summer—they fed him while holding him outside of a certain threshold. He learned how to sit at dinner and eat slowly, but he always forgot to fold his napkin in his lap, and it took him years to absorb that rice should be pushed onto a fork with the edge of his knife and not his fingers.

Mostly he felt like he was performing a trick at these meals, the spectators waiting for him to make a mistake. He was never comfortable until it was over, walking in the dark, the air from the desert on the land breeze, the sage reminding him of some mother's dish soap.

Even once he was alone with the girls, he almost liked the memory of them, breathing with their bodies, more than whatever they may actually be doing—the dimples in their backs, the shelf where the plain of the sacral plate formed a triangle, their hair brushing his neck as they lowered themselves onto him while he sat on the cool sand, knowing there would be marks on their knees from the friction.

It took him a long time to realize this, but they always seemed to sense it within a month. They also seemed to know that this was a part of him that could not be changed or instructed, like the knife with the rice, and that was why the smart ones left first.

He wondered sometimes if his mother had also sensed this in his father. He tried to picture what the kitchen had been like before she had left, and the bedrooms, and the bathroom, and imagined there might have been a rug on the floor next to the shower. He had only been four and couldn't remember. He had never visited her new house in Stockton, which would actually be an old house now, where she lived with her boyfriend, so he couldn't take that image and transpose it with the bungalow.

He had never asked her why she had moved to Stockton, and had never asked his father about her, because of some silent communion between them. Now he thought of the lymphoma and all the other things he would also never know.

The seat in the Tacoma was soft, and he was tired, and the fear he had felt earlier, which had seemed more like the memory of his fear from when he had been a child, was very old inside of him. Instead of exhausting itself, however, it seemed only dormant, and he knew if listened to the voice, which told him the oil pan could not be fixed, reminding him that he had not seen another man or vehicle since crossing the wasteland, it would continue to grow.

He turned on the flashlight and pulled himself up from the seat with the steering column. He gathered his tools and set them in a row on the tailgate and put the parts he had removed from the oil pan into a tray in the toolbox. He re-checked the tailgate and searched under the truck with the flashlight and found a washer at the edge of the oil. He rubbed it dry with his fingers and set it with the rest of the parts.

Out on the plain, he searched for a flat rock he could set under the tear to hammer it closed. As he walked, he panned with the flashlight and came across rabbits feeding in the chaparral and watched them scatter, their tails bouncing thinly in the illumination. Part of him wanted to climb into the camper shell and wrap himself in his sleeping bag—it would be easier, he told himself, to hammer the pan after the sun rose, except then he would have to wait, he said, staring at the roof of the shell, watching for the gray light, surrounded by the faint blood scent of his tackle box.

He discovered a flat volcanic slab on the hill behind the truck, larger than the Tacoma. He checked his watch. Only four hours had passed since the sunset. It was cold in the dark and felt much later. He oriented himself by aligning the place on the hill against a yucca. He returned to the tailgate and carried the pan out to the rock and knelt over it with a hammer.

Blood

So we go back to Pearl, and we get a new device, and we winch on a new cable, and we re-outfit the boat, and the new gear is working underwater. Then we take off again and we're out there towing. We don't know exactly where—it seemed like we were still getting the wrinkles out of the system, and it was still warm, so we definitely weren't in the Sea of Okhotsk.

About three weeks in, we have another malfunction.

The reel hadn't compensated fast enough for a seamount on the bottom or something, and the device hit an obstruction. I remember the whole boat shook. Everybody in the forward torpedo room felt it.

So they start to reel the thing in because the cameras are torn off the device and they don't have a bottom visual. And as they're reeling it in, the device is coming in sideways because, when it bounced, the cable fouled and basically tied itself into a half hitch.

So there's a knot around the device, and now, instead of coming in onto the reel straight, the cable has a roll to it, and the device is spinning while we're cranking it in, and the cable travels a little on the reel and scrapes along the bottom of the boat and tears off the new cameras that we mounted on the hull. Now we have no visuals of anything. And as the device is approaching the tube, the whole thing comes to a halt.

The outer door is open again, and they can't get the device in, so it's another one of those situations. We have to surface, and when we surface, I remember going into the captain's office, and the boat is rolling, and he tells us they just came to periscope depth and there's some swell running.

It was maybe thirty-plus feet, he told us, and it felt like it belowdecks, except the problem was they had to find out what was wrong, so here's where they throw two people in the water again—me and Ayers. So they open up the hanger door, which was a huge forward compartment, and we get all geared up. The boat had originally been designed to launch ICBMs horizontally, Regulus Ones and Twos, but now it's been converted, like I told you, for this bugging op, and we're using the hanger as a staging platform.

They tell us we're still equatorial, and we decide to go with just swim trunks, no wetsuits, and our tool belts and dive gear. The handlers and the shark watch are up on the deck, and they have these big canvas straps around their waists, and they're connected to a chain, and there's a way for them to hook into this rail, almost like a single railroad track, so they can walk up and down the boat in their harnesses.

Three or four of them are up there for us, and now we're coming out with our flippers on and our tanks, and they're supporting us, and the boat is rocking, and the swell is running like a son of a bitch. I don't know how big it actually was—the captain estimated it at about sixty feet later; he was downplaying it in his quarters. I remember there was no wind, so the surface was like a mirror.

There must have a storm out there somewhere, thousands of miles ahead of us. It was late afternoon, and coming outside again, everything seemed incredibly bright, and I blinked and looked up at the swell going by, like the buildings in Honolulu, and said to myself, holy shit, this is some bad shit here. Then the captain gave us the signal, and we jumped over the side.

Water

He finished the last mouthful in the last jug sometime late the third night, as he was drawing close to the saddle. He kept the containers dangling from his shoulders, hoping to find a spring somewhere in the pass, which he knew was unlikely.

The first liter of water that he opened from the backpack tasted incredibly cool and fresh, and this surprised him because he had expected it to taste like the water in the jugs, of sunlight and plastic. He drank three sips from the bottle and tightened the cap, closely watching his cracked fingers.

When he began to speak, it was near sunrise, a line of pink light spreading across the empty sky, deeper in color behind the mountains. He looked up for the dogs, but they were nowhere in his vision. Instead, in the growing light, he could see small clumps of greasewood on the ramparts and the fall line of a gully. A stack of boulders had settled near the base of the cliffs, and chollas were growing in a hollow beside the rock pile.

Watching the mountain, he had the same impression he often experienced in the F-150 while riding across so much open space, a sense of surprise that his father had caused a feature in the distance to grow so large and so immediate in the landscape.

What are you doing here? he said.

Don't stop walking.

How long can you stay?

Let's just dogleg along this arroyo and keep following the tracks from your Tacoma.

He wanted to turn to check if his father's face was as gaunt as he remembered from the hospital. Then he became aware that his father might know what he was searching for, and remembered how his father had often rolled away in the bed, close to the end, as if something about withering among the bright, clean sheets was embarrassing for both of them.

They were traveling easily and quickly, it seemed, and the presence of his father was very much like walking with the dogs except, instead of spreading around him loosely and pulling him deeper into the desert, his father was close and pushing him forward. The hour of the dawn, when the temperature equalized, seemed to arrive, and he was no longer cold, and he could not see his breath, and the deadness in his legs had receded.

He was still aware of his thirst and his own movement across the wasteland, the pass rising ahead to snake out of sight behind a saddle, but the latter seemed to be occurring without his control and entirely without effort. It reminded him of being six and riding on his father's shoulders.

Where have you been? he said.

Have you been talking to your mother?

No. Not since the funeral.

When they reached a place where the Tacoma's tread marks began to ascend with the land, the sun came up from behind the rim of the mountains. He scanned ahead for something that might cast a shadow, then thought if he could climb out of the valley, it might be cooler in the dry weight of the daylight and imagined a breeze alive above the wasteland.

It's not steep, his father said.

I want to lie down.

Go another hour.

I need to tape my sneaker.

You should keep moving. I'll tell you a story.

I've heard your stories, he said. He watched his legs,

the pebbles, and dust scrolling past at his feet, and the shadow beside him.

What about the one when I was overboard?

I'm not a kid anymore.

You're my kid.

This is the one with the whitetip, isn't it?

You're not listening to me.

You always tell that fucking shark story.

You remember this one too.

I'm too tired to think about it.

Well keep walking anyway. You can't last another day in this valley. You don't have enough water.

Blood

So we jump, and we immediately get sucked under the sub because of the boat moving up and down in the swell and the currents. I literally went from the surface to at least thirty feet of depth in an instant. And I look straight up at the superstructure, and then I look to my right to see what's going on, to see where the lieutenant is, and he's back by the stern, close to the screws, swimming for his life.

To keep the bow into the swell, one screw is turning in one direction and the other screw is turning in the other direction, and he's getting pulled toward the propellers, and there's the device above me with a perfect half hitch in the cable, and the outer door is open, and the whole mess is slammed up against the opening of the tube.

So I swim to the surface, and I'm maybe fifteen yards from the boat at that point, rising on this massive swell, and I yell to the handler that the device is athwart ships, all stop, and he says, "Where's Mr. Ayers?" And now suddenly he's way below me because I'm at the crest of the wave, and I don't even answer. I just dive back to the lieutenant.

I was a stronger swimmer than Ayers was; he was a good swimmer, too, and he was definitely UDT, except he wouldn't admit that he was UDT because that's how special operators are. Everything is a secret. What I'm trying to say is he was a better diver than I was, and more experienced even though I was a better swimmer.

So I kick down to him, and I can feel the wave action pulling on us, and I can also feel the vibration from the propellers. It was really loud back there with the screws beating the water and the drive still engaged, but then they put the boat into neutral, and it was suddenly quiet. I mean the blades were still spinning, and I didn't want to go anywhere near them, but I knew what would happen if I didn't get in there and help him, and that's never anything you want to see or something you want to think about every day for the next thirty years, what you could have done or whatever.

So I go in, and I grab ahold of him, and we both kick hard off to the port side of the boat, since we've drifted that way, even though we jumped to starboard, and we surface. And now we're bobbing around and we're both exhausted, and the submarine is rolling and it begins to back down on us.

When I was by myself later, I would go to the top of a wave, and there'd be nothing—no land and no lights and no spray and no whitecaps, just these huge, glassy rows of swell, like long, heavy columns moving in trains, and then I'd slide back into the trough, and it would feel like falling into a canyon that was totally silent. I'd be down in the bottom of this thing, looking up at the sky, and then it would get ahold of me, and I'd ride back to the top again, and I'd look all around, and it would be the same thing, just endless ocean to the horizon.

Anyway, at this point, we're on the surface and she gets close, and it's the whole problem of getting onboard again. The screws are turning, but they're turning slowly, so she wanders, and subs don't operate that well on the surface to begin with.

The steel ladder comes over the side, and my buddies Doc Fields and Red Lategan are at the top. I don't remember the names of the other handlers, but I do remember the waves were washing over the deck and running back toward the stern, plus the submarine was rolling all the way to the base of the conning tower. And I'm with the lieutenant, and we're holding the bottom rung, dragging in the current along the hull, and we're struggling to take off our flippers.

Every time the sub heels back, it rolls away from us and rides up with the next swell, and we lose our grip on the ladder. Then the whole thing snaps back, and we'd basically fall ten feet against the side of the hull and land on our knees, scrambling to get a grip on the rungs, and then the next swell would pass, and the boat would roll back again, and the whole thing would start over.

Well, we had a small argument there between the two of us, me and the lieutenant. The last time with the shark, he let me get out first, so this time I wanted him to go. He was completely finished and it was just one of those things.

"No," I said. "Lieutenant, you go first, sir. You go."

So he starts to climb, and he's taking a beating, and I decide to swim away from the hull to keep from getting hammered too. And the surf is taking the air tanks and jamming the regulator into the back of my head, so now I have a laceration there, and I'm bleeding from my knees, from slamming against the hull, and my fingers and palms are bleeding.

Anyway, they get him onboard, and they yell down to me that they're going to come in on the leeward side, they're going to run up swell a little and drift down on me. The only problem is a nuclear submarine doesn't turn on a dime, like I said, even at flank speed. They have to run off away to turn, and by the time they do, I've drifted and they've drifted, sixty-foot seas, remember, and within thirty seconds they're gone.

Oil

He set the flashlight on an angle along the face of the rock and laid the pan in the beam. Drawing his arm back, he caught himself breathing too quickly, then not breathing at all, and put down the hammer.

Listen, he told himself, you need to think for a second, and you need to be careful, and you have to be calm, and you need medium force, at least at first, otherwise you'll tear the edges, which are super thin, which will just make things worse, which is exactly what you'll do if you don't get your hands to stop shaking. Remember, if you can't peen this thing closed and line the reservoir with tinfoil, it'll be impossible to drive the truck at all, much less back across the caliche. So listen—if you can't get the truck running, you're walking out, and you don't like the odds on that idea, so take a breath and remember that slow is smooth and smooth is efficient and work slowly.

Then he picked up the hammer and struck the pan, and became aware, under the ring of metal on rock, of how quiet the plain had been just a moment earlier, in the dark, with no wind and his breath and the low surf occasionally hissing in the distance.

Blood

There were moments, his father said, when I'd look around and start to sink back into the trough, and the water was like a mirror. I could see a blur of color, of myself skimming by on the face of the water. I didn't know if I should panic, or if I should keep talking to myself, or just take it all in and slip down into the reflection.

I took off my tanks at one point, and that was a good thing because we carried double aluminum, ninety cubic inches apiece, and they were actually buoyant when they were full, unlike steel tanks. So I brought them around under my chest and used them for floatation. I'd dumped my tool belt, which was a mistake because my knife was on it. I was lucky, though, since I had something to float on.

I remember, after a while of going up to the crests of the waves and starting to get cold, thinking that maybe they weren't going to find me. You think to yourself you always wanted to be on a submarine and you always wanted to be a diver and well, now it's going to kill you. Then I just said hold onto these ninety-cubic-inch tanks and see what you can see over the next wave and deal with what you can deal with.

So I took off my face mask and started using the face-plate to catch the sun as a signal. There were these thin clouds in the sky, but it was mostly a clear evening. The real issue, though, was that the sun was starting to set, and I knew in the dark, in sixty-foot surf, I'd be nothing but a black spot on a black ocean.

Water

He climbed into the pass, and there was no breeze, but there were shadows in the early morning light from the angles of the peaks. The air still held the smell of the night, and it was cold in the shade, and he moved through it with his father, shifting back and forth into the sunlight.

They came to a growth of nopales in one of the hollows, and he took the knife from his backpack and cut away a cladode. The sap from the cactus was sticky on his fingers, and he shaved down the spines and squeezed the cutting from its base. Then he sucked the moisture that seeped from the pith, and sat on the ground, the taste of chlorophyll in his mouth, and peeled back the skin and ate.

Dead segments of the plant, which had withered and dropped from the main cluster, lay scattered around him. When he touched one, it broke apart, the skin flaking away to reveal capillaries, which also flaked to dust.

He finished a liter and a half of the water from the bottles in his backpack, all now half empty. His father told him he should sleep, and he carefully brushed the ground and checked the caps on the water bottles three times and lay under the cacti.

Tufts of scrub were growing in the shadow of a boulder at his feet, their branches curled inward, the same color as the earth, burned black at the tips and tangled like bird nests. In the winter he had seen these plants darken in the rain and open the same way a flower would blossom. Now they looked as dead as the capillaries in the cacti, though they were only withdrawn, protecting whatever life was wrapped inside them.

That's Jericho plant, his father said.

That's what they call it if you're not in Mexico.

What's it called here, then?

Siempre viva.

Look at you.

I'm just saying.

I'm glad I made you take Spanish.

What else would I take?

Your mother wanted you to take French.
That would have been pointless.
She thought it would make you cultured.
Then Latin would have been better.
She just wanted the best for you, that's all.
Whatever.
How's it translate?
Siempre viva?
No, *e pluribus unum*.
It means "always alive."
I like that, said his father.

Blood

It's hard for me to remember. I don't know what time it was. I remember looking at my watch and then at the angle of the sun. Things come back to you, and everything at that point— the reflection on my face mask, the blur of color on the water, the way I seemed to be going up and down, and how small the sky looked when I was in the trough—made me feel even more alone.

An hour at least must have passed, because it really was getting dark now. I gave up signaling with my mask, and I remember saying a few things to my mother, like she was listening. She did love your aunt and me—it was just hard for her, the way my father drank and all the rest of it.

Every teacher I had in high school who knew what was going on at home told me to join the service to get out of there. My swim coach helped me decide on the Navy since they were right in Coronado. Between him and the recruiter, we all decided, with Vietnam and everything, and the way I could swim, dive school would be the best solution. There were maybe a hundred guys in my class when we started, and eight of us left at graduation.

Anyway, I hadn't met your mother yet, or I would have said something to her when I was alone in the water. I haven't spoken to that woman in twenty years, except about you, or except through you, I guess that would be more accurate, but if I had known her then, I would have said something.

We used to fish together when we first met—I don't know if you know that. She liked being out on the pier in Imperial Beach at sunrise. She was from Point Loma, but she liked IB in general. She liked that it was a border town. Sometimes we'd cross over with a group of guys I knew from the shipyards, other welders and their wives, and we'd all go down to Tijuana. On Fridays we'd go out along Avenida Rev, and then on Saturday mornings we'd drive down to Puerto Nuevo and get some lobster.

Eventually on Saturdays I'd take you down to the pier instead, just so she could get some sleep in the mornings. You liked looking at the fish, at whatever anyone caught, and we'd sit and eat our burritos. Once I caught a sand shark, and you couldn't stop looking at its eyes; they were blue like yours were.

There was this girl from New Zealand whom I'd met in Honolulu, whom I used to call Kiwi. I thought about her for a little while when I was in the water. Ultimately, I realized that was counterproductive, and I remember I just accepted what might happen.

I remember coming to the crests of the waves and looking around and seeing absolutely nothing. I was catching the sun with my mask, then not catching anything since there was only the afterglow on the horizon, and I said it's okay. It's okay, I said to myself.

The thing about the submarine is she just appeared next to me. I don't remember seeing her in the distance, and I don't remember her drifting down on me. She was just there, and I think maybe she surfaced in the trough when I was on the top of a swell, and when I came down, we just met each other. I was probably borderline hypothermic since I'd lost a lot of blood, and a scalp cut will bleed like a son of a bitch. No one onboard seemed to be able to confirm if they'd submerged, and I never asked the captain. I was just on her leeward side all of a sudden.

So they throw some grappling hooks over, and I put my tanks on the hooks, and now I'm relatively light, and I only have one flipper at that point; I don't know where the other one's gone, and I don't have my tool belt. Sometimes I remember having the tanks on as I tried to climb up the ladder, except I know now that I never put them back on again—I know they took them with the hooks because they were having trouble grabbing ahold of me.

They had nothing to hold onto to hoist me up, no webbing or shoulder straps. I'd come up to the handlers, and they'd grab me, and I'd slip out of their hands and slam onto the hull, and then a wave would pick me back up and smash me against the ladder. Red Lategan at one point wanted to go in after me. He was my rotational dive partner for everything, except for working on the device, and he could swim like a fish, and I could hear the chief of the board ordering him, "Lategan, do not go into the water."

Finally, on the third or fourth time I tried to make it onto the deck, Doc Fields, who was a corpsman, reached out with his right hand, all soaking wet and strapped into the rail on deck in his harness. And I remember looking at his face, and he was totally focused on me, and I reached out, and it was one of those things where we're kind of grabbing the other guy's wrists and forearms, and we slid a little except he grabbed ahold of my elbow and then my wrist, right above my watch, which gave him an anchor, and at the same time, he grabbed me by the waist of my dive trunks.

Then he and Lategan, who actually grabbed me by the hair, dragged me up onto the deck, and the next thing I know, I'm being stuffed down a hatch, and then I remember being in the shower. I think I went to sleep at one point, and then I was in the captain's office with Doc Fields, and we had two brandies apiece, and the captain sent me back to my bunk with the rest of the bottle.

We turned around after that and went back to Pearl again, and as soon as we docked, I had to go back into the water. They put the winch in reverse and dropped the device into the mud, and we spent days taking it apart and unhitching it on the bottom. The pen was only about twelve feet deep, which made me really fucking happy.

We put a drape over the device underwater since it was classified equipment and it had to be concealed when they hauled it. They brought in a crane and slid it onto the bridle in the mud, where you can't see a thing, and then they loaded it onto a truck, and I heard they went back and tapped that telecom hub about a year later, except by then I was back in San Diego and out of the service.

Oil

He worked in the beam from the flashlight until the sky shifted. Then he stood and rubbed his eyes with the edges of his wrists, careful of the oil and dust on his fingers. At the base of the draw, he could see the ocean again to the west, which was slate colored.

The air was cold and smelled like kelp as he carried the oil pan back to the Tacoma and set it on the tailgate. The tear still ran the length of the pan except now it was much thinner, and the ragged edges were smoothed and spread inward, toward each other. He took the tinfoil from the container that held his cooking supplies, and felt the impulse to rush again, to lay the foil into the pan and cut the edges away and tamp them down under the gasket.

He climbed out of the shell and walked slowly around the Tacoma. He looked at the pan when he passed the tailgate but did not touch it and turned back on his footsteps, still looking at the gash, and walked once more around the truck.

Dew had coated the scrub overnight in whatever moisture had come inland from the ocean, and his footsteps knocked the beads loose, leaving dark ovals in the silver blanket. A network of trails led away from the truck through the condensation, and in places, rabbit pellets lay steaming in slick, green piles. He thought of his father's friend, another welder from the shipyards in Chula Vista, who had come with them once to camp, and the snares the man had set in the desert. He saw the box of dead rabbits he'd found under the back bumper the next morning, the blood on their coats maroon and clotted, a gray skim of fat rising to the surface as they'd boiled them in a pot over the fire.

When the sun rose, the dew burned off almost instantly, and the ocean shifted to turquoise along with the sky, and he sat in the cab for a while, resting his eyes, his face pointed toward the light, allowing his skin to loosen and his sweat to dry. He did not sleep, but he almost slept, seeing images against his eyelids, his fingers unthreading the bolts under the truck, the impact of the hammer in the beam from the flashlight. His knee bobbed with impatience, and his fingers ran across each other, tacky with oil.

He found himself standing over the tailgate again, looking at the peened scar of metal. He drank a bottle of water from the cooler and took off his shirt, which was still damp with sweat, and dipped it into the ice melt. The water in the cooler was pink with the blood of a halibut he'd caught two days earlier, and he used it to wipe his face and his neck even though it smelled like fish oil. Then he held the wet shirt under his armpit and shivered.

He repeated this process until the shirt was soaked through and his upper body was clean and cold and a sharpness had returned to his vision. He started a fire and cooked the fish and ate it blackened. Then pulled on another shirt from the camper shell and began measuring segments of tinfoil against the reservoir.

Water

When he opened his eyes, he was alone under the cacti, and the sun was shimmering white over the flatlands below him, draining the landscape of detail and color. A headache bloomed at the base of his neck and descended over his vision. The pain caused him to lie back down and remain as still as he could manage in the small patch of shade that remained under the nopales.

His mouth was throbbing, and his lips were pasted closed by a crust that tore softly and tasted like copper. He did not remember climbing into the pass and suddenly had a fear that he was no longer following the tread marks from the Tacoma. He reached for the liter of water remaining in his backpack and became terrified of drinking because he could not be sure if he would be able to stop before the bottle was finished.

The headache shifted with him as he leaned and took the knife and cut away another pad from the cactus. He shaved down the spines and sucked at the pith, which tasted like the blood running from his lips, and looked up, searching for his father.

He opened the liter of water and drank all of it and closed his eyes again and lay in the blinding light, not checking the Seiko or the progress of the shade around him. The dogs returned sometime after the moon rose. He allowed the animals to pull him eastward, the tread marks at his feet plain in the silver light, the track winding narrowly through the mountains.

The pass had been graded in the far past and was rutted and uneven. The incline was not steep, and he might have made good time if he'd had more water and something to eat other than the pith and the jerky. The backpack felt too light, and the empty jugs around his neck made the only noise as he climbed. He ran his tongue across the dried blood on his lips, and his saliva burned, and he nearly sat down but then continued.

When he imagined the plain on the far side of the range, inland and perhaps hotter than the bowl in the wasteland, it seemed impossible that he could cross it before the sunrise. The road would be close as soon as he exited the mountains, he told himself, and the plain was not nearly as wide as the caliche, but it was difficult for him to tell how far he had come since setting out that evening.

The lie of the pass made it so that he expected to see the flatlands ahead every time the track descended. Then it would climb again, lost behind another shoulder. His breathing was shallow, and he could not walk any faster, even with the dogs as company. He stopped often, and in the stillness, he did not know if he would be able to make his legs come alive enough to continue.

In a hollow, he crossed through a cloud of chiquistas. Bats cut through the moonlight to feed on the insects. His vision dimmed, and it took him a moment to realize it was only the swarm close to his eyes, followed by the flitting shadows.

A gnat landed on his lips while others crawled into his nostrils. He took the shirt from his backpack and wrapped it around his head and brushed away the chiquistas that were drinking from the corners of his eyelids. He saw himself in the bungalow, water running across his mouth from the sink in the kitchen.

He opened the closets in his father's bedroom and touched the fishing tackle and spear guns layered in a thin skim of dust, and then closed the door and looked at the photo of his father on the wall, cross-legged on the deck of the sub; then he returned to the kitchen where the last gallon of pumice soap sat empty on the counter. In the garage he felt something in his sinuses. His lips burned as he looked for the F-150 and the pack of Marlboros. He tried to read the watch on his wrist, but it was too dark to see the dials.

"Where did you go?" he said. "Dad, please come back. Where are you? I need you."

The gnats lay clustered around the open skin on his fingers. They moved across his mouth, and he wiped them with his sleeves, then shook them from his hands, wondering why he was still so thirsty after drinking from the tap, not quite certain of the reason he was walking, or where his father had come from when he returned at his shoulder.

Blood

Do you remember the beggar on the docks in Ensenada? he said. You liked that place down near the harbor for its mussels. I remember we were eating outside, and you saw him out by the patio. I think you were old enough to drive then, and I'd let you take the wheel in the backcountry and then all the way north until we hit the Santo Tomás Valley.

We'd stopped at the hot springs and asked that señora to fill the bathtubs. It had been maybe two weeks since we'd washed in fresh water. In the Navy, when we'd get into port, it would've been a lot longer than that since we'd had a real shower. We'd get cases of beer and drink for hours just standing under the nozzles.

It was nice like always to be sitting out in those tubs with the shacks the señora had built around them. They had tin roofs and open walls with a view of the hills, and we could see her grandkids down by the springs doing our laundry. They did all our clothes for us, and it was a hundred pesos for everything, and while it dried on the line, we had a beer together.

You were in a tub on your side of the partition, and I was in mine, and we talked about what you were thinking about doing after graduation. Then the señora came back with more hot water and these clean towels that smelled like Fabuloso detergent. Down there, every market we ever stopped in smelled like that stuff—I remember when I'd go into the 7-Eleven in Imperial Beach, if they've just mopped the floors, the soap would take me to all the little roadside places we ate in, or stopped for gas in, or that I'd gone into when I was younger.

Anyway, we kept driving north after that, and in Ensenada, when the beggar came down to our table, he was speaking Spanish, and I couldn't make out what he was saying, but you translated. He told us how he'd been an urchin diver until he'd been bent with decompression sickness, and he was skinny now, like those puppies, and he didn't smell great either.

You went into your pocket, and you gave him two hundred pesos and ordered him a plate of rice and corn sopes and two dozen mussels, and while he ate, you told him I was a diver, too, and he sat there and told us about when he was bent off Todos Santos. You asked him if he missed it, and you told him that I did, too, and we talked about how we both missed it, and then we talked about how we both were young and strong at one point.

I think you would have tried to save him like you wanted to with the puppies. It took you a while growing up to see not everyone can be saved and not everything can be put back together.

Oil

He drew a line in the tinfoil with a utility blade along the edge of the pan to trim each segment to fit against the housing of the gasket. Then he tamped them into a groove, which ran around the edge of the assembly, and threaded the bolts and poked them through the layers of sheeting, listening for the thin, metallic sound of the foil tearing.

When he was finished, the gasket had framed the foil into the pan like a lid. He took the flashlight and, in the sun, ran it around the entire edge of the pan and soaked a rag in fuel and cleaned the tear. Then he taped the excess layers of foil along the outside of the reservoir and drank more water.

He went into the chaparral and peed and came back to the truck and breathed, watching the ocean. It took him twice as long to mount the pan than it had to strip it the previous evening. He looked over at the stain where the oil had pooled and seeped into the ground, then across the curled bodies of the ant colony. It was hot now, even in the shade under the truck, and he kept finding himself watching the convection of the heat inland.

He tightened the final bolt, which was the one that had been bent by the impact, and this also took longer than he had expected. A pinacate beetle was moving through the chaparral, its long legs rising and falling, always in slow motion. It crept out of the sunlight into the Tacoma's shadow, where his tools lay spread, and he thought of how the last living creature to touch them, other than himself, was his father.

He lifted it with the blade of his screwdriver and carefully set it back into the sunlight. Then he rolled out from under the truck and set the five quarts of oil next to the jug holding the reclaimed lubricant. A sea breeze had come up, and the wind felt good against the back of his neck and along his temples. He poured the old oil into the engine, listening as it ran down into the oil pan, and lay on his shoulder and watched the outer patch on the tear as a thin hint of secretion coalesced at the edge of the foil.

The droplet bulged and vibrated in the wind, then fell away and was replaced by another. He moved quickly to gather the tools and loaded the cooler into the camper shell and came back to the front of the truck with the rest of the oil. He poured the five extra liters into the engine and climbed into the driver's seat and reached for the ignition.

A handful of quail shot up from the chaparral on the far side of the windshield, startled by the roar of the engine. At the bottom of the dashboard, a light flicked on, indicating the vehicle was low on oil, which he had expected. He ran to the front bumper and listened to the engine and looked once more at the lubricant under the truck, dripping away in time with the vibration of the motor.

He crossed from the chaparral into the wasteland and settled back into the seat and looked up at the mountains in the distance. Then the temperature gauge on the dashboard spiked into the red, and the engine became deafening and shrieked along for perhaps another ten minutes. After it seized, he stood beside the truck, watching the column of smoke that billowed back from the fender.

He walked in a circle and kicked in the grill, the engine radiating heat, smelling of hot metal and burned oil, and screamed into the silence.

Blood

The first time I brought you down here, it rained and pinned us in the backcountry. You know as well as I do that once these tracks get slick, that's the end of it. It doesn't make sense to pull stakes and try to get out. The only move is to hunker down and ride the front, and if you're running low on food, go fishing, and if you're running low on water, you collect whatever's falling from the sky to begin with. Then you hope the new water holds out until everything is dry again, or if you do run out of water, you roll the dice and see if you can make it.

We were down near the *faro* out at Punta Cabrillo, except the light was out and the *ejido* hadn't been out to change it. It was summertime and you were six or maybe seven. A tropical system had come up from the mainland somewhere, and the sky was so thick with clouds that at night, there was no moon and no stars; there was just the thunder and the lightning—you've seen it like that plenty of times since then.

After your first night in the tent, you were proud of yourself. You'd never slept outside before, and we had sun all that day, and it was clear ahead of the front, and you woke up the next morning like it was nothing. You slept right through the night, and you kept rolling off your pad, onto my shoulder, but you didn't wake up until the sun rose.

I could tell, though, with the storm coming in, the second night was going to be a little different. I kept telling you everything was okay, that we had a good spot in the cove, which would be mostly out of the wind, and we had plenty of everything. We'd caught some halibut, and there were Pismo clams all over the beach at low tide, and I couldn't get a real fire going, but we had my propane stove, and we made a little chowder and some fish tacos.

Anyway, this storm was the leftovers of a hurricane, and especially that second night, it was a pretty good light show. This was before I had the shell on the F-150, so we were down in the tent again, and the rain fell out of the sky like a river. I mean we were dry, sort of, but the tent was blowing around and leaking, and I turned off the flashlight eventually, and we got zipped into our sleeping bags, and you kept asking me questions about whether the surf would wash over the beach and get us, or whether the arroyos would blow out and wash us out to sea, or if the lightning might strike the truck. "It's the only thing metal out here," you said. Then you asked, "What about the tent poles?" and I'm thinking you're only about six, but you've retained everything I've told you from back when my uncle used to bring me down here. He taught me everything he knew about the backcountry, my mother's brother, Great Uncle Jack, you remember him, and now you were repeating it back to me, everything I told you.

So I tell you a few things about the storms I saw with Jack and how we came out okay, and eventually you get started on the wildlife. You're thinking about the coyote we saw drinking near the *presa* and the osprey eating a mackerel on the beach that morning. And you ask me, "What's the biggest thing down here with teeth?" and I said, "Well, a shark, but it can't get us on land." And then you asked about bears, and I explained the Mexican grizzly went extinct a hundred years ago.

Then you asked me what's the strongest animal in a hundred miles, and I thought for a moment, and I gave you the most honest answer I could think of—I said that the strongest animal out here is me, man is the smartest animal, which makes him the strongest, or at least the most powerful. "And you're going to be even stronger," I said, "because you're smarter than I am and because of everything I've shown you. You also have to remember to think." I said, "And use your brains, they'll keep you out of trouble, maybe not all of it, but most of it, until it's time to do whatever you have to."

I remember you dropped right off to sleep after that, and the next day, once the storm cleared, we caught a dorado off the beach, and we ate the rest of the Pismo clams with this wild garlic I dug up behind the campsite. Fear can be a good thing sometimes. It's your brain showing you that you need to pay attention.

A lot of things that happened in my life scared the shit out of me. There are other things that happened to me that I like to think about. I guess all of them are a part of why I am the way I am, and a part of you, indirectly. And I know what you're thinking now, you want to lie down and you're frightened. I also want you to know that you have to keep moving. Listen to me when I say this, just keep walking; the road can't be far now.

Water

He came down from the range and continued for perhaps an hour into the flatlands. When he laid down in the track, he did not bother to look for shadow. Instead, he simply folded his legs into the dust under the sun and pulled the shirtsleeves across his face. You should get up, his father said. You need to get up.

He felt the heat of his sneakers on his feet and the grit in his socks and wondered when he had fallen asleep. He moved his legs through the sand in his sheets and rose, and they passed through the kitchen and came through the garage and climbed into the truck and backed down the driveway.

At the edge of the empty lot off Palm Avenue, they took a sack of food from the bed of the truck and walked out to the puppies. The dogs came from the chaparral to meet them with their heads bowed, wagging their tails in submission. His father poured three mounds of food onto the ground, and the puppies collected at his feet and began to eat, nipping at each other.

Let them figure out who gets what, his father said, and lowered his arm to keep him from separating them over the piles.

Maybe they're thirsty, he said. We should go find some water.

They climbed back into the truck and drove to the freeway and turned south and came to the border. They crossed over together and left the road south of Ensenada. The fishing tackle in the camper shell rattled as they bumped across the empty plain to the ocean. It was so dark inside the cab that he couldn't remember where they were headed.

He saw his own reflection in the windshield, and the face of the Seiko flashed, and he looked over at his father. It's okay, he said. It's okay. We'll finish this last part together.

Alex Webb Wilson is a writer and editor who lives in California. His short fiction appears in *Tin House*, *StoryQuarterly*, and the *Southwest Review*, among others. He is a graduate of The New School University's MFA program and the recipient of a Tennessee Williams Scholarship from the Sewanee Writers' Conference.

Printed in Great Britain
by Amazon